ACES & EIGHTS

ACES AND EIGHTS

BY PHILIP GARLINGTON

M. EVANS AND COMPANY, INC.
NEW YORK, N. Y. 10017

M. Evans and Company titles are distributed in
the United States by the J. B. Lippincott Company,
East Washington Square, Philadelphia, Pa. 19105;
and in Canada by McClelland & Stewart Ltd.,
25 Hollinger Road, Toronto M4B 3G2, Ontario

Library of Congress Cataloging in Publication Data

Garlington, Philip, 1943
Aces and eights.

I. Title.
PZ4.G2343Ac [PS3557.A7163] 813'.5'4 75-14191
ISBN 0-87131-191-7

Design by Joel Schick

Manufactured in the United States of America

9 8 7 6 5 4 3 2 1

CHAPTER 1

Officer William McCann was a large man even for a cop. He was 6 feet 5 inches tall and better than two hundred and thirty pounds. He had a huge head and spiky red hair poking out from beneath his uniform cap. His face and neck were pitted with acne scars; his forehead and nose were covered with blotches of freckles; and his entire face was so scarlet his skin almost seemed to burn.

Although McCann was only twenty-eight years old, the malevolence of his face seemed to add decades to his age. All his features were congested near the center of his face, small malicious blue eyes close-set over a bulbous nose, and lips that habitually sneered. His whole bearing was threatening. He had a menacing way of standing too close to smaller people, glaring down in a way clearly meant to intimidate.

Shortly after 7 P.M. on the first day of August McCann and his partner, John Roosevelt Henry, were having canned cocktails in a squad car parked across Haight Street from the Argonaut Hotel. McCann had finished his third old fashioned and was fishing around in the ice chest under the seat for another. His partner, meanwhile, was muttering to himself and wiggling the fingers of one hand in front of his lips.

Since the evening had turned chilly McCann started the engine to get the heater going, and the radio immediately sprang to life.

"Park units," crackled the dispatcher's voice. "A report of three two-eleven suspects casing a liquor store at fourteen-oh-nine Hayes. Suspects described as NMA's, early twenties, wearing dark clothing. One of the suspects is reported to have a long-barreled revolver under his coat. Units responding? Park Two? Park Four? Park Ten? CP Four? CP Six?"

"Nuts to that," said McCann. "I don't want to hassle anybody."

Henry had been still for a minute except for his loud breathing. He was recovering from one of his periodic attacks.

"We should answer some of these calls," he said.

"We don't have the time, Henry. We have to wait for our eight-oh-two."

The radio continued its monotonous racket. "No response from any Park or CP unit to the two-eleven complaint at fourteen-oh-nine Hayes, KMA four-three-eight, San Francisco police."

"I'll tell you what," McCann said, glancing at his watch. "It'll take Mrs. Smith at least another hour to get good and hysterical. We'll take the next reasonable call, no matter what it is." The giant policeman smiled in the direction of his partner, whose coal-black face was invisible in the darkness.

2

"I know you don't feel well," McCann added. "Maybe a drink would cheer you up."

"Do you have any margaritas?"

"I certainly do. I put some in because I knew you like them." McCann fished in the ice chest for a margarita, pulled the tab, and passed the drink to Henry.

"Thanks," said Henry, taking a swig and wiping his mouth with his sleeve. "You know, don't you, Bill, that it isn't me."

"I know it's not you, Henry, because I remember what you were like before these people took over. So it couldn't be you."

"That's right," said Henry. It was his belief that sometimes other people spoke out of his mouth.

To take Henry's mind off the ventriloquists, McCann would tell him stories. Somehow Henry had slipped like a sprat through the fine mesh of universal education; he had never learned to read, but like most illiterates he loved stories, and McCann happened to be good at telling them. Moreover, a story soothed him and took his mind off the voices. Henry's favorites were about King Arthur and his knights, Richard the Lion-Hearted, the Crusades, and Julius Caesar crossing the Rubicon.

Sometimes Henry would interrupt to ask a question.

"What's chain mail, Bill?"

"It's like a flak vest."

Henry would nod and the story would continue: Caesar, landing on the shores of Africa at the head of a woefully small army, trips and falls on his face while getting out of the boat. Instantly realizing the effect this accident will have on his superstitious and omen-conscious soldiers, Caesar improvises.

"So Julius gets up, see, and he turns to his men and shouts out, 'Africa, I embrace you for Rome.'"

"That was damn smart," Henry had to admit.

The two officers sat quietly in the squad car parked in

3

the shadows across from the Argonaut. They drank and listened to the radio as it rattled out a stream of numbers, names, addresses, complaints, inquiries, advice, and instructions.

"In the Park district," said the radio, "a unit to abate a nuisance at six-forty-seven Cole Street. Nine-ten an X at that address."

"Abating a nuisance sounds about right to me," said McCann, picking up the mike. "Headquarters, this is Park Four coming ten-eight from an assignment. We'll handle the nuisance at six-forty-seven Cole."

"Ten-four, Park Four."

"This shouldn't take long," McCann told his partner. "We'll be back in plenty of time to handle Mr. Smith." He replaced the mike, revved the engine, threw it in gear, and the car jerked forward.

The two officers rolled along, drinks in hand, McCann occasionally swerving into the wrong lane to pass slower drivers. They drove down Haight to Masonic, took a right, and then turned into the 600 block of Cole.

Halfway down the block a Ford Mustang was parked in a driveway. The light was on inside and McCann could see two figures, a man and a woman, sitting in the front seat. Even as they turned the corner the two cops could hear the stirring strains of a military march, a cacophony of brass and drums, emanating from the parked car.

"I guess that noise must be the nuisance," McCann said.

After double-parking, McCann put his old fashioned back on ice and slid out of the car. His idea simply had been to shush these people, but after taking a second look he realized they weren't strangers.

"Could it be?" McCann said to Henry.

Actually, McCann could see for himself that it was

Barry Howitzer, editor of *The Clenched Fist*, one of the few underground revolutionary tabloids to have survived the sixties, a feat it had accomplished not as others had, by jettisoning all principles and accepting advertising from massage parlors, nude encounter studios, and other sleazy oppressors of women, but instead by a barnacle-like adherence to the rock of journalistic excellence, along with the large inheritance that accompanied the timely demise of Howitzer's mother.

Barry Howitzer had long been a figure in radical politics. In the late sixties he had been a regular on the back of flatbed trucks at countless marches and rallies, waving his arms and denouncing imperialism for all he was worth in staccato bursts of eloquence that seemed just right for one of those metallic, echoing portable public-address systems everybody used. And when the amplifier inevitably failed, it was Howitzer who would mount to the roof of a car and yell himself hoarse.

His arrest record in those heady days was the envy of every college student: he had been jailed in Mississippi, jailed in Alabama; he had done three months on the Alameda County farm for inciting; and he knew the inside of the San Francisco Hall of Justice better than he did his own apartment.

But now the wheel had turned, and the revolution, the same revolution that he had predicted a thousand times would rise like a colossus tomorrow, had somehow overnight sunk into the ground like a petulant Rumpelstiltskin. Yet unlike those sunshine traitors who had slunk away into back-to-the-land communes or guru promotion, Howitzer, perhaps aided by his comfortable inherited income, had remained true. As he pointed out endlessly in his *Fist* editorials, there was a palpable force in the world called Historical Inevitability, and it would have the last laugh yet. History would exalt those who remained firm just as it would bury those who fell away.

Although leaving Howitzer's convictions intact, the passage of time had nonetheless exacted a price. As a platform firebrand he had electrified audiences. His bearing had been stern and unyielding, his chiseled face set off with a Pancho Villa mustache like an exclamation point, his fluent exhortations rushing like a cataract over his stunned auditors. Now, slouching listlessly in the car, the former spellbinder, long past thirty, seemed aged and deflated; pouches of gunpowder flesh sagged under his eyes, his mouth was no longer taut, his teeth were gray in the meager light, and his milky face shone like radium.

"I'll tell you what," McCann said to Henry. "I'll chat with brother Howitzer. You can talk to the complainant."

Then, whistling along with the martial air booming into the night from Howitzer's car, McCann marched over to the Mustang and leaned his hands against the door while he looked inside. Howitzer, to celebrate McCann's arrival, turned up the volume of sound from his tape deck. The woman in the car McCann recognized as Howitzer's wife, a former beauty now sadly plump, who served the *Fist* as chief photographer when not working as an office coordinator, which is what Howitzer called the people who had to do the typing.

"Good evening, Mr. Howitzer," said McCann, nodding also to his wife.

"A good oink to you," said Howitzer. "I always like to address people in a manner they're likely to understand."

"Well, then, you ought to print your rag in Braille." McCann liked to talk with Howitzer and always made a point of bantering with him a little whenever they met on Haight Street.

In fair payment for this, McCann and Henry figured occasionally as gestapo in the pages of the *Fist*.

Henry bounded down the steps from the building next door and stood alongside McCann.

"Who's the complainant?" asked McCann.

"It's an old cunt who says the music bothers her; she's trying to watch TV."

"I can't understand that," said McCann. "This is a very catchy tune. What is it, Howitzer?"

"Chinese martial music," Howitzer said. "This selection is the Peking Symphony Orchestra playing *Red Banners Over Asia.*"

"I like it," said McCann. "Ta-ta-te-tum-tum. I admire a composer who's not afraid of a few trumpets."

"But," said McCann, continuing in a more businesslike voice, "I can't let my feeling for art conflict with my duty. I hereby accuse you of disturbing the peace. That's a crime, you know."

"Come on, McCann, we're not disturbing the peace," Howitzer said peevishly.

"Now don't get testy, Howitzer. Everybody knows the *Fist* is the same to me as a conscience, and God knows I don't want to deal with its editor harshly, but the least you could do, considering that I'm a fellow music lover, is tell me what brings you here tonight."

"It's none of your beeswax," said Howitzer.

"Or I could put it another way. Either you tell me why you're here or I'll book you for disorderly, and have the jailor put you in the tank with a bunch of fags and winos."

"Oh, McCann," Howitzer said, lighting a cigarette. "You're such an asshole."

McCann sucked a Clorets and gazed over Howitzer's car at the streetlamps marching down Cole to the Panhandle of Golden Gate Park, a black void over which a few stars somehow managed to penetrate the reddish glow of city lights reflecting off the smog. Then he turned and surveyed the empty tenement windows while he allowed Howitzer to weigh his options.

Finally, Howitzer sighed and said, "We thought you had come about . . . somebody we're interested in."

"Who might that be?"

"We heard there might be a raid tonight; we want to be here to protect our people."

"Oh, ho," said McCann, grinning as he suddenly understood. "This is one of your famous surveillances."

Since the revolution in the streets had flickered out, the *Fist* had sustained itself on a steady diet of gossip and rumor about various cells and collectives that had reputedly gone underground to set up munitions works in the basements of deserted buildings.

And since at the moment San Francisco was suffering a rash of terrorist bombings of toilets and restrooms all over the city, the *Fist* was having a heyday printing communiqués from the terrorists. Howitzer liked to parade his intimacy with the bombers in the pages of the *Fist*, suggesting obliquely in his editorials that he was fairly palsy-walsy with the underground cells and that they always took him into their confidence before they kayoed another john. Moreover, Howitzer stoutly defended the bombings as the only real revolutionary activity then going forward, other than, of course, the publication of the *Fist*.

Lately, McCann knew, he and his wife had taken to prowling the streets at night in their Mustang on a sort of patrol in which they passed by all the houses where they thought terrorists might be holed up, to make sure they were all right. They did this because the police, harried by public indignation, had been pressured into a couple of ill-planned, clumsily executed, and totally ineffectual swoops on apartment buildings where somebody had heard there might be some bombers lurking around.

Nothing had come of any of this, except that Mrs. Howitzer had got some nice shots of completely innocent people being dragged down the stairs to a waiting paddy wagon.

Now, whenever Howitzer got the notion the police had their eye on some building, he put it under *Fist* surveillance, an act of nobility that he had mentioned more than once in his newspaper.

"Gosh, Howitzer, you really think there might be a terrorist around here?" McCann said, pushing his hat back.

Howitzer turned off the tape deck and it was suddenly very quiet in the street. "Now, do you *really* think . . ."

"Okay, Howitzer," McCann said, straightening up. "Here are your rights: You have the right to remain silent, you have . . ."

"Now wait a minute," said Howitzer, squirming uncomfortably in his seat. "I don't *know* this person is affiliated with any liberation group."

"Honest to God," McCann said, "we were just sent here to abate a nuisance."

"Well," said Howitzer in a low voice, "you know that slumlord agency, Sanders Associates?"

"An upstanding firm," McCann said. "The only place that provides better accommodations for hippies is the morgue."

"I know they're trying to evict this guy. Supposedly it's because he's on rent strike until they fix the heat and water . . . but I heard that something else was going on in his apartment."

"He's making bombs," said McCann.

"Now, I don't know that."

"Okay," said McCann. "Tell me his name and I promise I won't arrest him or you either. Not only that, I promise

I won't tip over any more of your vending machines for two weeks."

"So *you're* the one doing that," said Howitzer angrily. "What's his name?"

"Clayton Thomas," Howitzer said. "I don't think you know him, he's not political." Despite himself, Howitzer had allowed a note of distaste to creep into his voice.

McCann nodded and smiled. Howitzer's politics tended toward the puritanical. He disapproved of drugs, alcohol, sexual license, or any other distraction that might delay the day of reckoning for corporate capitalism. Mr. Thomas, then, while surely a bona fide victim of the system, evidently was not a perfect prole hero suitable for representation on a three-color Chinese wall poster.

A little fire glowed inside McCann. He asked Henry to bring the ice chest and they had drinks, Howitzer and his wife both accepting martinis. McCann's head, his whole body, was under a pleasant pressure; his frontal lobes, his nasal cavities, felt as if they were hardening in concrete. He felt large, confident, strong, standing in the night air in the shadow of a tenement, conversing with the docile enemy.

"Let's go see this rent striker," McCann said. "Howitzer, I swear I won't jug him, I don't care if I find him buggering his mother."

"We should pacify the old lady first," Henry said.

"Oh, that's right, that's right; we'll see the cunt first, then Thomas. Wait'll I load up." McCann bent over and filled the inside of his leather jacket with canned cocktails.

They rang the bell of the complainant's first-floor flat. A set of eyes belonging to an elderly woman peered through a crack in the door, which still had its chain lock in place. From what McCann could see of the parchment face, the woman was in her late fifties, with tufts of gray hair springing out from beneath some kind of shower cap.

"Thank God for the police," she said, seeing McCann's uniform and badge. "I'm supposed to see my sister but I'm afraid to go up to Haight to catch the bus with those people out there. They've been sitting there all night. I can't sleep, I can't watch television, I can't go see my sister, and all they play is Sousa.

"I live in constant terror in this neighborhood," she went on. "My neighbor, Mrs. McGregor, was mugged walking her dog in the park today. Two kids knocked her down and stole the dog. Last week a little pickaninny stole my purse in broad daylight." She saw Henry standing behind McCann and told him, "I meant no offense by that."

"By God," said McCann, "we'll put a stop to this harassment. And after we're through with these cretins we'll give you a ride to your sister's."

"Thank God for the boys in blue," she said. "No offense," she added to Henry. The door closed, a lock clicked, and the bolt shot into place.

"Now for Mr. Thomas," McCann said. The two officers walked over to the next building and Henry beamed his flashlight on the mailboxes.

Thomas was on the second floor, and as they trudged up the stairs McCann opened an old fashioned for himself and a margarita for Henry. It was a narrow flight, with dirty frayed carpet and stained wallpaper. They stopped at the door to Thomas' apartment. Swaying slightly, McCann drew his revolver and gave a kick to the bottom of the door. Henry drew his gun and stood back.

"Who is it?" said a nervous voice.

"Chicken Little," McCann said. "With a message."

"I don't know no Chicken Little."

"Knock, knock," said McCann.

"Who's there?"

"Goring," said McCann.

"*Who?*"

"No, no, no," McCann said. "*Goring* who."

"Goring who?" said Henry helpfully.

"Goring to getcha," said McCann, grabbing the nozzle of Henry's gun and shaking it.

"Is that the police?"

"Police to metcha," said Henry.

"We aim to police," said McCann.

"I'm prepared to defend myself," said the voice.

"Now, wait a minute," said McCann, rubbing his blazing face. Preparations for home-defense in the Haight typically focused on shotguns rather than on burglar alarms. And it was not McCann's policy to intimidate or insult a suspect to the point of valor.

"We'll have to use restraint with this one," he stage-whispered to Henry. Then, louder, "Listen, sir, this is just routine, nothing to get excited about. But we do have a search warrant."

"Slip it undah the door then."

"Okay." McCann slapped his pockets until he came up with a small booklet of blank arrest slips. He bent down and slipped the corner of the booklet under the door.

Stepping back a pace, McCann chugged the old fashioned and flipped the empty over his shoulder, enabling him to transfer the Colt to his right hand. The arrest slips wiggled; with a tremendous kick, McCann battered open the door and lunged inside.

The room's occupant, who unwisely had been bending over to reach the paper, now was seated on the floor with his feet in the air and a surprised look on his face. McCann put one boot on the stock of the foreign-made carbine lying beside the dazed defender and extended the muzzle of his pistol until it touched the tip of the man's nose.

"Ding dong," McCann said cheerfully.

The defender, a young black, would have been described in any police report as an NMA, approximately twenty years old, 5 feet 10, one hundred and forty pounds, slim build, medium Afro, wearing dark trousers and a three-quarter-length tan patent-leather coat. In other words, exactly the sort of person who gets in trouble with the police.

A more complete description, however, would add that the man was wearing yellow alligator shoes, four or five rings studded with semiprecious stones, a light blue silk shirt with a ten-inch collar, and a gray Stetson of the kind once favored by Lyndon Johnson.

This young man, staring up with yellow eyeballs in which the brown blood vessels stood out prominently, soon realized he wouldn't be killed instantly and began to take offense at the sudden entry of these intruders into his room.

"What *is* this shit, mahn? You can't come bustin' in heah without no warrant, mahn; I mus' be some no-count chump niggah to you, mahn, but I got mah rights like anybody, mahn. And shame on you brutha," he added, addressing Henry. "Shame, shame, fo' doin' the mahn's work."

"We have ways," McCann said, "of making you talk normally." He hoisted Thomas to his feet and spun him across the room onto the bed. "Besides, haven't you heard of no-knock?"

Holstering his own weapon, McCann picked up the carbine and began working the action. A few cartridges popped out on the floor. Looking around, the giant policeman took in the contents of the room: the dresser covered with perfumes and cosmetics; the dark velvet curtains; the empty liquor cabinet; the hanging plants; the lavender bedspread across which Thomas was sprawled.

Everything about the place spoke of a woman's presence. Even the air was scented.

"This doesn't look like a bomb factory to me," said McCann. "I think Howitzer is having another of his delusions. Listen, Thomas, are you an incendiary?"

"A wha'?"

"Are you trying to overthrow the system?"

"I wouldn't do that," Thomas said, grinning.

"Then you're a credit to your race." McCann pulled up a straight-back chair next to the bed and straddled it to get a better look at Thomas in the poor light.

Thomas, he saw, had coolly propped himself up in bed with a heart-shaped pillow and was giving his long manicured nails some serious attention with an emery board picked up from the nightstand. He was now perfectly at ease, except every once in a while he tossed a glance at the double-eagle-sized Seiko he wore stylishly on the inside of his wrist.

"The old paddy hustle," McCann said, smiling. "You're waiting for some poor john to come up here right now. Or do you dump them on the way out?"

"Hey, *sold* brother," Thomas called out at Henry, "whutch you doin' theah?"

As a matter of fact, while McCann interrogated the suspect, Henry had been conducting a methodical search of the apartment.

"Bureau drawers over here are full of junk," he said, "wallets, cuff links, tiepins, rings, money clips; here's even a pair of suspenders."

"Now what do you want with all that garbage, Thomas?" McCann said. "You're not a junkie, are you?"

"Whutch you say. Only chumps take that line."

14

Actually, McCann could surmise that Thomas came by his collection of men's accessories by having his whore lure would-be customers into alleyways where her pimp unburdened them at gunpoint.

"Your woman's out hustling tonight, huh? No, don't give me that shit," McCann added, when Thomas wet his eyebrow with one finger. "I know what you're doing. Listen, is she white or black? You got a picture?"

"Whutch you say, *offi-sah*. You look roun' and then you scoot. Ain't no *bomb* heah and ain't no junk. En-cinder-ary! Mah black ass."

"I suspect you of being a pimp, Thomas."

"Whutch you say."

"So I don't blame you for taking precautions. You be careful when you open your door to strangers from now on, you hear me?"

In the past month or so, McCann knew, several young pimps had had their expensive hustling attire ruined by repeated shotgun blasts at close range. Some little problem in the ghetto was sorting itself out, but in the meantime Thomas and his ilk would have to step carefully.

Thomas indignantly glanced at his watch again. "Ah'm clean as clean, *offi-sah*. Now lookah heah, mah girl goin' be comin' home shoatly. . . . Lookah heah, you'n brutha Bones jus' take this considah-ration, an' then you run 'long." Thomas brought from his pocket a wad of twenties and began peeling off a few.

"What's your rush?" McCann said, absently putting sixty dollars in his jacket pocket. "This is a police interrogation, not premature ejaculation night at the Moonlight Ranch."

Henry came over and showed McCann a sap he had found lying in a candy dish on the television set.

"Brutha wan' some a this action?" Thomas held up the wad of bills to Henry.

"Listen, Henry," McCann said. "Does it make sense to you that a young man like this, successful in every way, who probably drives a Lincoln with a phone in it, would only have a measly couple of hundred cash. He must have some more stashed around here someplace. This kind of guy doesn't use a bank."

"Muthas."

"We'll ask the suspect." McCann took the various liquor cans out of his jacket and put them on the floor, selecting and opening another old fashioned for himself.

"Drink, Thomas?"

"I'm not immune." Thomas pointed at a martini.

"Now, how about it," said McCann, after emptying his can in a gulp. "Where do you keep your money?"

"Key-*iss* mah ba-*LACK ass*."

"Well," said McCann, slapping his knee. "Okay for you."

Jumping to his feet, McCann tossed away the clip from the rifle and began pacing back and forth, brandishing the weapon like a bat. He stopped in front of the door, tapped the butt of the rifle against the carpet and took a series of practice swings. Then he put one hand to his cap and peered at Henry, who had taken a seat next to Thomas on the bed and was having a drink.

"Now, gentlemen," McCann said, "I am well aware that I may appear to you up there in the bleachers as nothing more than a half-snozzled Irish flatfoot pig cop oppressor of the people who weighs two hundred and thirty-seven pounds and has a face the color of a baboon's ass. Put that thought away, gentlemen, put that thought completely out of your mind, because I want to conjure you with a deeper vision.

"When you look at me, gentlemen, I want you to see none other than that wonder-boy all-star primitive out-fielder Willie Everett" (a ballplayer, McCann knew,

16

much admired by Henry). "Yes, fans, it's Willie Boy himself, dumb spade, aging champion, seducer of teen-age white girls. And please note carefully, gentlemen, if you will, the way this paragon of bye-bye babies approaches the plate. Look at him, gentlemen: he wiggles his sassy hips in a manner reminiscent of the jungle; he taps the dust of kings from his outsize subhuman feet. And God Almighty, can you hear it? The predominantly black crowd roars with savage delight as this possibly over-the-hill champ takes a few warm-up swings. Then, cunningly, he eyeballs the young smarty pitcher in da way dat da *King*fish look at Andy, and he rub da chinbone and he say to himself, 'Hmmmmmmmmm.'

"There's the smarty pitcher standing on the mound," McCann went on, "with his hands tucked behind his back and his head cocked forward like a parakeet. And he is eyeballing the aging champ right back. Now who is this pitcher? I'll tell you who: some punky spic lout from the barrio, his throat all dried up with ambition, his eyes afire with dreams of glory, lean as a wolf, dumb as an ox. He takes a quick look at first while he speculates on whether he can undo the aging champ with a lightning curve.

"But the champeen, insolent as only a rich nigger can be, wets his lips, takes his stance, cocks his bat; the pitch is made . . ."

To Thomas' surprise, he found himself suddenly being propelled toward McCann by Henry, who had dragged him to his feet by his belt and collar. As the startled pimp came within range of the impromptu bat, McCann took a wild cut, catching Thomas across the mouth and knocking him abruptly to the floor, where his landing raised a small cloud of dust.

"The champeen sends one smartly down the third-base line, creating a sensation with the black apes in the stands. The young lout from the barrio, humiliated beyond hope, has to bite his tongue, bury his fist in his glove, and look the prospect of the Iowa City Corn Dodgers *straight in the eye.*"

Thomas, still stunned, looked up with his mouth open, blood welling from his cut lip. Henry wrenched him to his feet again, while McCann pranced around the room swinging the rifle and shouting, "Batter up, batter up." He lunged toward Thomas and jammed the rifle butt into his stomach. Thomas said "oof" and bent over; McCann slapped him again in the mouth, but without much enthusiasm.

"You dumb motherfucker," McCann said, shoving Thomas back on the bed. "Henry, see if you can find his stash. Now listen, you asshole, tell my partner if he's warm or cold."

Henry looked around. After a few minutes he found a roll of fifties in a Donald Duck orange juice can in the refrigerator.

"No imagination," McCann said, opening the last of the drinks. "I guess you realize it's our duty to confiscate these bills as evidence. For all we know you may be a counterfeiter. No, don't bother asking for a receipt because . . ."

Later, McCann would remind himself again that it was never wise to kid around too much with pimps, junkies, violent queers, or anybody else who looks unstable, until you give them a good pat-down. McCann suddenly was looking at a wicked little Browning automatic that a moment before must have been reposing inside Thomas' shirtfront but was now pointed at the policeman's heart.

Fortunately, Henry, standing to the pimp's right, had learned to act decisively while serving his country in the Army. He swung the sap he was still holding smartly against Thomas' arm; the pimp found himself not only in agony but unable to press the trigger as well.

18

The pimp's pain lasted only an instant, however, because Henry's next blow fell on the back of the neck and Thomas collapsed in a heap.

"You gave him a pretty good wallop," McCann said. "I hope he doesn't arrest."

McCann put his hand underneath Thomas' shirt to feel his heart, which was jumping around like a mouse in a paper bag.

The two officers tossed the unconscious pimp on the bed, then settled back against the wall to finish their drinks in a silence broken only by the rattle in Thomas' throat.

"This creep wanted to kill me," McCann finally said. "I don't think I can let that go by."

Tears streaming from their eyes, McCann and Henry were dragging Thomas toward the landing when they met two black-slickered firemen, their axes at the ready, who had just come pounding up the stairs.

"Mattress fire," McCann managed to say despite his fit of coughing. "Gent here was smoking in bed." The two firemen shouldered past for a quick look at the burning room, then turned and rushed back down the stairs. When they met again on the first landing, the firemen were pulling a fat canvas hose.

Outside, McCann became aware of the sirens. He and Henry laid the toasted pimp on the sidewalk just as the city ambulance screamed up. An elderly attendant hopped out, opened the rear doors, and wheeled over a stretcher. He knelt down and quickly checked Thomas' pulse.

"Smoke inhalation," McCann said. "I don't think he's too crisp."

"Hard to tell on a coon," the attendant said. "Excuse me," he added, seeing Henry.

"It was lucky we got to him in time," McCann said, helping the attendant work the stretcher underneath

Thomas. He noticed the cops had gotten Howitzer to move his Mustang to make room for the fire equipment.

Some glass came crashing down on the pavement; the fire fighters had knocked out a window, and the pleasant smell of woodsmoke scented the air. Several hoses snaked into the building from trucks pulled up alongside the curb. The fire lieutenant, a walkie-talkie in his hand, stopped by the stretcher.

"Mostly smoke," he said. "How's the victim?"

"Just dandy," said McCann.

The fire lieutenant wandered away until he was stopped by a newspaper reporter standing beside one of the engines. With a sort of heavy, preoccupied air, Mc-Cann began moving in that direction himself.

"That officer could probably tell you more about it," the fire lieutenant said, and a moment later McCann found the reporter plucking his sleeve. Giving the reporter a big smile, McCann related how he and Henry had saved the man from burning to death.

Then the two officers went to offer the old woman next door a ride to her sister's. They had to hurry, of course, because in a few minutes they were due at the Argonaut Hotel to investigate a homicide.

CHAPTER 2

Charles Brannon of the San Francisco *Examiner* stood in
the empty corridor outside the press room waiting for the
elevator. He was a man of medium height, wearing the
kind of hat men regularly wore in the forties. He had
heavy jowls, a chin or two over the normal allotment,
and a coarse fleshy nose with painful-looking blue veins
in bas-relief. His ruddy alcoholic's face seemed animated
by inner merriment, the result, no doubt, of his unstint-
ing consumption of gin.

Below his beltline, the lower part of his stomach jutted
out like a prognathous jaw, the unfailing sign of long
dissipation and its repellent companion, alcoholic gas-
tritis. The bulge of the gin bottle pulled down heavily
on one side of his coat, the triangular tip of a notebook
peeped out of the other pocket.

With better than a quart of gin inside him for the day, Brannon experienced a glowing sense of health. But the rawest intern would have recognized him for what he was: a sick man who in all probability would be dead within a year from bleeding ulcers, cirrhosis, or, if he was lucky, a fast coronary.

Brannon was a reporter of the old school. He had been a Hearst man all his life and had grown up in the rough, tawdry world of Chicago journalism in the thirties. In Chicago he had covered the police beat, played the ponies, drunk to excess, hobnobbed with the mob, called a hotel room home, and given, in his own opinion, Ben Hecht some of his best lines. Although his true age was fifty-seven, he claimed to be sixty-three, and his looks helped corroborate the lie. He had a vivid recollection of the old days, when newspapers were in competition with one another, and teams of newsmen rushed through the downtown streets to every barroom cutting and hotel mattress fire. He frequently reminded the bored young men who drifted in and out of the press room at the Hall of Justice that the police beat was once the mainstay of the newspaper, and not a dumping ground for incompetent punks who couldn't hack it in the city room.

"Back in the days of flash powder," he liked to say, "a reporter didn't think twice about standing outside all night in subzero weather to get a two-hour beat on a rival."

In those days, every reporter had been a housebreaker, and the contents of a jimmied desk became a lurid story in five minutes flat. In the days of flash powder, a reporter was expected to do a little more than accept a handout from a thirty-thousand-a-year flack. Back then, a newsman cultivated sources, and a tip from a gambler friend might result in an exclusive front-page photo of a notorious rackets figure slumped behind the wheel of his phaeton with a bullet hole neatly between the eyes.

That was reporting. Nowadays, a reporter was just another bureaucrat, particularly the police reporters, who seldom left their desks and took everything straight from the turgid and laughable police accounts.

But, being a reporter of the old school, Brannon occasionally did more than just English the police blotter. If some incautious copper stopped a bullet and became a hero in one of the continuing skirmishes between the People and the Law; or if there were, say, cult overtones in a hippie dope murder; or if the victim or the suspect or anybody else involved happened to be a pretty blonde, brunette, or redhead, then Brannon would not hesitate to get the facts himself.

This was not because he had hopes for finding the truth. He was fifty-seven years old. It was his romantic ideas that prompted him to scout around on major stories himself. Added to this, he actually enjoyed the company of cops, many of whom he knew personally. He also liked to go out to Mission Emergency to chat with shooting victims, or to drop down to the basement morgue at the Hall of Justice for a cup of coffee with the duty coroner over one of this gentleman's foolish-looking charges.

In a word, Brannon prided himself on checking things out for himself. It was Brannon's willingness to occasionally leave his desk at the Hall and plunge into the streets that made him, even in his advanced state of alcoholism, an asset to the *Examiner*.

In fact, that was why Brannon was waiting for the elevator. He was going to check out a call from an anonymous tipster. In this case, the caller had seemed to be an elderly woman, either drunk or senile. She had given Brannon some garbled message about a dead man at the Argonaut Hotel on Haight Street.

Having been a police reporter in San Francisco for many years, Brannon knew the Argonaut; it was a converted tenement, now a transients' hotel, catering to freaks, junkies, welfare mothers, and other trash.

In his time Brannon had viewed thousands of dead bodies, and he would not have walked across the street to look at a no-class fatal. But there was something about an anonymous call, about a stiff in a seedy hotel, that could still charm his senses. Like all reporters, he had a taste for the sordid.

Besides, you never knew. There might be something to the story; a good reporter never pissed on anything until he had checked it out.

"It's my man," the woman had said. "He's been there ten days. They're going to break him if they take him down the stairs."

"He's been dead for ten days?"

But the woman had hung up.

Brannon drove into the Haight, relishing, as always, another chance to rub elbows with night managers, rheumy-eyed winos, cops, and coroner's deputies.

Parking in the 1500 block of Haight, he stepped onto a sidewalk fouled with dog excrement and joined the meager traffic along the bleak, ill-lighted street, passing dark figures huddled under Army blankets in doorways and the inevitable pair of spade men outside a corner liquor store, drinking cans of beer still wrapped in paper bags.

A less-experienced man might have been apprehensive about the withered young flowers who approached out of the darkness in their tattered Levis and fatigue jackets in their morose quest for spare change. Brannon, however, could tell the dangerous from the pathetic. Not that there wasn't some danger.

24

Despite interference from City Hall, Haight-Ashbury still had a respectable number of murders, rapes, and strong-arm robberies; only Hunters Point and the Fillmore could do any better. On the streets at night, a frightening collection of sickly addicts, motorcycle thugs, and diseased hippies wandered disconsolately along the filthy sidewalks. The drug traffic flourished in every crumbling tenement, and a knock on the door at night signaled the arrival of a couple of ragged, bleary youths with a few dollars and a great need.

True, the Christers at City Hall had put their oar in. Neighborhood committees had been formed, street lighting had been improved, police patrols stepped up, and some of the worst of the condemned buildings, once such an attraction to depravity, had now been torn down. And on Saturday mornings along Haight bearded kids with paint buckets and mops were running around like a bunch of Seventh-Day Adventists.

Yet, Brannon was glad to see the gutters along Haight were still full of broken glass, and every once in a while the stillness of the night was punctuated by the sound of a smashing bottle. It was the reporter's belief that for some reason or another nothing pleases the poor and dispossessed more than breaking glass in the street. In the Haight, the bottles broke all night.

A late-model pastel-blue truck was double-parked outside the Argonaut as Brannon entered a lobby as narrow as a kitchen. He sensed immediately that something had happened because of the two jabbering crones seated together on a battered couch, their liver-spotted hands fluttering in their laps. A hubbub of voices floated down from the second-floor office. Brannon slowly huffed his way up the dogleg stairs.

In the office two young cops, smiling, their hats pushed back, stood over a seated old woman, who was alternately sobbing and talking excitedly. A compact little Italian, evidently the manager, angrily interrupted the woman's narrative every few moments with a loud *"Jesus Christ!"*

"The *Examiner*," said Brannon, showing his press card. He was breathing heavily after the walk upstairs.

"The old bellows ain't too good," he wheezed to the cops. "Snuff of gas in the Big War." Brannon, of course, had been a newborn baby in 1918.

The two cops, one a giant, red-faced Irishman, the other a wiry, bitter-looking black, stared at Brannon suspiciously. The Irish cop raised his eyebrows and shrugged. But the little manager threw up his hands and shouted, *"Jesus Christ!"*

The old woman (Brannon assumed she was the one who had tipped him) leaned forward, her hands, clasped, her head wagging, the tears running down her cheeks. "No, no, not the newspaper. I don't want John in the newspaper."

The cops had a laugh at that one.

"She's crazy," said the manager, stepping out in the hall. "She come in every day for a week and she don't say nothing."

"Where's the coroner?" Brannon asked.

"He's not here yet," said the big Irish cop.

"I saw his wagon outside."

The cop smiled and wiped his mouth. "Room seven-twelve. But you'd better take a clothespin. The guy's been dead ten days."

"I don't want you to go up there," said the manager, putting a hand on Brannon's arm. Brannon shook him off and walked down the hallway to the elevator, which gave him a creaky lift to the seventh floor.

Deputy Coroner Jerold Keating and a helper were in the hallway smoking cigarettes.

"Hiya, Brannon," said Keating, who knew Brannon from the days when the press rode the ambulances out of Central Emergency. "We're letting the room air a bit I don't know why you're interested in this cheap shit."

"My only chance to see old friends."

"Not many of the old ones left."

"Have a bite." Brannon pulled out his gin bottle and unscrewed the cap.

"Can't do it," said Keating, making a face. "I've got these fucking ulcers."

"Too bad. What else can you tell me?"

"Well, if you're really interested, here's the deal. The deceased is a guy named John Smith. That's his real name. Him and that old broad—did you see her in the office?—had a little thing going. She lives in some other rattrap, but she comes over here every night to watch TV and drink a little wine and milk, which seems to be the staple fare for these old coots.

"Anyways, she comes over here for *I Love Lucy* one night and finds her boy friend has croaked. He's lying there in bed covered with puke. Now, as you may have gathered, the old broad is not too well up here . . ." the coroner tapped his skull, "so she cleans him up, fluffs his pillow, pours a little juice, and flips on the tube. I guess old John was about her only friend, and she didn't want to admit it was *all-l* over.

"Anyways," Keating continued, "when she goes home she doesn't say dickshit to nobody. The next night, it's the same routine, except she brings her supper. She says howdy to the manager and comes up to see John. This goes on for more than a week until I guess somebody finally got a noseful. She'd been keeping the windows closed."

Then, with a wink, Keating took Brannon by the elbow and pulled him to the door numbered 712. "Now get a load of this," he said, kicking open the door.

On the bed in the center of the small room lay the

corpse of John Smith. Strangely, the right half of his face was well-preserved, while the left side was black and swollen. More remarkable, however, was the fact that the body was wrapped from neck to toes in strips of newspaper.

"Ha, ha," said Brannon, remembering the woman's remark in the office. "She doesn't want him in the newspaper."

Along with the unmistakable smell of putrefaction, Brannon thought he caught the suggestion of another sour odor. He scratched the back of his neck for a moment.

"Is that vinegar?"

"Right," said Keating, giving Brannon a squeeze on the arm. "When he started to go bad, the old broad wrapped him up in newspaper and then soaked him in vinegar."

Brannon slapped his knee. "That's a cream," he said. "Christ Almighty, the infallible nose," he added, pointed to his own diseased example. "I can actually make something out of this. A Jack and Jill story . . . vinegar and brown paper . . . the poor shit breaking his crown in this sleazy dump."

"I've got to admit, you've made up some pretty good stuff," Keating said.

"They don't make 'em like me anymore," Brannon said, taking a long swallow of gin. "They broke the mold after me." As he looked down at the papier-mâché mummy on the bed, he wondered if the desk would really go for a Jack and Jill angle.

In the old days, of course, they would have banged it on page one, with a cut of the old cunt weeping at John's feet. And the photographer, if he was worth a shit, might even make a picture suggesting that John had been wrapped in old *Examiners*. Now the story would probably show up as eight paragraphs next to the truss ads.

Brannon took another swig. Back in the days of flash powder it meant something to be a reporter. People made way. But times had fucking well changed! At the last big fire Brannon had covered, some pickaninny had hopped up and asked him what channel he was with. What channel! Fifty-seven years old, three chins, a paunch, an unpressed suit, and not so much as a Kodak Instamatic around his neck.

In the old days newspapers had clout, the cops cooperated or else, and police chiefs came and went at the whim of the *Examiner*. Those old cops were gone now; dead, retired, cushy jobs in the warrant bureau. The new cops, like the two punks in the office, had no respect for newspapers. That lying Irish orangutan had even told Brannon that the coroner wasn't on the scene when his wagon was parked outside the front door. The new breed either lied or dummied up when the press was around. Too many cases blown out of court because of pretrial publicity; too many stories about police brutality—it was giving the department a tight ass.

Nowadays, it was impossible to even get a suspect's picture in jail. Ten years ago the cops would drag the bastard out of his cell and hold his head to the camera. But it was different now; everybody was serious.

In the old days the business had been fun. When Brannon had ridden the ambulances, it was jokes and drinks night after night. One morning he had woken up handcuffed to a corpse, and he had retaliated by putting a pound of Limburger cheese on the engine of the prankster's car. The cops, reporters, ambulance drivers— they were all pals.

Now suspicion had crept in, and cops no longer trusted reporters, not because reporters had changed but because the world had changed: court decisions, clamoring minorities, the humorless young, monopoly journalism, everything.

Brannon moodily finished the bottle and tossed it into the late John Smith's wastebasket.

He said good-by to Keating and shambled to the elevator. Passing the second floor on the way down, he caught a brief glimpse of the two young policemen in the office, laughing about something. On the street, he shivered in the swirling fog, pulling his overcoat tighter around him as he surveyed the dismal boarded-up storefronts. Then, in the car, the gin took hold and he brightened, he hummed a tune, and by the time he got back to the Hall he had composed the Argonaut story. It appeared the next day on page 27.

Senior's Tryst Pad
ELDERLY HAIGHT WOMAN DENIES REAPER

"Till death do us part—and then a little longer," seemed to be the motto yesterday of Mrs. Alice Harris as she sat beside the body of her long-time friend and companion, John Smith, 60, of 1605 Haight St., who died almost two weeks ago of a heart attack.

Tears bedewed Mrs. Harris' wrinkled cheeks as she told the *Examiner* of her tragic refusal to give up her loved one to the grave.

The story went on for six or seven more paragraphs. The desk had cut out the Jack and Jill angle.

CHAPTER 3

The two young cops Brannon saw in the office of the Argonaut Hotel were part of a new departmental policy to racially mix the units working the high-crime districts of Haight-Ashbury, Fillmore, and Mission. This new policy was the result of numerous blue-ribbon studies undertaken in the wake of this or that crisis; and these studies had convinced a lot of important people that an Irishman and a black in a squad car went down better in the ghetto than the usual two Irishmen. On the other hand, these same people reasoned, a balanced unit would be at least 50 per cent more responsive to the wants of society than the other racially enlightened possibility of two blacks in a squad car.

Although lauded as far-sighted, this policy was undermined by a shortage of earth colors in the department and by an abundance of brick-faced Irishmen. The big problem during the Phase One Implementation Period had been to figure out which officers were actually going to have to suffer a black partner. Some bureaucrats had suggested a lottery.

But, since it was not the policy to force integration on the unwilling, a tacit understanding had developed: a white officer had to volunteer to take a black partner and could even pick the one he wanted. Happily, the number of officers willing to make this sacrifice almost exactly coincided with the number of colored cops in the pool.

This is just to say that it was not true the two officers in the Argonaut had been thrown together by the machinations of a pointy-headed bureaucracy. Rather, they were working together because they wanted to. These two cops, in fact, had known each other for several years, having met during the war, where, although assigned to different outfits, they had collaborated in the removal of an unpopular officer.

The two former warriors were now lolling in the office of the Argonaut Hotel, their thumbs hooked nonchalantly in their cartridge belts. Out of the corner of one eye McCann noticed the pink, leering face of Brannon flash past the elevator window. McCann stepped out of the office and leaned over the second-floor railing in time to see Brannon stagger out of the elevator and weave toward the door, obviously drunk.

The reporter was singing: "Jack and Jill went up the hill, to fetch a pail of waa-ter, Jack fell down and broke his crown . . . excuse me, ladies." Brannon touched his hat to the two withered crones in the lobby, and then his shabby coat disappeared out the front door.

McCann nodded to Henry and the two officers went up to see Keating. When the deputy coroner saw the two uniforms striding toward him, he sent his helper to get the sheets and stretcher from the wagon.

"You told him a good story, I hope," McCann said.

Keating looked up at the huge policeman's blazing, congested face and shifted his feet.

"Brannon used to be one of the best."

The three men were standing at the foot of the bed. Under the naked bulb Smith's remains looked like some object d'art or a papier-mâché memento mori, placed in the room merely for a cheap effect.

The dead man, it was true, had run into some bad luck he really didn't deserve. A junkie and small-time dealer, Smith had been a responsible person, as junkies go, and had never left some blue-faced little teen-age runaway stuffed in a closet. But for the last few months he had been appropriating more and more of his merchandise for his own use. Ordinarily, this would have occasioned no more than a visit from a couple of heavies, who would have admonished Smith and perhaps given him a good shake.

Unluckily for the deceased, his petty transgression coincided with McCann's first efforts to find and arrange some business with the shadowy figures controlling the heroin traffic in San Francisco.

These efforts had culminated, two weeks previously, in an anonymous telephone call at his apartment. The caller had a droll, fruity voice.

"Officer McCann?"

"Yes."

"There's a man named John Smith living in the Argonaut Hotel on Haight Street. It will be your job, should you choose to accept it, to arrange for him to self-destruct." With that, the caller had laughed and hung up.

Henry had shrugged when McCann told him about the call. They both could see it was a test. Together they had gone straight over to the Argonaut, and while Henry, who had gained experience in these matters in the Army, took care of Smith, McCann had detained the little manager in his office, amusing him with a number of quick draws, including a new variation of the Road Agent's Spin. Then McCann took the perturbed manager up to 712 to see Mr. Smith.

He made the little Italian touch the corpse, feel the lack of pulse, tap the eyeballs, and in every way assure himself that Smith was indeed thoroughly lifeless.

"Now look here, Mr. Plate-of-spaghetti," McCann said. "I want you to give a message to the people concerned with Mr. Smith's health. You say this room is open for inspection for one week."

"Who am I going to tell?" said the little manager, raising his bony shoulders.

"Also, I'm afraid you'll have to sit on Mrs. Smith for a week or so. You'd better keep her in your room, I guess."

"No way," said the manager.

Unbidden, Henry's arm moved so swiftly that even McCann was startled, and the little manager was suddenly on the floor with blood dripping from his nose. Henry's leg flashed in a short arc and the manager yelped in pain. Nobody in the hotel paid any attention to this because it was not the kind of place where people upset themselves about sudden screams in the night, or about any of the other noises that go with cheap accommodations.

McCann dragged the manager to his feet, brushed him off, and in the end, the Italian agreed that he would sit on Mrs. Smith for a week, that he would deliver McCann's message, should anybody ask, and that he would try to preserve the remains as best as possible with the old G.P.'s trick of vinegar and newspaper.

It was more or less as a last macabre fillip that McCann decided to throw in the story of geriatric passion to ensure that Smith's demise would not pass completely

34

unnoticed. He assumed it would have just enough sentimental value to get a few lines in the *Examiner*.

"Have you looked to see if his tracks are gone?"
McCann said.

Keating wrinkled his nose. "Don't worry, they're gone.
Besides, nobody is going to do an autopsy on this one.
And the university won't want him."

The helper came up with the stretcher and he and
Keating set to work wrapping Smith's remains.

"Let's talk to the wop again" McCann said, touching
Henry's arm. When they got back to the office they
found the manager at his desk reading a magazine.

"Where's Sally?"

"She's in my room," said the manager, unable to
conceal his disgust. Sally Smith's long life of addiction,
hepatitis, and gonorrhea had addled her brains somewhat. When she was under the influence of smack, she
usually thought she was still appearing at the Black-
hawk Theater and sang snatches of forgotten songs
in a hoarse, broken voice. When she was straight, as she
had been that evening for Brannon's benefit, she was
liable to the hysterical. Sally, of course, believed her
husband had died of an overdose.

"It's up to you to keep her supplied with whatever she
needs," McCann said, sitting on the manager's desk.
"And I just want to make sure you understand what
happened tonight with that reporter."

"Nothing," said the Italian.

"But what if somebody asks you a question? What do
you say?"

"Nothing again."

"What a sweet place you have here," said McCann,
smiling at the manager. "Vinegar-soaked carrion and
garlic."

CHAPTER 4

August is the worst month in San Francisco. An evil, bad-smelling fog squats on the city day and night; perverse squalls, blowing out of nowhere, scatter the tennis parties in Pacific Heights; and a kind of monsoon sweeps out of Oakland, raising goose bumps on the naked arms of the bewildered nonresidents huddled under leaden skies at Fisherman's Wharf. The tourists just can't seem to understand why on August 1 the thermometer won't budge past 47 degrees.

The natives, of course, are another matter. They go about their business as if nothing were wrong. Out at the beach, for example, oblivious as corpses or madmen to the whirling rain, the members of undoubtedly the most insolent tribe of surfers in the world parade along the strand in their wet suits, then paddle out in the bitterly cold water to bob up and down on the miniature waves. The very existence of these robust teen-agers is like a slap in the face to the passer-by on the wharf, who, coughing and sneezing in his handkerchief, prays that God will send one of His most impenitent sharks inshore for a light snack of teen-age insolence.

This is merely one of a thousand examples, and there is no point in citing the others, because everybody already knows that August is the worst month in San Francisco. And this August was particularly severe because the city was in the grip of revolutionary terror.

Time bombs, planted perhaps by the Weather Underground, or by the Black Panthers, or by God knows what extremist group, exploded frequently and with impunity in almost every district of the city. Nobody seemed to know much about these occurrences but it became obvious after a while, even to the police, that the bombs always exploded in public lavatories of those buildings most symbolic of American decadence.

San Franciscans are reputed to be complacent people, their city being to them what a plate of beans and a hammock are to a Mexican, but this incessant bombing of restrooms finally aroused their indignation, and there were predictable results, both political and editorial. Big headlines in the late editions helped enflame public opinion. So did television news bulletins, which (regrettably, of course) always seemed to interrupt prime time.

San Francisco's two newspapers, editorially distinct but owned and operated by the same company as a monopoly sanctioned by Congress, scrutinized the crisis daily and assigned some of the biggest reputations in crime reporting to the story, as a public service and as a comfort to the police. But the homeowner and property-tax payer was not comforted. Instead, he was increasingly alarmed by the spiraling number of explosions, which, though low in mortality, were high in sensation.

Adding to the tumult, the alternative press, particularly one strident guttersnipe of a rag called *The Clenched Fist,* rushed to print the names of a dozen exotic affinity groups, all of which, after nocturnal visits to out-of-the-way mailboxes, vociferously took credit for the vengeance rapidly closing in on smug America.

These revolutionary gangs, with such names as Purple Noon Conspiracy, Mao's Marauders, Wounded Knee Tribe, Gun Sisters, Inc., all claimed, simultaneously, the onus and the laurels for the broadcast destruction of metal stalls, tile walls, and ceramic fixtures, in letters reeking of proletarian earnestness and cordite.

It was also becoming apparent that the incapacity of city agencies to deal with the crisis was unsettling the average citizen's faith in the efficacy of government. In fact, this year being an election year, the incumbent mayor was, as the pols say, taking his lumps on the terror issue from his Republican opponent, who was accusing the city administration of being, basically, pro-anarchy.

It would be unfair, however, to depict the city administration as idle. On the contrary, the mayor, acting with unexpected speed, had made his position clear at the outset by forthrightly condemning the bombers.

And the police department, not far behind, had established strict security in the Hall of Justice and increased its undercover surveillance of those bookstores and movie houses that the Inspectors' Bureau had long suspected of catering to malcontents. Moreover, the chief of police, feeling Draconian measures were justified, initiated door-to-door searches and okayed a stop-and-frisk policy against those pedestrians who had previously walked around unmolested. While none of this curtailed the bombings, it did bring in a volume of handguns, knives, and saps that the department could display during Police Appreciation Week.

A feeling remained, however, that further steps were necessary.

Thus it happened on the morning of August 1 that the mayor and the chief of police put their heads together and came up with the idea of forming a special police unit, comparable in its freedom and mobility to the vice squad, to investigate cases involving politically motivated terror. For starters, the chief and the mayor had what was described by the media as a frank and wide-ranging talk at the Hall of Justice. Later in the day the two of them voluntarily faced a battery of cameras and poised pencils that had been gathered together by the mayor's press secretary for the purpose of making public the mayor's new plan to combat the terror.

When the reporters were finally settled, the coffee cups set aside, the lights fixed, the cameras trained, and when the newspapermen had crossed their knees the better to center their notepads, the mayor made a brief address in which he declared at once his contempt for the bombers and his vow to see them rot in San Quentin for fifty years. Following this measured statement, the chief of police brought forward a veteran officer who had served with a secret branch of Army intelligence before coming to the San Francisco department in 1960. The chief explained that this person, Lieutenant Michael O'Riley, would be the first officer-in-charge of the new unit, which henceforth would be called the Anti-Terror Unit.

As Lieutenant O'Riley closed in shoulder to shoulder with the chief and the mayor, the cameras started to roll, and the cameraman for Channel 7 exchanged an approving nod with the cameraman for Channel 5. And, in fact, all the television people were pleased with the choice, because the lieutenant had a lean, ascetic face, with inset eyes, a sharp nose, and prominent cheekbones, all of which would photograph perfectly on the fast Tri-X film used in television work.

But the newspaper reporters were less pleased, because the lieutenant turned out to be monosyllabic and evasive, saying only that he would bend every effort to end the terror. He did not elaborate, drop hints, or get flustered, even when he was pressed relentlessly by the most persistent and least respectful of all the big-name crime reporters, Charles Brannon of the *Examiner*, a man whose rude manners and impertinence often reduced city functionaries to jelly. The only detail Brannon managed to wrest from the taciturn lieutenant was that the unit would be fleshed out eventually with several young patrolmen, picked from those whose higher-than-average intelligence might be expected to give them rapport with the terrorists.

To further speed an end to the terror, the new unit was given an office in the Hall of Justice; and the noisy crowd of cameras and notepads trooped along as O'Riley was formally installed.

As the TV crews bustled after O'Riley down the hallway, Channel 7 found a chance to comment to Channel 5, "What a head on the guy; it looks like the mummified head of Rameses II."

Crowding into the tiny office, the reporters stood around as the cameras zoomed in first on O'Riley shaking hands with the chief and then on O'Riley transferring some pipes and pipe cleaners from his briefcase to the top desk drawer.

"What's in the bag, lieutenant," asked a camera, pointing to the brown paper bag in O'Riley's case.

"I usually eat my lunch at my desk," O'Riley said.

"What you got today?" persisted the camera, getting

ready to roll some footage. O'Riley obligingly poured out the contents onto the desktop: three walnuts, an orange, a Baggie full of cherry tomatoes, a hard roll, and a chunk of rock candy.

Brannon, still piqued, apparently, at the new commander's reticence, sneered at this lunch.

"Who packs your lunch for you, lieutenant? Santa Claus? I haven't seen a lunch like that since I opened my last Christmas stocking in 1922. No wonder you look like something that crawled out of a grave."

The mummified head of Rameses II swiveled on its stem and the dry lips peeled back a mirthless grin. Brannon, meanwhile, boldly picked up O'Riley's briefcase and began to poke through it.

"Do you have a bottle in here, Lieutenant?" asked Brannon. "I don't suppose a monk like you would ever take a drink."

"I'm Irish, aren't I?"

"I don't know what you are. The people of San Francisco will settle that argument when they see how fast you can put bomb throwers in the slammer. Oh, my God. Look at this!" Brannon held up a slim, leather-bound volume he'd removed from the case. "Can you believe it? *The Moral Discourses of Epictetus*. Is this your idea of a nooner, Lieutenant? Christ Almighty, a philosopher flatfoot."

O'Riley's smile had frozen while Brannon rifled his case, but now the bloodless lips began to work again. "If you'll excuse me, gentlemen, I'll go to work," he said, and Brannon was forced to use that for his clinch paragraph in a generally favorable article about the new Anti-Terror Unit boss. His story had to have a new lead the next day, however, because after the *Five O'Clock News* on Channel 5 and 7 the bombers became aware of O'Riley's installation and obliged everybody by blasting another john.

CHAPTER 5

It was past midnight when McCann entered his apartment. He went straight to the kitchen for a drink, took down a bottle of bourbon and filled an orange juice glass to the brim. As he raised the drink, he heard a rustling from the living room and a pointed cough.

"Remember me?" said Rose Stein.

"The tuberculosis ward?"

Wrapper in a terry-cloth bathrobe, McCann's mistress entered the kitchen. She sized up his spiky hair and flaming nose.

"Drunk again," she said reprovingly.

McCann raised his glass and saluted her. He had met Rose almost six months before at San Francisco State College when he had been on the campus with a squad of police searching students' lockers for explosives, after the men's room at the Air Force ROTC building had gone up one night.

Some of the students had taken umbrage at the police pawing through their personal belongings without permission, and there had been some joustling in the hallway. In the midst of this, McCann had met Rose. He was going through the contents of her purse, which, naturally enough, he had found in her locker.

"Just think of me as Art Linkletter," he had told her. In return, she had called him a few names from the usual radical naturalist's phyla: pig, running dog, hyena.

McCann had laughed—she was such a little thing, barely five feet tall. But indisputably she filled out a pair of Levis; mere words, however violent, could not detract from that.

As it happened, an explosion the next night in the faculty lavatory of the International Relations Building caused the college president to request a police guard for a while longer, and McCann stayed on campus with his squad for a week. To pass the time he amused himself by courting Rose, making blunt advances, threatening her with arrest, exchanging barrages of lively or obscene remarks. In short, after a thousand vicissitudes, she was living with him. She was twenty-three or twenty-four, with jet-black hair, a low convex forehead, the smooth dusky skin of a Southern European, small breasts, a sharp, rather pointed nose, and, of course, a Jewish heritage. She was now in her senior year in the psychology department.

Rose came closer and looked up at McCann's burning face. "I've been thinking about our conversation last night," she said.

Like all couples, they were always having little talks in bed. Rose's favorite exercise was to examine their relationship, or her relationship with professor so-and-so, or with her parents, or with her gynecologist. She also liked to examine McCann on his true feelings, despite six months of hitting nothing but a brick wall of sarcasm. But a relationship meant communication, she said.

"You know I like to talk with you." McCann extended one huge hand, nipped her lapel between finger and thumb and drew her over.

"I thought habitual drunks lost interest in sex."

"I'm just not shy around you, Rose." McCann put his hand inside her robe and caressed her smooth shoulder. "I *do* have tender feelings for you, no matter what you say."

"I've noticed you like to ball me sometimes, but I haven't noticed this tender feeling, which I now find out is supposedly responsible for your *brutish* behavior."

"I've a sentimental heart."

"You're heartless."

She stood next to him in the kitchen, one of her hips pressed against the drainboard, her head cocked up at him. McCann pulled a dishrag from the rack and mopped his neck and face.

"You smell like smoke," she said.

"A mattress fire. Henry and I saved some jig so that next month he can stick up a liquor store and kill one of my benefactors."

"You saved him though."

"Well, to be honest, I didn't know it was a nigger; I just thought the guy was burned up."

The hulking officer laughed and drank off the bourbon. In his blue serge, with his burning and congested face, his spiky red hair, huge red hands, and pendant revolver, McCann struck a nice contrast with little Rose, her coffee-with-cream-colored skin covered partly by the white robe.

Rose moved closer to him and tucked her small hands inside his belt. "McCann, just tell me one thing. Do you really love me at all?"

McCann laughed and poured another drink. "Do jackals love carrion?"

"McCann!"

"Listen, Rose, in my deck, you're the ace of hearts."

"I want to have a talk."

"Oh, Rose."

"A talk!"

"All right, all right," McCann said. In accordance with a procedure that had been worked out over the months of their cohabitation, McCann drew out his .357 Magnum Colt revolver and handed the heavy weapon, grip first, to Rose. They had these talks frequently, in which Rose would worry the various problems besetting their relationship. At first McCann's penchant for sarcasm so infuriated her that she would rage for days. Now, however, to keep peace, McCann, before embarking on a talk, would hand her his loaded pistol, thus giving her an extra option, that of blowing his brains out. Seeming so much like fair play, the device worked; with the heavy, outsize pistol in her hand, Rose's temper seldom hit the higher registers.

Taking the revolver in one hand and pulling her robe more snugly about her, Rose pattered off into the living room. They sat together on the well-worn couch, under the small circle of light thrown by a table lamp.

"Now," she said, pressing the muzzle of the pistol against McCann's heart, "I want you to be serious."

Since her sixteenth birthday, Rose had been active in the Movement. While other students frittered away their hours in senseless teen-age pursuits, Rose had demonstrated against imperialism and mass murder. During her high school years every Thursday afternoon found her painting antiwar placards. And on Saturday, rain or shine, she had paraded in the marches, chanting slogans denouncing United States atrocities in Vietnam. "U.S. Get Out Now" had been her A, B, C, and D.

By 1973, of course, most of the students had sunk into a drug-induced apathy, but Rose and a few other puritans doggedly continued the struggle to heighten the contradictions. Consequently, it troubled Rose more than a little to be giving her body to the oppressor, the only mass murderer she had ever met. But for some inexplicable reason she had hope for McCann and still thought it possible to win him over. The first step, she felt, would be to wring from him a confession of his crimes. But so far he had been reticent about his participation in the genocide.

The pressure of the pistol barrel against McCann's rib cage grew insistent.

"McCann. Please tell me what you did in the Army. Where were you? What was your job? How many men do you think you killed?"

"We were given clear instructions, Senator. Kill only women and children. That was company policy; I remember the notice on the bulletin board."

Rose sighed. She would have liked to supply her comrades in the Women's Caucus with some inside information, particularly since her duties included a position on the leaflet-writing committee. But McCann refused to cooperate and, worse, made a joke of everything. It might be possible to be more aboveboard about her private life if he would only show some remorse for his actions, or if he would at least join the Veterans for Socialism. It was impossible, of course, for Rose to confide in any of her friends about McCann, for she was afraid they might regard her liaison with a hyena as some kind of quislingism. At college she reddened whenever the police arrived to search the lockers; her hoots and catcalls no longer carried real conviction. And it was horrible to recall the day when she had recognized McCann among a squad of policemen sent to protect industry and government recruiters from being mobbed by a swarm of job applicants. She had gone quite cold when she saw McCann's red face underneath a helmet, and she didn't know what to do when he caught her eye. But McCann treated her as he had in the old days, before they'd started living together. Putting on his fiercest expression, he had brandished his club at her in a suggestive way, bringing down on himself a scornful look from the Dow Chemical representative.

Now, looking at his pitted red face, his squinting icy eyes, and malevolent grin, Rose couldn't understand how she had fallen in love with a person so redolent of American decadence. But his blue uniform, his spiky hair, the ever-rushing flow of sarcasm, had somehow overcome her defenses with a completeness and rapidity that a succession of intense, nail-biting young activists had never been able to accomplish. And they had all been correct politically.

She put her arms around his neck, the pistol resting on top of the couch.

"Be serious with me, McCann, I love you so much."

McCann put his hand inside her robe and stroked her back. "Speaking of seriousness, I ran into Comrade Howitzer tonight, editor of the *Epileptic Fit*."

"Oh, Christ, what happened?" Rose asked, nestling under his arm.

"What's a lackey to do. I saw an opportunity to grind his face and I took it."

"All right. What happened?"

"Oh," McCann said, peeling away the robe from her shoulder, "nothing much really. Howitzer was making a lot of noise and bothering some old cunt. Henry took care of it. You can't imagine how valuable it is to have a coon along when you're dealing with white radicals."

"You really like Henry. I don't know why you pretend to be such a racist."

"Did you hear the one about the old nigger who took

his black dog to the vet to get it fixed. The old coon says to the doctor, 'I wants my dog desexified,' and the doctor says, 'Brother, why not call a spayed a spayed."

"You told me that one before," Rose said, kissing his cheek. She put the gun down, opened her robe and climbed on top of him. "Don't stick me with your badge," she said.

"I do have some news to tell you. Henry and I are being assigned to new duties. I may have to go plain-clothes, so you might want to see if you can find my suit."

"You're becoming a nark," Rose cried, drawing back.

"Worse," said McCann. "We've been assigned to the new Anti-Terror Unit."

"Christ," Rose said, grabbing him by the arm. "I saw that on the news. They interviewed some Jew who's going to be in charge of it, to stop the bombing."

"He is not a Jew," McCann said. "He's just a very skinny Irishman."

CHAPTER 6

McCann's participation in the genocide had been colorful but brief. He had not asked for the Army, of course; rather, in the waning days of the lottery, the Army had asked for him.

Assigned to the Americal Division, McCann saw his only day of fighting forty-eight hours after getting off the plane at Long Binh. Following a massive, noisy, and apparently futile assault on a deserted rubber plantation, elements of McCann's division were making a lazy sweep through some grasslands and rice fields north of the Assau Valley, in a free-fire zone along the Cambodian border that by that time included most of the district.

The objective that day, as far as anybody could remember from the briefing the night before, was some nondescript hamlet lying within the arms of the approaching division. On the map, the villages were called Tango Charlie One and Tango Charlie Two; the hills commanding them were named TC-845 and TC-846; nobody knew the local names for these places and certainly nobody cared. The purpose of the assault was to confiscate, or rather, interdict, any rice or munitions found in the villages and to kill or capture anybody who looked Vietcong. To the discriminating grunts of the Amer-ical Division, a Communist affiliation was considered proved if the suspect was found in possession of an epicanthic fold.

McCann's platoon was commanded by a twenty-year-old Shake 'n' Bake second lieutenant and a typical lifer sergeant. The platoon had been momentarily diverted from the main thrust of the assault to check out a lone copse of trees across a rice field heavily scored by saturation bombing. Several gunships were already at work prepping the trees with rocket and machine-gun fire when the men turned off the dirt road and trudged down a narrow dike that passed some three hundred yards to the right of the trees. As always, the distant sound of machine guns had a lulling, reassuring effect, deepening the trance of men as yet unclimatized to the scorching heat of the Asian boondocks. A command helicopter carrying the brigade colonel circled a mile away, directing various little sideshows, including the attack on the trees.

The radioman was getting a message from the command ship.

"The colonel wants us to get off the path five hundred yards from the objective," the radioman said.

"On the right or on the left?" asked the lieutenant.

"Let's keep it open," said the sergeant. "The right side of the dike is more likely to be mined. So if we don't take any fire we might want to go off on the left. I don't think anybody's in there."

"If we get off on the left we might be enfiladed," said Shake 'n' Bake.

"That's right, Lieutenant, but I don't think we will. For the simple reason that there ain't nobody in those trees. For the simple reason that there ain't no exit route from them trees."

"How about a tunnel?"

The sergeant looked around at the surrounding miles of muddy rice fields. "Pretty wet for a tunnel."

"How about an underwater cache?"

The lifer mopped his brow with his sleeve. "Do you want to get off on the right side, Lieutenant?"

"Let's wait and see."

Strung out for fifty yards on the hard-packed dirt path atop the dike, the platoon straggled along, glum and silent, behind their officer and noncom. Dragging their feet, soaked through in the 100 degree heat, the troopers kept their eyes fixed on the ground, except when taking frequent swigs from their canteens, several of which dangled from every belt. Used to the temperate California climate, the men making up McCann's platoon felt as if all the air had been let out of their tires, as if their blood pressure had dropped to zero over zero. The heat was so enervating that every step was an effort; the mind gradually fogged and went blank; and all interest in life was sucked out of the pores. Only the veteran in the platoon bothered to glance around from time to time, as he mechanically fingered his shirt pocket for the Dexedrine he would pop into his mouth should a fire fight break out.

"Halt," shouted the sergeant. They had stopped some five hundred yards from the trees while Shake 'n' Bake and the lifer argued about something.

McCann, turning slightly away from his superiors, took a long pull from the flask of whiskey he carried in his shirt, chasing the liquor with some tepid water from his canteen. He gave the flask a shake. It was early and he had already polished off better than a pint. Heat burned alcohol right out of a man.

McCann removed his helmet, massaged his spiky red hair, wiped his brick-red brow. The climate was awful. Large, blue-eyed men were not designed for this heat. Little brown men with matchstick limbs thrived like maggots. Irish giants, no. McCann was a large man and suffered in hot weather.

"Fuck the war, right," said a blond kid next to McCann, grinning and pushing back his helmet. The kid, eighteen or nineteen, was from New York and wore a wooden peace-symbol medallion on a chain around his neck. All through training he had had arguments with people about whether war was right or wrong. At night he argued in whispers with the guy in the next bunk. He circulated copies of Fort Ord's illegal antiwar newspaper, *The Ord Deal*. He was a pest, a pain in the ass, and McCann had never spoken a word to him.

"Well, this could be it," said the kid, smiling imbecilely. "Not too late to change your mind."

"Button up, back there," shouted the sergeant.

"Just supposing there is a sniper in there," the lieutenant was saying, "he could scrag the whole platoon in one burst, if we got off on the left."

"Practically speaking, sir, it's far more likely that one of these bozos will trip a mine if we get off on the right —for the simple reason that the gooks *always* mine the far side of a dike from an obvious objective."

"The colonel wants to know what's the holdup," the radioman said.

McCann took another swallow from his flask before returning it to his shirt. He stared glumly at the clump of trees, some of which had started smoldering from the rocket attack. It was his third day in the field, two hundred and seventy-seven and a half days to go. The black smoke hung motionless in the breathless air; McCann sweated in the heat, dumbly, apathetically waiting to be told what to do. He began fumbling in his shirt pocket for his roll of Tums.

"All right, girls," shouted the sergeant, "I want you to follow me. If we take any fire, haul ass over the bank to the other side. Try to keep your heads below the embankment."

The platoon filed off the path into the muddy ditch on the left side of the dike. Their boots squished and slid as they stumbled along, bent forward. McCann, walking listlessly, tried to think. His mind had seemed stiff and unworkable all day, like an engine with its piston stuck. He couldn't follow a coherent train of thought and he had been paying absolutely no attention to what was going on around him.

Nonetheless, when the machine gun opened up on them from the trees, he acted automatically, without hesitation, bounding up the dike and tumbling into the ditch on the other side. Flat on his back in the mud, he heard the staccato bursts, the crackling of bullets overhead; he heard a squeal of pain from the other side of the path, some cursing, and then the sound of men rolling into the ditch around him.

The sergeant appeared on the path. "Get up here and fire your weapons," he yelled. Those were the sergeant's last words, for an instant later his head disintegrated in a splash of blood. Then something exploded to McCann's left and mud showered down on him. A trooper, scrambling around in the ditch, had tripped a Claymore; his uniform from knees to nipples had been torn to shreds. There was more screaming and shouting.

"Mooney's still on the other side," somebody yelled.

"Medic, medic, medic," another trooper was shouting

in behalf of the soldier who had stepped on the mine, although, of course, that hero was beyond help.

To McCann's complete astonishment, he saw that his leg was bleeding slightly; he had actually been wounded; and as he stared down in bewilderment at his leg he felt a stinging sensation, as if iodine was being poured on the cut.

"Well, I'll be Goddamned," he said aloud, taking out his flask and unscrewing the cap.

Shake 'n' Bake, his face ashen, his uniform spattered with mud, came crawling frantically along the ditch.

"McCann, Hallman, get over on the other side and get Mooney."

Mc Cann took a good-sized swallow of whiskey. "That's nonsense," he said.

The lieutenant's face went a shade whiter. "That's an order, McCann."

In reply, McCann picked up his rifle, thumbed off the safety and pointed the weapon at Shake 'n' Bake's chest. The lieutenant, on his knees in the mud, stared wildly around at his command. Nobody showed any enthusiasm for exposing himself again to the sniper. The radioman, who also had been hit by shrapnel from the mine, crawled over and tugged on the officer's sleeve.

"Don't anybody move," shouted Shake 'n' Bake, giving the one order that, temporarily at least, saved his men from mutiny.

"It's the colonel," said the radioman. "He says somebody is still alive over there." Which meant that Mooney must be flopping around as well as shrieking.

"Tell him we're pinned down," said Shake 'n' Bake, looking up at the helicopter as it went wop-wop-wopping over their position.

"He wants to know why we don't pick up our wounded."

"Tell him we're unable to do so at this time."

A certain stillness had returned to the area. True, Mooney's cries for help were still faintly audible; and the radio burbled static or, intermittently, a tiny voice; and the helicopter beat overhead. But despite these minor distractions the platoon felt sleepy and peaceful in the Asian sunshine. They lay in the mud panting, bathed in perspiration, but somehow contented, experiencing the same sense of ease and restfulness that comes over all soldiers when they take a break during a march.

McCann put aside his rifle and peeled back his ripped trousers to examine his leg. He found he had received a superficial shrapnel wound; the blood had already dried into little black beads. He settled down with his back against the dike, had a drink of whiskey, followed by a swallow of water, and basked in the sunlight.

The radioman was plucking at Shake 'n' Bake's sleeve again.

"The colonel says he's going to send in a dust-off to pick up the wounded. He says he's going to order another air attack on the objective. He says we're supposed to assault the enemy position when the gunships come in."

The men lay in the sun dozing, their eyes shaded under their helmets. Flies, thick and buzzing, had settled on the hero who had tripped the Claymore. McCann thought he looked very foolish. In the distance they heard the sound of the approaching gunships, and a minute later the sputter of Maxim guns and the thump of rockets. There was a louder racket overhead, and a giant med-evac helicopter, a huge red cross on its white flank, plumped down on the path a dozen yards from the platoon. Two medics with a stretcher hopped out and ran over to Mooney. In a minute one of the medics, a black, naked to the waist and wearing a Mets baseball cap, came over to talk with the lieutenant. The other medic took the empty stretcher back to the chopper. The medic in the Mets cap hunkered down next to Shake 'n' Bake.

"Your man bled to death, sir. We're leaving him for Graves Registration. Any of the others here hurt?"

"Me," said McCann, sitting up and raising his hand. The medic turned and with two fingers parted McCann's rent trousers. "Shit," he said, and pulling out a small-sized field dressing from his pocket, tossed it on McCann's lap. Seeing that the radioman had been hit a couple of times, he motioned him with a thumb to get in the dust-off. Then, rising and brushing some mud off his fatigue pants, he sauntered back to the ship, which immediately pulled into the sky and headed back to Long Binh.

A tiny voice came from the radio. Reluctantly, the lieutenant picked up the receiver and listened.

"Yes, sir," he said. "Yes, *sir!*"

Shake 'n' Bake carefully returned the receiver to its cradle. "That's it, men," he said brightly. "That was the colonel on the horn, and, um, he wants us to go over to the woods there and make sure that gunner is knocked out. It's kind of, um, a *formality,* really, because it's obvious that, um, nothing could have withstood that rocket attack. So, um, let's just walk over there for a look and then we can have lunch. And remember, the colonel says to remind you that today's Wednesday, pizza and beer day."

Shake 'n' Bake got up and took a few steps up the side of the bank. Nobody else got up. McCann drained the last of the whiskey and put the empty flask back inside his shirt. They all stared bleakly out at the heat shimmering on the flooded paddies. They had all noticed, too, that there was beginning to be a very bad smell in the air.

Shake 'n' Bake had been on active duty less than three months. He racked his brains but could not think of one argument for going over to the trees that made any sense. He realized, however, that he was supposed to do something to make the men move. He tried to remember what they had told him in the ROTC classes on platoon leadership. All he could remember was the precept, "Set an example." But he knew that if he was to set an example by walking over to the trees by himself, his men would continue to sit right where they were. Besides, the sergeant had set an example and now his head looked like the pulp of a rutabaga.

Obviously he had to threaten them with court-martial; it was a grave military crime to refuse to obey a lawful order in the face of the enemy. But somehow he really didn't blame the men for refusing to follow him. He didn't want to go over to the trees either; however, the colonel had ordered him to do it. A tear suddenly rolled out of Shake 'n' Bake's eye and trickled down his grimy face. He sat down again, completely at a loss. He heard the tiny voice from the radio, but this time he didn't answer.

Ten minutes later another helicopter landed on the path, several hundred yards away. A jaunty figure in starched fatigues jumped out and started for them at a brisk trot, his M-15 balanced on his hip. Looking at this figure, the lieutenant's heart sank. Several others who recognized the newcomer groaned aloud. For the man trotting toward them was none other than Sergeant Frenchfries, from brigade headquarters, a notorious character in the division, having the reputation of being the general's most valuable trouble-shooter, with an uncanny talent for persuading recalcitrant troops to go into combat.

The sergeant was a short, wiry bantam, with a hooked

nose and bulging eyes. Even at high noon in the field, he looked crisp. He strolled along the path above their heads with a springy step, as if his greatest pleasure was to promenade in front of an enemy machine-gun position when the temperature stood at 120 degrees.

When he came abreast of the platoon he looked down at the men and a surprised expression came over his face. But then his features broke into a smile, as if it was really quite a treat to see the platoon sitting at the bottom of a ditch.

"Greetings, gentlemen, I'm Sergeant McDonald, from brigade headquarters. Thought I'd drop by to see how you guys are coming along. How are you, Lieutenant?" The sergeant's alert little face took in the situation at a glance: the three mutilated heroes; the prostrate and frightened soldiers; the young officer with the tear-stained cheek.

"I believe this is Sergeant Conway up here," said Frenchfries, pointing with his toe toward the trunk of the hero who lay sprawled across the path. "Of course, I'm just guessing. I remember that Conway and I served together in Europe during War Two. I didn't know him personally but he had the reputation of being reliable."

Frenchfries was just talking to be saying something. As he spoke, he shaded his eyes and peered toward the clump of trees. Obviously, the young lieutenant had got the platoon into trouble by taking them into the ditch on the left side of the path. The enemy gunner had simply waited until the platoon drew abreast of the mined section of the ditch on the right side, fired a burst, and forced them over right on top of the mines. Frenchfries looked again at the lieutenant.

"Sir, the colonel would like to speak with you a moment. He's in the chopper." Frenchfries smiled benignly as Shake 'n' Bake clambered out of the ditch and trudged down the path toward the waiting machine.

The sergeant, meanwhile, took another look at the trees. Three hundred yards was a little far for a .30 caliber; and the Cong gunner clearly was a smart cookie, judging from the way he'd handled the platoon. If he were still there, and Frenchfries had no confidence whatever in air strikes, he would hold his fire until he had a group to shoot at.

"Frankly, the colonel is upset with you guys," Frenchfries said after Shake 'n' Bake had gone, "because you guys are holding up the overall operation. The overall operation is bigger than one clump of trees, you know." Frenchfries paced back and forth on the pathway, trying to sense what argument might appeal to the confused troopers cowering below him.

"You know, gentlemen, nobody cares about one gook more or less. If it was just one gook under a tree we'd say, 'Fuck him; leave him there.' But our mission is to interdict supplies. In plain fact, gentlemen, there's rifles and mortars over there, and we have to fish them out before nightfall, or the Cong will just move them someplace else. If we don't get those weapons today, they'll be used tomorrow to kill Americans; maybe your buddy, maybe you. You see what I'm saying? If it was just another gook we'd say, 'Fuck him,' and go about our business. But what it really is, gentlemen, is a whole company of American soldiers whose lives are being held hostage in that clump of trees. And you guys, in effect, are saying, 'Hell with 'em, I don't care, let 'em die.' You see what I'm saying?"

Frenchfries stopped his pacing and stared down at the platoon. Some of the men had sat up and were picking at the mud with their fingers.

"Now, I know. Some of you are thinking to yourselves: 'It's stupid to assault a position from three hundred yards, through a muddy field in ankle-deep water. That fucker will cut down every one of us before we get halfway there.' Let me tell you one thing. When you begin in this business, as you guys are, you tend to exaggerate the skill of the enemy. You think to yourself, I'm scared, so he must have his wits about him; you think, I'm confused, so he must have his shit together. Well, let me tell you something from thirty years' experience: that ain't the case. Ninety-nine chances out of a hundred that guy over there is dead. But say he ain't dead. You know who he is? He's some fourteen-year-old kid who learned how to fire a machine gun last Thursday afternoon. And you know what he's going to do when he sees you guys running at him? He's going to haul ass just as fast as he can go."

As he paced back and forth on the path, Frenchfries had been watching the men from the corner of his eye. Now he noticed that one of troopers, an ugly, red-faced giant, was slowly inching his hand toward his rifle. The sergeant leaped into the ditch, kicked the rifle away from the man's hand, jumped back onto the path, and resumed his pacing. The others were responding a little; all of them were sitting up now, except the ugly one.

"Besides, you guys, that grove of trees just took an awful shellacking from the fly-boys. That Charlie has been incinerated eight times over. Hey, you don't believe me? Watch this."

Making his left hand into the bird, Frenchfries bent down and starting from the tip of his boots raised it upward until it was stretched at full length over his head, accompanying the gesture with a tremendous raspberry. "How about that, motherfucker?" Frenchfries yelled at the trees. "Wait a minute. You want some more?" The sergeant unlimbered his rifle and sent a burst of fire into the trees. "How about that, cocksucker?"

Frenchfries danced around on the path, firing shot after shot into the trees. "You fucking slope, take that."

When the magazine was empty, Frenchfries quickly reloaded and came back to the edge of the path.

"You see what I mean? He ain't nothing but a little spot of grease. Now come on, let's get over there, pick up the weapons, and get out of here."

After a moment's hesitation, a few of the men started to get up when McCann said, "Why don't *you* go over there, if you want to go over there?"

Frenchfries glared down at McCann. The men who had started to get up sat down again.

"I can see now what I didn't realize before," Frenchfries said. "Some of us here are worried about our precious bodies. Now, it's one thing if a guy doesn't want to fight because he's got a problem about the rightness of the conflict. You see a lot of that these days.

"This black trooper here might say to himself: 'Why should I risk my ass fighting for gooks when there's prejudice at home?' Or somebody who's been reading the newspaper might think it's all a matter of capitalism or imperialism or forty different other kinds of isms. Now you can reason with a man who sincerely holds a different viewpoint.

"But you can't reason with a man who's only thinking about his own skin," said Frenchfries, looking straight at McCann.

"Now, you happen to be looking at a career soldier," he continued. "I've been in the U.S. Army thirty years and I don't regret one minute. It's not for everybody, I know, but it's been good to me. When I joined up things were pretty bad in the USA. I mean tough. My generation experienced hardship. None of you have ever experienced hardship. Oh, some of you may have burned your mouth on a Frenchfry, but that doesn't

61

mean you've known hardship. All your lives you've had it real easy.

"And now, when you're asked to do a little job, what do you say? 'Glad to help, it's the least I can do'; is that what you say? Your *ass*! You say, 'No thanks, buddy, I'd rather have a Coke and look at TV; I'd rather take a ride in my Ford; I'd rather go roller-skating; in fact, I'd rather do *anything* than bear arms for my country.'

"All your lives you've jammed around from parties to dances to movies, singing, 'I'm a hotrod,' and grabbing everything you could lay hands on, and not giving one fucking thing back; and then *finally* your country says, 'Look, I need a little help'; and all you can say is, 'Fuck off, I'm too busy having a good time.'"

Sergeant Frenchfries danced along the top of the bank, doing a characterization of callow youth bent on pleasure.

"Now, I know what some of you guys think. You think that because war isn't popular anymore you don't have to do anything. You say to yourselves, 'If this was War Two, sure, I'd fight; if it was the Germans or the Japs, I'd fight because everybody hated the Germans and Japs. But nobody likes war now, so why should I do anything?' Well let me tell you something from thirty years' experience: bullets kill people just the same whether the cause is just or unjust. Your daddies who went in after the Japs and Germans had to do it exactly like we do it today. What do you think happened in 1944? Do you think that when the assault boats got to the beaches of Normandy your daddy scratched his head and said, 'Gee whiz, maybe I'll feel better about this next week.' Your *ass*! Your daddy went in and did his job."

Frenchfries glared down at the men in the platoon.

"Let me ask you guys one thing. Do you really believe you can fuck up today and feel good about it when you get home? Do you really think it won't make a difference

62

to your parents and your friends? Do you really think you can get up on a platform at some college and tell the punks how you became a conscientious objector right after the shooting started? Well let me tell you this: Jane Fonda can kiss your ass from coast to coast and you'll still know in your heart you didn't act like a man.

"Sure, some of your friends might say, 'You did right not to fight,' but you know damn well what they really think. One big word is in their minds, just like it's in your minds right now. Oh, they might not say it, but they're going to think it. They're going to say to themselves, 'That man's a big chickenshit.'

"And what about your wives and girl friends. Sure, your old lady might be glad to get you back. But which one of you would *dare* tell her about what happened today? And don't be so damn sure she's going to want you back. If you can't act like a man today, what makes you think you're going to be able to act like a man with her?

"Do you see what I'm getting at? It doesn't matter what's right or wrong or upside-down and backward. You're here, you have a job. If you fail, everybody is going to know why. Nobody will ever really believe anything else. In the final analysis, you've got to do it; not for flag, or country; not for me or the Army; but for yourselves and your own feelings as men."

Frenchfries stopped pacing, rested the butt of his rifle on the ground and wiped his brow with his sleeve.

"Now," he said, "how about it?"

One after another, the men got to their feet and sheepishly fidgeted with their weapons. The only person who didn't move was McCann.

"What about you?"

"I'm wounded," McCann said.

Frenchfries, seeing the rip in McCann's trousers, bent

over for a look. The blood had long since dried on the scratch. Straightening, Frenchfries cast a quick glance at the other men, who were tentatively peering over the rim of the dike at the grove of trees.

"This is worse than it looks," Frenchfries said. "I wouldn't be surprised if the shrapnel had gone clear to the bone."

"It has," said McCann.

"Much pain?"

"I'm in agony," said McCann, without the slightest expression.

"I think you'd better stay here. The rest of you, follow me." Frenchfries and the platoon (except for McCann, Shake 'n' Bake, and the three heroes) disappeared over the rim of the bank. McCann could hear their boots splashing in the water on the other side.

Resting his back against the bank, McCann worked an emergency half pint out of his back pocket. He took several swallows, following the whiskey with a chaser from his canteen. Several minutes passed in silence except for the beating of the helicopter overhead. Then he heard the rattle of a .30 caliber machine gun. The faint sounds of shouts and curses drifted over to him. Overhead, a gunship swooped across his field of vision; he could hear the Maxim guns, the crunch of exploding rockets, the pop-pop of small arms. It went on for a few minutes, then stopped.

McCann felt almost a sense of bliss as he lay in the sunshine taking sips of whiskey. A quarter of an hour later he became aware of another helicopter hovering overhead. The machine landed and more soldiers with stretchers came running along the pathway. They were from Graves Registration, coming to collect the heroes.

"Hello there," one of them said to McCann. "You missed the fight."

"Really. What happened to my platoon?"

"They got their ass kicked."

"Did they capture any weapons?" McCann, grinning up at the soldier, tossed the empty half pint to one side.

"There ain't nothing in them trees. They can't even find the gook. How did you get hit?"

"Shrapnel," said McCann, "That guy over there tripped a mine."

The soldier looked down at McCann's Purple Heart, which was fresh and running bright red. "Gosh," he said with a grin. "That sure looks like a bayonet wound."

"That's what I said, wasn't it?" McCann scrambled up the bank and began to hobble along the path. "Mistah Dillon, Mistah Dillon. How does that look?"

"Perfect," said the soldier. "You can ride back with us if you don't mind riding with these guys." He indicated the heroes.

"I don't mind at all," McCann said. "Did Sergeant Mc-Donald get killed by any chance?"

"Ha. You got to be kidding. No such luck. I see they got one lifer up here though."

"Yeah," said McCann. "That's one good thing."

On the way back to Long Binh McCann rode with the argumentative kid from New York. The kid, of course, had nothing to say.

CHAPTER 7

Shortly after the so-called pre-monsoon counteroffensive, McCann was recuperating from his wound at Long Binh. McCann's wound actually had not been sufficient for hospitalization, but he had immediately told the doctors that he was suffering from chest pains and dizziness, and they had put him in the hospital for observation.

During this period he had the good fortune to meet the Armenian surgeon who was the major heroin outlet for the I Corps region. It was this energetic and capable physician, in fact, who arranged for McCann's assignment to the post office at Long Binh in lieu of further combat duty. In return, McCann helped the Armenian by introducing contraband into specified pieces of mail arriving from the States. It was a fortunate and well-timed meeting, because the doctors did not believe there was anything wrong with McCann's heart or any other organ. The tests were negative and the electrocardiograph machine just couldn't be fooled; and the doctors had trouble anyway in believing in McCann's ill health because he was such a large, robust-looking man. Despite all McCann's avowals, he was suspected from the start of being a malingerer.

It was during this same period, while McCann was elaborately hobbling to work holding his chest, that he came across his future partner, John Roosevelt Henry. It was at the height of the Cambodian invasion, and Henry, like many of his brothers, had volunteered for the airborne troops and had seen combat continuously with the 101st in the Mekong Delta.

A capable soldier, Henry had distinguished himself again and again, collecting more in bounties than any man in his battalion and twice winning the divisional "Zero Defects" award. Less than a month after getting his second ZD, he won the Bronze Star with clusters for (as the citation stated) "steadiness in the face of the enemy and above average utilization of firepower." His Purple Heart came with a bayonet thrust administered by a seventeen-year-old sapper one dark night during a confused skirmish with a North Vietnamese company somewhere on the perimeter of the Da Nang airfield.

It was also during this period of McCann's convalescence that the troopers of the I Corps Black Soldiers' Affinity (BSA) took up a collection to terminate w/EP a certain Major Chisholm from Camden, Arkansas, who bore the double onus of being an overt racist and an aggressive combat officer.

Somehow Henry learned of this; and although still listed in serious condition, he immediately offered himself for the purse, feeling perfectly confident after his training and experience that he could climb down from the second story of the hospital, walk a mile to officer territory with a grenade in his pajama pocket, settle with the major, and then get back safely to his bed, all without anybody being the wiser. Negotiating through an intermediary, Henry did not specify his reasons for seeking the prize money, but it might be surmised that while languishing in the hospital, his thoughts had turned to his future. After a year of outstanding service, he had collected a jug of ears, representing enemies of all ages and sexes, as well as other trinkets and souvenirs. He had satisfied some of his deepest urges. But the bounty money had disappeared in the back streets of Saigon, and thus it might be assumed that John Roosevelt Henry felt anxious about his returning to the world without so much as two pennies to rub together.

In any case, his qualifications, his good record, and above all his ready-made alibi made an impression on the BSA screening committee. His application for the bounty on Major Chisholm was approved.

To be honest, Henry, after a year of patrols and ambushes, at first had had a certain amount of professional contempt for the BSA undertaking. He assumed it would be an hour's work. He was disabused of this notion, however, on the first night he walked over to the officers' compound to visit Major Chisholm and saw the precautions taken by the racist officer, who apparently knew his faults and calculated the esteem of his colored troops accordingly. The major had posted a sentry outside his tent, a fellow Southerner who knew duty lay in keeping an eye out for spooks bearing hand grenades.

As Henry, dressed in his hospital pajamas, lay motionless in the grass outside the compound, watching the dark bulk of the sentry outside Chisholm's tent, he realized that he might have to recruit an accomplice to draw off the sentry.

68

McCann's name came up a day or two later when Henry had wondered how a brother could maintain his fifty-dollar-a-day heroin habit while confined in the hospital's detoxification center. Plum cake, the junkie said. Every week he got a plum cake from his sister. There was this giant red ofay named McCann who brought all the mail and packages for patients in the detoxification center. The mail went straight to the administration office for a thorough search before it entered the ward; but somehow that little sack of white powder was always there beneath the cake. And it was all gratis, because either the Armenian surgeon or somebody looked upon the detoxification center as a bad omen and was determined to resist it.

McCann, for his part, perked up his ears at Henry's hint of a bounty. That was because McCann had a need that very moment for venture capital. Putting capsules and hypodermic kits into cookie tins repaid the surgeon's favor of keeping him out of combat. But his participation in the war, his observation of his fellow troops and the conditions under which they lived, had aroused in McCann a feeling for the potentiality of smack. At that time, narcotics in Vietnam pretty much were held in the jealous hands of a clique of lifer sergeants in the Office of Special Services. The so-called Golden Triangle in Laos and Cambodia, of course, was fabulously rich in poppies, but, remarkable as it seems in light of later developments, at that time only a trickle of opium came into Vietnam from the Triangle, and that was primarily for native use, that is, for the use of expatriate Chinese in Saigon and Da Nang.

Most of the heroin in Vietnam then was of Turkish manufacture and came into the country from France. This state of affairs, naturally enough, made heroin expensive. But accurately sensing the coming boom, the

Armenian had put out a signal for a trade pact with General Lon Pak of the Royal Laotian Army. General Lon, of course, more or less controlled the Triangle and used the proceeds to finance the sputtering, irregular war with the Pathet Lao in the matted jungles and treacherous ravines of the Emerald Mountains.

"With the help of General Lon," the Armenian told McCann, "I'm going to found a *family*. I don't mean Corleone, either. I mean *Ken*-nedy."

With fluency in several Asian languages and with the business acumen common to his race, the Armenian surgeon opened negotiations for the smuggling of pure Double O Brand heroin, which was just then beginning to be manufactured as a sort of cottage industry in some of the larger villages across the Laotian frontier. The drug would have to be smuggled south, out of Laos, along the Ho Chi Minh Trail into Vietnam. The deal was vastly complicated and involved bribery on a titanic scale, starting with huge sums for General Lon and ending with a few piasters for the Pathet Lao guerrilla who called a temporary truce when units of the Royal Laotian Army passed into Cambodia carrying raw opium.

The Chinese, whose material aid was crucial to the continued struggle of the liberation forces, also had to be dealt with. Here, money was not as good, and the Armenian turned to ideology. Meeting with a group of incognito Chinese and North Vietnamese Army officers over a pot of herb tea in a private dining room of the Sheraton-Saigon Hotel, the Armenian cogently reminded the officers that a plentiful supply of heroin doubtless would continue to have a demoralizing effect on American troops. Answer attrition with addiction, the American said.

Raising money was another almost insurmountable problem. Most of the cash generated by the black market was controlled by the same clique of sergeants who controlled the narcotics trade. It would be suicidal to so much as hint of his plans to the sergeants, since their response would not be cooperative. Thus, the money had to be raised in the States. It was here that McCann felt he could play a role.

By establishing a Pacific beachhead for Asian heroin in San Francisco or Los Angeles, McCann told the Armenian, they could undercut the price of European smack arriving from the Atlantic seaboard. In a word, McCann was seeking the West Coast franchise, in return for which he would channel money back to the Armenian in Saigon. He would hook up with the existing distribution network, raise money on a first, relatively small shipment, then plow the profits back into the operation. The Armenian saw the sense in this, but insisted McCann front some earnest money to cover the expense of bringing in a shipment from Cambodia. The Armenian wanted five thousand dollars.

When, for no apparent reason, a strange, mean-looking coon with a stab wound in his belly had delicately suggested there was "prejudice" within the BSA against a certain field-grade officer at Long Binh, McCann's eyes opened and he had shaken off his customary lethargy. Although McCann at this time was in the habit of declaring himself a racist whose only hope was that someday all niggers would be burned on a bonfire, he nonetheless took the first opportunity to invite Henry to have a glass of milk with him at the hospital canteen.

A tortuous conversation ensued until McCann finally realized that the entire purse being offered for the officer was less than three thousand dollars. And Henry certainly was not offering an even split, meaning McCann would have something considerably under a thousand to add to the five hundred or so he had borrowed from parents foolish enough to send cash through the mail. On the other hand, McCann suggested in the second installment of this meandering parlay, if Henry would care to go partners, the Armenian in all likelihood could be persuaded to accept an offer of four thousand in cash, a sum they could probably scrape up between them. And that's what did happen: McCann and Henry struck a bargain to frag Major Chisholm for the BSA purse; and the Armenian in turn accepted an offer from the two of four thousand up front.

Now the fragging itself wasn't much by the standards of that time. It went off without a hitch, being greatly simplified by the topography of the Long Binh reservation. Long Binh was thrown up overnight by the Army Corps of Engineers in the spring of 1966 on flat, somewhat marshy ground five miles northeast of Saigon. An abandoned rubber plantation had been bulldozed for the airstrip, and all other irregularities in the sprawling base had been filled and leveled. Prefab buildings were plumped down squarely in the middle of the cleared patch: headquarters buildings, the movie theater, the various messes, the commissary, the swimming pool, the snack bar, the bowling alley, and the EM club and the Officers' Club—all had been dumped in one cluster. Some prefab barracks, however, the living quarters for headquarters' staff, had been arranged with great care to one side; and the hospital and the stockade, built a year later, had been erected half a mile to the east.

Long Binh at that time was not the major city it had once been. Mostly, it was the principal staging area for replacements arriving from the States, a truck park and a supply dump, with acres of equipment surrounded by miles of barbed wire and machine-gun posts. The troops passing through Long Binh—just then it happened to be the 23rd Infantry Division—slept under canvas, sweating by day in a landscape as dusty and barren as the Texas

Panhandle and taking their gritty meals from field kitchens. Only one hill at Long Binh had escaped the bulldozers. That hill, overlooking the central complex of buildings, was officer country, off-limits to enlisted personnel. This was the home of Major Chisholm, West Point, '60.

McCann liked to drink beer as well as other spirits, and it was therefore not unusual that on one moonless night in April he appeared at the EM Club, because he appeared there every night. He got drunk and that too was normal. What *was* unusual was that McCann that night wore a misleading uniform, the insignia being that of the 82nd Airborne, a contingent of which was also passing through Long Binh. The great majority of drinkers that night were from the 23rd, but a small knot of airborne, keeping to themselves as befits elite troops, were drinking at one end of the bar. The noise was awful, everybody yelling and laughing at once. McCann immediately joined the little group of replacements for the 82nd and somehow managed to create the impression that he had served with that badly mauled division before being wounded himself. He congratulated the soldiers on having the courage to volunteer for a fighting outfit, emphasizing the spirit of loyalty that pervaded the 82nd from top to bottom and demonstrating what he meant by buying two rounds.

Then, and this too was a little out of character, McCann announced in a booming voice that while the men of the 82nd were certainly fine fellows, on the other hand, anybody who belonged to the 23rd Infantry must be some kind of queer or pervert as far as he could tell from looking at the examples present. He followed up on this generalization by pouring a pitcher of beer over the head of the nearest member of the 23rd. And then he kicked another one in the butt. In the brawl that immediately started, McCann stepped back to give his comrades in the 82nd a better chance; and a moment later, when six or seven drunken soldiers tried to rush him, he pulled the tab on a jumbo-sized CS cannister he happened to have with him. Now, all military authorities agree, when they say anything on the subject, that tear gas is hard on anybody, but it's particularly hard on the inebriated. Several hundred men, shouting and weeping, tumbled out the door at once and continued their interrupted battles in the dust.

It became noisy so suddenly that many people thought the base was under attack. Dazed soldiers rolled out of their tents and grabbed for their rifles; jittery sentries at the outposts sent off streams of tracers into the darkness; the siren atop the headquarters building began wailing. The point of all this, however, was that the commotion diverted Major Chisholm's sentry long enough for Henry to bounce a grenade under the flap of the officer's tent. The major, disturbed by the noise, had just put his bare feet on the ground and was rubbing his eyes when the grenade rolled against the side of his cot. Only a scant ten seconds or so elapsed between the time Henry lofted the grenade and the time Major Chisholm became a hero, but it was long enough for Henry to disappear into the night.

It seems likely that the investigators of the tragedy linked the two occurrences, but it turned out to be impossible to determine who started the brawl or who threw the tear gas; for the witnesses, all from the ranks, had been drunk and were not disposed to talk anyway, since enlisted men at Long Binh, as enlisted men everywhere, felt unanimously that officers ought to be killed and rejoiced when it happened. In the end, the investigating team attributed the incident to racial unrest.

CHAPTER 8

At home in his small apartment Lieutenant Michael O'Riley, newly appointed officer-in-charge of the Anti-Terror Unit, prepared his simple evening meal: one half cup of health cereal mixed with wheat germ and covered with brown sugar, skim milk, and dried apricots. A teakettle bubbled on the two-burner convenience stove and a volume of history by Polybius lay next to the cereal bowl on the small wooden table. The lieutenant's dark face, looking more than ever in the harsh overhead light like the mummified head of Rameses II, showed nothing but sockets, lines, and ridges.

Waiting for the tea and moodily cracking a few walnuts, O'Riley experienced a sharp pang of nostalgia as he sat there, a walnut shell in his bony fingers. The walnut shell reminded him of his dead wife. Once, for their first wedding anniversary, he had sent her a note saying *"My Love is Yours Forever"* sealed inside a walnut, along with a pair of nutcrackers. "My heart must have gone dry since then," the lieutenant mused. He was prone to somber thoughts in the evening.

O'Riley presented the appropriate human figure for an apartment that was small, cramped, and Spartan. The living room, with its bare white walls, contained only an armchair, a neat writing desk, and a bookshelf overloaded with eclectic works on philosophy and history. Light was supplied by a single floor lamp with a fringed shade.

Sitting there in his little kitchen moodily crackling walnuts, O'Riley suddenly became aware that the doorbell had been ringing for almost a minute.

The lieutenant had a habit upon returning home in the evening of hanging his shoulder holster in the closet next to his coat. Despite a hatred for any kind of show, he appreciated that his new position in life had made him more conspicuous. It was for this reason that he now took the trouble of buckling on his gun before answering the door.

But it was only his old friend and next-door neighbor, Brannon of the *Examiner*.

"Hi, Iron Mike," Brannon said. "I thought I'd drop by for a quick belt."

"I have some wine."

"I brought my own," said the reporter, who knew O'Riley was practically a teetotaler, allowing himself during his rare celebrations only a thimbleful of wine at the bottom of his dinner glass.

"That's a good idea," continued Brannon, nodding toward the revolver O'Riley was returning to the closet, "You're going to have to be more careful. That bomb tonight at the Irish-American Soldiers and Sailors Hall was meant as a threat against you, you know. And if I were you, I'd take my name off the mailbox."

O'Riley lowered a tea ball into the boiling water, then sat down across from Brannon and began filling his pipe. The cereal bowl had been pushed aside.

"What's doing at the Monarch of the Dailies?"

"Oh, Christ, I had a peach this evening." Brannon leered and lit a cigarette. "An old stiff at the Argonaut Hotel on Haight Street." He briefly recounted the story told him by Deputy Coroner Keating. "You can see the pathetic situation: this guy was her only friend and she couldn't stand the thought of losing him. She'd rather watch TV with a stinking corpse." His voice broke into hoarse laughter.

"Do a piece?"

"Oh, sure, a few paragraphs. But you can never get into the paper anymore what the real story is. Nowadays, they want the guy's name and address; can't waste space on color. The last thing they want is a description of what it's really like to be in on something like that."

Brannon paused as he pulled a pint bottle out of his coat pocket. He hadn't bothered to take off his hat or his stained overcoat. His pants were much too short, and his ankles glowed luminously beneath the kitchen table. His belt cut in sharply on his narrow chest while his stomach bulged over his lap. He unscrewed the cap and poured a large dollop into the coffee mug O'Riley gave him.

"For instance, the cops that were there," Brannon continued. "Two pups playing at being hard. A black and white number; or I should say red and black, because one of them was a big red Irishman, ugly as they come. But there they were faced with a grotesque situation, and what do they do? They react by slapping on an extra coat of toughness.

"You see, Mike, although they'd sooner die than admit it, at some level that scene must have engaged their compassion. But that kind of feeling is confusing and alien to a youngster; so they swagger around and grin at each other and poke fun at this jabbering old lady.

"If I could get in the paper how they walked or the angle of their caps, then I think the reader would get the idea. But that kind of color stuff doesn't go in the newspaper anymore."

O'Riley poured out a cup of tea and put the pot back on the stove. His face was like a mask.

"I think you might be talking about my two new helpers, McCann and Henry from the Park."

"They didn't seem too bright," Brannon said.

"I don't know. They seemed to be the most intelligent of those who volunteered. I'm afraid it's not an assignment that draws the best sort. I tried to weed out the obvious misfits and sadists. Also, I thought younger men might have more rapport with the terrorist element; and the fact that it's an integrated team also influenced me. It indicates some awareness of social trends."

"I hate to say it, but I think one of them might have been drinking."

"Yes," said O'Riley, holding up a spoonful of tea to cool. "That's McCann. It's Black Cat, of course, but there are several complaints in his folder about alleged drinking on the job. On the other hand, he's an outstanding officer and a decorated combat infantryman. If he drinks occasionally, it doesn't seem to influence his work. And between you and me, Charlie, I think it might be helpful to have a man on this job who can hold his liquor; he might have to spend time in company where it would be inappropriate not to drink."

"Gee, I don't know, kid. It might be bad PR if the guy's a lush. Couldn't you find a Boy Scout?"

O'Riley's lips peeled back from his stained teeth. "There are few Boy Scouts in our pool. Some Hitler Youth, yes. No Boy Scouts. What kind of man do you think becomes a cop these days anyway? Do you think healthy, sane people become cops?"

"I know some sane cops, including present company."

"Old men, Charlie, all old men. You damned journalists —not you, but members of your tribe—you're always carping about the behavior of policemen, how their repressiveness is pushing the country toward a police state. And I admit you're partly right, because it's regrettably true that most cops are more interested in administering a taste of the club than in meting out justice. It makes it appear that our heritage of law is being trampled under for the sake of a bloody and ephemeral order.

"But what you journalists and the public fail to realize is that society today *must* have this kind of enforcement. True, people are no longer marching in the streets, the campuses are quiet, but this is merely a lull before America and the world will be plunged into a stormy period that will make the trivial upheavals of the last few years look like a joke.

"It's my belief that by the end of the decade ten per cent of the population will be out of work, money will be worthless, and the military will be running the government, while abroad the underdeveloped nations will be swept by all Four Horsemen at once. Then, literally, nothing but authoritarianism can hold the fabric of society together. Force, Charlie; minimal and intelligently applied, one hopes; but force. Why? Because there is no cohesiveness. Custom and tradition no longer have any weight. Conventional morality has lost its gravitational pull, and people feel free to do anything they want. When that situation arises, then nothing stands between chaos and anarchy but force.

"But where are the enforcement officers to come from?" O'Riley put a match to the bowl of his pipe and sucked loudly on the stem. "The truth is, we literally take anybody we can get. And since no sane, well-brought-up young man today would ever consider becoming a cop, we have to use those instruments chance and circumstance put in our hands. Sometimes, admittedly, these instruments are flawed; we have no option but to use them. When the river is rising and the dike in need of repair, we don't ask that every shovel be new and clean.

"It's pointless, Brannon, to waste time worrying about the lack of perfectability of individual policemen. Officer A drinks too much; Officer B roughs up hippies. Of course, we step in if we can; but we can't expect every patrolman to be a paragon. Paragons are in some other line of work. The essential thing is that those in command retain an overview, a feeling for history and tradition, an appreciation of the vital balance between the demands of society and the rights of the individual . . ."

"Jesus, this is a civics lecture," said Brannon, frowning and moving restively on his chair. "All I said was this guy of yours looks to me like a juicehead. Why don't you tell me something I can use?"

O'Riley's bloodless lips again revealed his teeth. "Well, let's see, do you want to hear my theory about the toilet bombings?"

"Sure."

O'Riley picked up a copy of the latest *Clenched Fist* and spread it open in front of Brannon.

"On the letters page. Read the first letter."

Brannon adjusted his glasses and looked down at the smudgy newsprint.

. . . *Sister Speaks Out* . . .

This is to correct the sexist line taken by *Fist* staff reporter Remington Rand in the last issue, in which (in the article headlined "Intensified Bombing Kayoes Enemy Targets") he stated that "all evidence thus far gathered from the bombed-out washroom in the Southern Pacific Terminal would indicate the bombing July 28 was the work of one *man*" (emphasis supplied).

Nowhere in the article does writer Rand demonstrate any inside knowledge as to the gender of the bomber(s), and it should be pointed out to him, should he prepare future articles, that there now flourish many exclusively female collectives dedicated to a revolutionary line.

The notion that every blow struck against imperialism *must* have been dealt by a male hand is an outrageously chauvinist line, especially in light of the revolutionary male's political impotence over the last decade.

Yours for smashing the state,
Gun Sisters, Inc.

After reading the letter, Brannon shrugged. "You can't make anything out of this. Everything in this rag is alike, full of bombast and innuendo."

"Listen, Brannon, this is Black Cat, of course, but I think the whole answer to the bombings is in this paper." O'Riley waved his hand at a stack of tabloids in the corner. "*The Clenched Fist,* or some publication like it, is going to lead us straight to the people we're after. Talk about a compulsion to confess!" The lieutenant made a stiff gesture with his arm. "A firecracker can't go off in Chinatown without half a dozen affinities claiming credit for it. That Gun Sisters letter is just one minor example of the alacrity with which these people will cuddle up to any violence that seems revolutionary to them.

"Now ask yourself, Brannon, why would anybody take the risks involved in bombing public facilities? Obviously, the people responsible think of themselves as heroes; they know their peers aren't doing anything except worrying about finding a job; only those who have given up everything to go underground are carrying on the struggle; hence, they regard themselves as heroes; and as heroes they share in common with all celebrities the overwhelming desire for recognition. Unconsciously at least, they demand it. And one of these days an article will appear in *The Clenched Fist* or a paper like it that points the finger right at the culprits.

"My job, Brannon, is to understand that message when it appears."

Brannon doubtfully toed the pile of papers with his scuffed brogan.

"But can you actually read this shit?" He shook his head and poured the rest of the bottle into his coffee mug.

O'Riley, as a matter of fact, had been assiduously collecting alternative press papers for several weeks, ever since learning of the new assignment. Already he had spent a dozen evenings puzzling over illiterate jeremiads and pompous expositions; he had pored over impossibly tedious political tracts, over slangy, introspective eyewitness accounts of this or that rock star's home life; over florid essays on Earth shoes, sexual improvisation, or communal nesting; he had even studied that portion of the papers devoted to utterly incomprehensible phenomena, stories of spiritual mystery, hallucination, and ecstasy.

And from his reading O'Riley could see that something might be afoot. All these papers! *The Clenched Fist, The New Dawning, The Hard Line, The Tribal Bard,* and a dozen more. Some, like PLP's *Hard Line,* were consistent throughout, every article expressing the same politically correct position.

In other papers, however, each issue was a jumble of conflicting sentiments. One issue of the *Bard* alone featured a psalm composed by a Jesus freak, a paean of beatific Christianity, which was followed by a hilarious confession on the tribulations of group marriage and a blood-drenched screed against the police, with violent death the deserved fate of pigs and their assassination the highest virtue. The *Bard* also exulted in orgiastic promiscuity and promoted unlimited drug experimentation, amid a welter of massage-parlor ads.

Some papers preached specific cures, such as the recondite *Pleasure Garden,* which damned all power- and head-trips in favor of getting it together through a new technique discovered by a liberated Beverly Hills movie executive who had pioneered a new mixture of Transcendental Meditation and gestalt therapy called Paneceavision. The *Fist,* on the other hand, was mainly political, banishing all sentiment and flaying all bourgeois indulgence in drugs, music, and art and all sensuality other than strict monogamy in the missionary position.

Concurrent with the bombings, which the *Fist,* of course, editorially applauded, there had begun to appear on its letters pages a number of anonymous letters, ostensibly composed by terrorist groups—Purple Noon, Blue-Steel Colts, Che's Revenge—that boastingly took credit for the terror and promised, like Johnny Carson, more to come. The letters were all signed, "Death to Imperialism," or "Yours for Armed Love."

O'Riley had made a careful study of these letters, searching for any telltale sign, any repetition of phrasing, that might point to a single author.

But whether the letters were written by authentic bombers, by cranks, by mischievous collegiates, or by the editorial staff of the *Fist,* O'Riley at this point was at a loss to say.

From his knowledge of literature and history, and to a degree from his police work, O'Riley knew that there is a compulsion in criminals to confess. He knew there is also a human inclination to parade in virtue. A bomber, he thus reasoned, must be dangling between the dictates of cold intellect, which counseled him to lie low, and the deeper, unconscious stirrings of guilt and glory, which pushed him toward the limelight and the gallows. For it would require nothing less than an act of self-revelation for a bomber to gain just recognition from his peers for his skill and courage in giving a hard thump to a monolithic government that through the very effective means of co-option and repression had confined most revolutionaries to college cafeterias, their hands growing more accustomed to coffee cups than to Molotov cocktails.

A hissing on the stove as the teapot overflowed brought O'Riley to his feet. He turned off the burner and sinking back on the hard wooden chair stared across the kitchen at the room's one spot of color, a map of the Roman Empire under Trajan. Brannon was still leafing through various copies in O'Riley's collection, muttering the words "unmitigated garbage" from time to time.

"This kind of thing repeats itself in history," O'Riley said, holding up a copy of the *Pleasure Garden*. "There's a return to mysticism and superstition when life, government, society, become too large, too complex, and when the individual is swamped and overwhelmed; then there's a groping toward the supernatural for meaning, a quest for idealized purity, which our callow young today believe might be found in the arms of Eastern religion or beneath the banner of some fantastic brand of Pepsi communism."

"Sure, kid," Brannon said, draining his cup. "A jerk is a jerk whether he sports a hair shirt or a bandoleer."

"When the individual is smothered, he struggles to throw off the blanket," O'Riley said. "Would you care to try some of the wine?"

84

"No, no, no," said Brannon, staring down at his empty coffee mug.

"We are dealing with some very exotic blossoms. We have a spiritual revival hand in hand with incipient anarchy, and a cult of terrorism coupled with growing street crime that is increasingly hard to distinguish from political disorder."

O'Riley's dark eye gleamed as he gazed at the map on the wall. Did he resemble a Roman administrator, confronted with the ragged superstitious bands of political criminals calling themselves Christians? No matter. Regardless how much the future might criticize the short-sightedness of the present, the present had to act according to its best lights. The American procurator could only try his best to balance freedom and order, realizing always that imperfection is inevitable. He must recognize the importance of encouraging different styles along with the equally important task of pruning them. He must recognize that it was not a bad thing to have revolutionaries as long as there was no revolution, good to have fascists without fascism, good to have all stripes, because unwittingly they contributed to balance. Yes, but just try proposing to a beat cop that occasional irruptions of indignation were good, just as it was good to suppress these irruptions with minimal force, so as not to kill the bud entirely. There, that was the nub: to keep a firm reign on the ranks and a feeling for the mean at headquarters.

Brannon had got to his feet and was attempting to force the empty pint back into his pocket.

"If I don't carry a bottle there, I walk with a thirty-degree list," he said.

"I can make you some soup, if you're hungry."

"Fuck no, I don't want any part of your puny diet, Marcus. I want the big steak and the baked potato and the sour cream and six or seven gin and tonics. How am I ever going to live up to tradition and be found slumped over my typewriter if I start getting healthy? A few drinks, a few laughs, a quick jolt, and darkness. And none of your fucking philosophy. I'll see you at your dinner if you can get along without any dumb press conferences until then."

O'Riley got up and accompanied his friend as he lurched toward the door.

"Be careful," O'Riley said.

Examiner, August 2, Section B, Page 18.

MAN INJURED IN HAIGHT BLAZE

A Haight-Ashbury resident narrowly escaped death last night in a smoky two-alarm fire that raced through an apartment at 645 Cole St.

Clarence Thomas, 20, was treated at San Francisco General Hospital for second-degree burns and smoke inhalation after a fire raced through his second-story apartment.

Park Station police officers William McCann and J. R. Henry were credited with carrying the unconscious Thomas to safety after finding him lying on a burning mattress. The two patrolmen were investigating a disturbance at the address when they smelled smoke, according to police reports.

Officer McCann said a neighbor had complained about the noise made by a car radio. "In a way, it's a good thing it was noisy or a man might have burned to death," McCann said.

Fire Lieutenant Maurice Esposito said 25 men and 4 pieces of equipment responded to the blaze. Esposito speculated that Thomas may have been smoking in bed.

CHAPTER 9

Henry's illness had complicated everything. It was true that the war had held them together for a time; but now, back in the real world, he was undergoing a full-blown schizophrenic break. In such cases, of course, it's impossible to know exactly when it started or how it happened, but shortly after being mustered out of the Army, Henry realized his life was not his own. His life, instead, was in the hands of a demonic cabal whose members persecuted him night and day. They were a group of noisy, rude, watchful, omniscient imps, possessing strange ventriloquistic powers, for they could project their voices out of Henry's mouth. Largely, it seemed the work of one devil, a big, powerfully built middle-aged man who wore a derby hat and smoked a cigar. But others were involved.

Henry could see them. They were sitting around a

card table in a smoky room, drinking boisterously as they played stud poker, slapjack and crazy eights. There was a constant bubble of talk and laughter and the sound of cards being shuffled and dealt. But there was only one topic of conversation and that was Henry. The cardplayers were always talking about him behind their hands. They laughed at him, ridiculed his movements, abused him in the vilest language. Henry, however, refused to say, even to McCann, what the gamblers said. But it was more than just ridicule, for frequently one of the players would turn on Henry and tell him he had to die. And the words came out of Henry's mouth.

It might happen, for instance, that the big man in the derby would turn over a card, perhaps the eight of spades and say "eight"; and the word "hate" would come out of Henry's mouth. Or the man might turn over a diamond flush and say "diamonds," while the word "die" would explode from Henry's lips. It was the big man's voice that issued most frequently from Henry's mouth.

Although this cabal tormented Henry night and day, it was not fully in possession. Sometimes the cardplayers were not at the table, and Henry assumed they were out mingling with other society. But they always came back somehow; Henry thought through the tap water, or perhaps through the electricity in the lamp. It was Henry's belief that he could exterminate these people if he could just catch them outside his body, while, say, they were taking a walk, or tormenting another victim, or getting their shoes shined, or something like that.

The emergence of this demonic activity did not surprise McCann. He had already guessed that Henry was unstable. It was understandable that blacks should be a little unstable after three hundred years of oppression, or four hundred, or whatever it was. Nevertheless, the demonic uprising had made things more difficult, because Henry might break into a chorus of, "Jack, Jack, die, die, die," at any moment. In fact, Henry almost had not been accepted by the police department because of some of these peculiarities. And this, coupled with his inability to read or write, had put his future with the department in jeopardy for several weeks.

Fortunately, there was the affirmative-action program. Henry got twenty points for being a minority. Then he got another ten points for being able to press his weight, and another twenty points for his service with the Army. That was the necessary fifty points right there.

McCann, of course, had easily won appointment to the police academy, because he had had the foresight to pay a clerk at Long Binh a hundred and fifty dollars to alter his military records. Instead of reflecting two years of drunkenness and malingering, they showed a commendable history of military accomplishment, including two Purple Hearts and the Bronze Star, the last borrowed from a hero who had been recommended for the honor posthumously.

After the police academy, where McCann did the work for both of them, it had been easy to get assigned together to the Haight-Ashbury. The Haight wasn't an assignment many officers wanted, because the people there had a dislike for police that they frequently acted upon. But McCann wanted the Haight because with so much violence and crime in that district the police were allowed to do as they pleased. And that, after all, was the reason they were cops, so that they could do anything, with immunity from the law. The police, McCann realized, had all the freedom denied other citizens. McCann and Henry didn't want to be molested during their efforts to find a buyer for their shipment of heroin.

If this first step was easy, the next step was more ticklish. They had to recruit a confederate in the coroner's office. To do this, McCann employed what he considered a good trick. Everybody knows that in police work officers occasionally stumble upon stolen goods. It is also pretty well known that not all recovered items find their way to the property room in the Hall of Justice. Thus a valuable necklace recovered from a burglary might wind up adorning the neck of Sergeant So-and-so's wife, although, practically speaking, it would be much more likely to turn up around the neck of some other woman. In any case, one such item that resisted a return journey to its rightful owner was an expensive gold wrist watch. McCann kept the watch for several weeks, waiting for the right opportunity, which came one morning when he and Henry discovered the body of a derelict curled in an alleyway.

McCann slipped the wrist watch on the corpse's wrist, pushing it high up the forearm under the soiled cuff. Later, checking the deceased's effects at the Hall, he found they included a hotel key, a Medi-Cal card, and thirty-five cents in change. No wrist watch. McCann learned that the body had been handled by Deputy Coroner Jerold Keating.

Keating was a squat, timid-looking little man with a toothbrush mustache and a seedy uniform several sizes too large, making him look like a conductor on the Penn Central. His natural timidity was overshadowed by almost boundless greed, and his cowardice consequently bowed to every temptation. Corrupt yet timid, he was exactly right, although McCann had known from the start that finding an amenable accomplice in the lower echelons of the city bureaucracy would be about as difficult as forcing a campaign contribution on an assemblyman. The deputy coroner, of course, was more than glad to become part of McCann's scheme to smuggle heroin into the country.

Usually when a soldier is killed in Southeast Asia the body is flown to Travis Air Force Base, across the bay from San Francisco. Then the hero is trucked to San Francisco International and moved by commercial air-lines to wherever the family wishes to take receipt. But it happens from time to time that a soldier dies who has no next of kin. In these rare cases, the body is taken to the San Francisco morgue in the basement of the Hall of Justice, where it is stored for a few weeks just in case a relative shows up.

If not, then on some slow afternoon at Golden Gate National Cemetery, it's the flag-draped caisson, the bugler, and the burst of rifle fire. This simple and dignified ceremony, so preferable in every way to the vulgar caravans put together by neighborhood under-takers, ought to be the rule rather than the exception, particularly since the family of the sort of person who gets himself killed in Southeast Asia usually would be more than pleased with a free plot in a national cemetery.

In any case, after the appropriate arrangements had been made in San Francisco, the Armenian surgeon would see to it that the next unclaimed hero going home via Travis would carry in his stomach cavity a load of Laotian Double O Brand heroin of the finest quality. Then, in the gray hours of some dogwatch at the morgue, McCann and Keating would perform a quick Caesarean.

That, at least, was the plan.

With the death of Smith, McCann had delivered evidence of his good faith to the shadowy powers in San Francisco. Serious negotiations could begin.

CHAPTER 10

A picnic had been Rose's idea and it had taken tenacity of purpose amounting to fixation to convince McCann that he ought to forsake his usual holiday, a leisurely slide into oblivion over a couple of newspapers, for what seemed to him the most desperate kind of catering to popular taste.

"Can't you see, Rose," McCann kept saying, "they'd love that, the international banks and cartels. They'd love lulling us into forgetting the real enemy. That's why the cartels *have* parks, Rose, and movies and ball games and franchise restaurants. You've got to resist sentimental propaganda."

But it was no good. Despite McCann's sound, albeit mocking, analysis of the motives of global financiers in encouraging mass opiates, and despite her own strict principles informed by a wakeful intellect, Rose in truth possessed a heart that mutinously ached for gondolas gliding in the moonlight, for taxis speeding to some secret rendezvous, for hansom cabs clattering over cobblestones. Even a hayride and a few folk songs wouldn't be too bad. In a word, she was determined that her romance would have some of the trappings guaranteed by *Cosmopolitan* Magazine, and she refused to allow McCann's mock-pious moralizing on the duties of a revolutionary to balk her design.

To get her picnic she campaigned like the Duke of Parma in Holland, and in the end she carried the day.

Not only did Rose wrest from McCann his promise to take her picnicking, but, more importantly, she extracted from him his solemn oath that while he was with her in the park he would not foment any trouble or untoward incident or uncomfortable situations like those that had blighted their outings in the past. She demanded scrupulous behavior, with every word and act in conformity with good manners and pretty much in character with what other people were doing in the park, that is, strolling hand-in-hand, visiting museums and commenting on the exhibits in a low voice, urinating in the intended facility, and so forth. There would be no clowning, buffoonery, or embarrassing scenes with strangers; there would be none of the drunkenness that in the past had given Rose second thoughts about ever venturing out-of-doors with McCann again.

"Do you *promise*?"

"I promise."

"I want you to pledge your sacred honor bright."

"Okay, all that."

"Can I trust you?"

"Of course, Rose."

When Sunday came, she packed a basket of cold

chicken, along with a loaf of fresh bread, wine, and pastry. She wore her most becoming outfit, a close-fitting dress of red velvet, over which she wore a light cape with a hood.

For his part, McCann wore an old overcoat, ragged sweater, slacks, and his revolver. Despite the incongruity of their appearance, the hulking, red-faced McCann next to the dusky, petite Rose, or perhaps because of Rose's red dress and the wicker basket under her arm, the two of them might have been viewed, from a distance, as an attractive young couple as they entered the park at Lincoln and Ninth Avenue and sauntered toward Big Rec baseball diamond, where the employees of a car-rental agency were challenging a storage-company team.

"I know a hell of a lot about baseball," McCann said. He was leaning against the iron rail above the bleachers, an unfinished half pint of bourbon in one hand. "I size up a player just by looking. For instance, the man at bat . . . wait a minute, it's coming to me now . . . yes, he's definitely a weenie. I bet he strikes out."

The pitcher unwound, the bat cracked and the batter laid down a neat double.

"What did I tell you," McCann said.

As a result of the ceaseless dews and damps of August, Golden Gate Park this Sunday was as lush, green, and chill as a head of lettuce in the supermarket. Wisps of fog still clung to the trees, and a low gray overcast rolled in from the sea.

It all *looked* pretty, McCann reflected as they walked through the eucalyptus, but it was really a sham park, built by a madman greengrocer out of sand dunes. And now it had become sort of a continental isthmus, artificially postponing and thwarting God's obvious intent, the inevitable intermingling of the two great seas of single-

94

family dwellings lapping on either side, the rolling Sunset and the wine-dark Ingleside.

As usual for a Sunday, the park was overpopulated. If they had waited a day, they would not have encountered a soul, except maybe some high school miler jogging past two freaks with a frisbee. But on Sundays everybody seemed to wind up in the park. The throng had caused the city administration, once again capitulating to whim and fad, to close all the park entrances to auto traffic on Sunday, a lick-spittle act but of protean consequences, in that it instantly engendered clouds of bicyclists (all trailing balloons or triangular orange flags) who floated all day up and down Kennedy Drive attended on by a symposium of yapping mongrels.

Family life was strident and abundant and in evidence everywhere. Big families prevailed; lots of Italians, and Irish and Chinese, gathered in planetary array around a barbeque, the master reclining in a lawn chair swilling a cold one, while at his elbow his lady fenced with rubbery little doggies steaming in a pan; a few paces away infant satellites orbited erratically over God-knows-what filth; and, more distant from their sire than Pluto from the sun, a couple of cryptic teen-agers lazily tossed a ball and yawned.

On this fecund Sunday of self-satisfied toddlers cruising in perambulators, there must have been just enough watery sunshine to stir the yeast in unvintaged blood, for the lovers were on parade, promenading by the hundreds; and while the odds were really against it, it did seem that every couple boasted a handsome man in his ski sweater to complement the pert girl in her knit cap. Fingers intertwined, they nuzzled, smiled for no reason, and watched their bicycle-borne opposite numbers flash past in double blurs.

Some of the lovers had thrown plaid blankets on the

grass and were lying side by side with wan faces tilted skyward; others covertly embraced under dripping trees, or sat close together on the green benches facing the band shell, or went rowing in tiny boats over the placid, cloud-dappled waters of Stow Lake, trailing a hand behind or leaning languidly across the gunwales to catch their own rippling reflections pacing them as the boat coasted in silence and solitude along a verdant shore.

"I hate that sort of crap," McCann said.

He had abruptly halted Rose in midstride and was glaring at the scene before him.

It was a yellow 1963 Chevy with the curb door open. Two speakers set out on the grass were connected by wires to a tape deck under the dash. Music, repetitive and poorly reproduced, assaulted the passers-by.

"Get on up, ah, ah, I said, get on up . . ."

By the car were three hoodlums somewhat beyond high school age. Two of them lounged on the grass working on beers while the third, apparently the vehicle's owner, polished the right front fender with a rag.

It was one of those cars, McCann realized, that a man put his soul into. He tinkered with the car, pampered it, refined it; until finally, in a way, he was the car and the car was him. In this case, the owner had improved the looks of his heart's delight with the help of a lot of decals; red flames leaped back from the hood, lightning bolts crackled on the doors, a black Maltese cross topped the trunk, and on the rear fender, in gothic lettering, were the words, "Gas Rhonda."

McCann stopped, thumbs hooked in the pockets of his overcoat, grinning happily at the tableau of car and punks, noting that, as far as he was concerned, the three of them were just about right in greasy looks and insolent deportment to deserve being present on the eve of Judgment Day, having as they did sallow faces, lank hair, dirty, broken fingernails, and identical blue wind-breakers. McCann could tell these guys had not so much dropped out as been thrown out, and their hopes for the future pretty much narrowed down to a career choice between the Army or the Marines.

"Come on," whispered Rose, tugging at his sleeve.

McCann shook his head. Displeasing as it might be to Rose, he was in no mood to hurry. He wished to contemplate this at his leisure. After all, he had had his usual breakfast of eggs, steak, pancakes, and a pitcher of screwdrivers. He had fortified himself against the weather with several brandies; and lately, to keep his spirits from dropping, he had been nipping some bourbon.

Consequently, despite the narrow and secular mission that had driven him to the park, that is, a picnic with Rose, the Jewish sentimentalist, he found he was not now disposed to forgo the pleasure of a little company.

The two youths on the ground were taking advantage of their position to examine Rose's legs as she stood fidgeting with the picnic basket. And in another moment Gas Rhonda's owner, sensing that he had attracted attention to himself again, carefully turned his head to pose a question that a school psychologist might say neatly summarized by implication Gas Rhonda's attitude toward the attentions of the larger world.

"Hey, ah, yagazum kind of problem?"

"Hi, guys," said McCann, smiling benignly, "I sure hope you fellows don't mind if I just stand here a minute while I'm admiring your swell car. It's a hell of a car; well-maintained, clean, all the extras, radio and heater, power, air, mag wheels, fuel injection, not to mention the traction and steerability of disk brakes and wide-tracks. . . . Say, I was just wondering, would you guys mind if I went around and kicked the tires?"

Gas Rhonda dropped his rag on the fender and turned

fully around. First, he nodded his head at his companions; he could have been Paul Newman, incredulous over some idiot's blunder. Then he quickly folded his arms and squinted; here, he was obviously Clint Eastwood in an Italian western.

"If I was you, my man, I wouldn't mess with *this* car."

"Just kick the tires," McCann said.

"Hey, my man, I told you no. You go kick somebody else's tires. Or if you don't like that, why don't you kick a tree with your head?"

"Ha, ha, ha," said the kids on the ground.

"Listen, you don't understand," McCann said, "I'm not just *looking*. I'm in a buying mood."

"McCann!" Rose said under her breath. "You *promised* me. I don't want you to talk to these guys."

"Not talk to them?" said McCann, looking at her as if he couldn't believe his ears. What do you mean? I just want to know what this bozo here wants for his car."

"Are you calling *me* a bozo?" Gas Rhonda said, his eyes opening in disbelief.

"Well," McCann said, "if the clown suit fits, you might as well wear it."

"McCann," Rose said, "please don't get into a fight with these guys."

"Fight?" said McCann. "There won't be any fight. All we have here is a harmless bozo and two bimbos."

The kids on the ground, now characterized by McCann as bimbos, painstakingly got to their feet, looked at each other as if they were getting their signals straight, and began examining the grease under their fingernails. At the same time, Gas Rhonda went around to the driver's side and got a tire iron from beneath the seat.

McCann hunched his shoulders, dropped his arms and planted his feet apart. "I'm Matt Dillon at the start of *Gunsmoke*," he told Rose.

"Don't, McCann."

Gas Rhonda came back around to the curb, lightly slapping the tire iron against his palm.

"Hey, my man. If you got any smarts at all, you're going to back away from this. Like, now."

"And if you've got any smarts, Bozo, you're going to *trade* in that turd of yours," McCann said. "At *night*."

"Okay, asshole," said Gas Rhonda. He and the other two had taken a step forward when McCann suddenly threw up his hands and shouted, *"Wait a minute!"*

"This is no way to settle anything," McCann continued, "What we need here is an unbiased outside opinion."

With that, McCann bounded down the sidewalk and grabbed a young man who happened to be passing with his girl friend. McCann or anybody would have described this newcomer loosely as a hippie type, in that he had long hair tied in a ponytail, wore a beard, a pair of patched and carefully faded Levis and an earring, smelled of incense, and was indistinguishable from a million other kids in San Francisco.

He was also a little startled when grabbed from behind for no reason, but this was nothing compared with his discomfiture when he found himself placed between his captor and an obvious hoodlum brandishing a tire iron.

"This is weird," said the hippie.

"We just want your opinion," said McCann, raising his voice to make himself heard over the shouts for help coming from the hippie's girl friend, "When a person is trying to unload a car on you, do you or do you not have the right to kick the tires.

"You tell me," McCann went on. "Does this *Bozo* have any right selling me a turd in a poke?"

"I can sense your anger," said the hippie.

"Motherfucker," said Gas Rhonda, raising the tire iron.

"But I can dig where this dude is coming from."

"Oh, that's right, that's right," McCann said bitterly, addressing the crowd that was beginning to form around the Chevy, "Don't get involved. Sure, my friend and I are about to be assaulted . . . but that's no concern of yours."

The screams from the hippie's girl friend at last attracted help in the person of a mounted policeman, who now came cantering over to see what the fuss was about. With his arrival things subsided, the girl stopped screaming, Gas Rhonda lowered the tire iron, and McCann released his captive.

The cop was the jovial sort of Irishman the department likes to put in the park, a man of middle years, of even disposition who saw the futility of being too hard-nosed, a man with a reassuring paunch and full cheeks covered with a fine mesh of exploded blood vessels.

"And now then," said the cop, smiling down on the group from astride his chestnut gelding.

"Now, that's horseflesh," said McCann appreciatively, slapping the gelding on the flank. And when nobody seemed willing to take the lead, McCann went on to say that, coincidentally, he too was a police officer.

"Are we now," said the cop, bending down in the saddle to look at McCann's badge.

"Yes, and I regret to say you've kind of blown my cover. I'm working out of NARCOTICS, and we've had some of these people here under surveillance for quite a while."

For some reason the crowd, composed mostly of young people, began to thin out with remarkable rapidity.

"Oh, Jesus," said Gas Rhonda.

"Hey, wait a minute," said the hippie's girl friend. "Even if you are a cop you can't go grabbing somebody off the street."

"I apologize for a case of mistaken identity," McCann

100

said. "I wouldn't blame your friend in the least if he wanted to come to the station and make out. Say, what's that in your pocket?"

"Nothing," said the hippie, who had automatically put a telltale hand to his coat and then instantly realized his mistake.

"Of course, as a formality we'd have to run his name through the computer for parking tags and so on, but . . ."

"There's been no harm done," said the hippie. And when his girl friend got the picture she shut up too.

After surveying the tranquil scene before him, the mounted cop said: "A word with you, Officer McCann."

McCann obediently walked alongside the horse for a few paces.

"Sure now, all's well that ends well," he said, beaming down from the saddle.

"Praise be for that," McCann said.

"But you'll not be thinkin' me hard if I say you've supped a wee much today."

"Sure, 'tis a harsh world and few the pleasures."

"And isn't it the truth. But I'm thinkin', Officer McCann, that it may do to slacken up a bit."

"Sure, an' I'm thinkin' you're right."

The policeman smiled, touched his cap, clicked his tongue, and the chestnut clip-clopped away down the path.

"Phony-baloney mick," McCann said to himself as he waved good-by to Gas Rhonda.

At noon Rose and McCann found themselves strolling along the footpath by Stow Lake. They stopped at the concession stand to buy a red-striped bag of peanuts, then sat on a bench to watch the traffic along the shore. On closer inspection, the couples resolved themselves into the hodgepodge of human types that reason would expect: sailors and fat girls, paunchy clerks and dowdy wives, acne high-schoolers reeking of potato chips, and every once in a while a healthy, tailored couple taking a democratic stroll when they could just as well have been on some verandah in Sausalito. Up close all they had in common was a sort of peaceful radiance brought on probably by light exercise, scenery, and companionship.

McCann, eyeing these innocent pedestrians along the pond, felt his own blood turn poisonous with murderous impulses. With difficulty, he mastered an almost irresistible desire to run up and kick one of the strollers in his complacent behind. Instead, he drank more whiskey and listened to Rose prattle on.

"McCann, admit it," she said. "This is a lot better than sitting at home. Why can't we do this more, why don't you ever want to take me anywhere? You see those two at the concession stand, how happy they look. Why can't we be like that? I mean, we *are* like that, except you never say you love me unless I hold the gun on you, and I think it should be more spontaneous. I was telling Professor Haines about you (you know, the one who conducts my advanced social psych seminar), and he was saying that Fenichel says in the *Psychoanalytic Theory of Neurosis* that spontaneity can only be the result . . . Oh, McCann, look at the duckies!"

A flotilla of grimy ducks had rounded an island of reeds and was cruising along the shoreline toward the bench occupied by McCann and Rose. Opening the hamper, Rose went rummaging after the bread, to tear off a few treats for the duckies.

McCann looked at the ducks, at the happy couples, at the children; he looked at Rose, so attractive in her red dress with her shapely legs crossed under the bench and her jet-black hair falling over the hamper as she tore up bits of bread. He felt so profoundly depressed

102

and bored that he seriously doubted whiskey would do much, although all he could do was try.

"Help me feed the ducks," said Rose.

"No," said McCann. "It will just make me more depressed."

The very thought of getting up and throwing bread to ducks made his whole body ache with boredom. "We've had enough fun in the park, Rose. Let's go home. Let's get out of here."

"What about our picnic lunch?" said Rose, biting her lip.

"Well, why not throw the whole goddamned thing to the ducks. I just want to get out of here."

Rose's lip quivered and she started to cry. "I've had enough of you, McCann," she said quietly, trying to stop the tears.

"Why don't you cool it."

"I'm *not* going to cool it," Rose said, her voice rising and getting high-pitched. "You're a selfish, self-centered, egotistical asshole who only thinks about himself. Doctor Haines was right about you; you're so *consumed* with yourself that you're the only real thing in the world; everybody else is made out of cardboard . . ."

Rose got up, took a few steps, and faced him. Her face was contorted and she was sobbing and wiping at her tears with trembling fingers. Several people at the concession stand had turned to stare.

McCann jumped up, grabbed her roughly by the shoulders, and shook her hard.

"I don't *care* what Jesus told you," McCann shouted. "I don't *care* that He told you to renounce the world and your family and live in a commune. I'm taking you home to your parents in Topeka."

"Oh, fuck off, McCann," Rose screamed, trying to struggle free.

"It's my duty to restore this girl to her family," McCann

told the people in line at the concession stand. "She's been bamboozled by a religious charlatan."

"Admit it," he said, turning back to Rose. "You are *not* the Virgin."

"Fuck you, McCann, you fucking bastard motherfucker creep asshole. All I wanted was a fucking picnic."

"She thinks she's the Virgin Mary," McCann explained to the onlookers. "We're going to reprogram her for a normal life."

"I'm through with you, McCann," Rose screamed. "You're a heartless, insensitive son-of-a-bitch without one spark of decent feeling. I hate your disgusting, pus-filled guts, and I only hope to God one day you're tortured one-tenth as much as you've tortured me, you rotten dirty cocksucker . . ."

"Please don't fence with me," McCann said.

"Get the *fuck* out of my life! I've had it up to here with you . . ."

"She exaggerates," McCann said modestly.

". . . and I don't ever want to see your goddamned ugly face again, so just take a fucking *hike*, buster, because from now on I'm doing what *I* want, and if you don't like it, you can just take a fucking flying jump at the moon."

With the tears wetting her dusky cheeks, Rose wobbled over to the shoreline and began throwing bits of bread to the ducks. She had turned her back on McCann, and although her shoulders heaved spasmodically, she was obviously trying her best to control her feelings, despite an occasional muffled sob.

"She's upset," McCann told the puzzled little group clustered around the concession stand. "It'll probably help if I talk to her."

But before he could reach Rose a man rushed between them.

"I'm sorry," he said, "but I can't allow this to continue."

In appearance the newcomer seemed a most unlikely knight-errant, being small of build, thin, and dressed in an enormous Army-surplus greatcoat that fell to his shoes. He had sparse damp hair atop a colorless pinched face. Although the man was trembling slightly, either from fear or anger, and seemed the victim of some inner turmoil, he resolutely stood his ground even as McCann loomed over him.

"I wouldn't interfere," McCann said. "This woman is capable of anything."

"It can't be helped," said the man. "This has got to stop."

"I guess you think I ought to leave her alone. Well, if you only knew . . ."

"Oh, I don't care about that," said the man. "But she's got to realize she mustn't feed the ducks."

With that, the man threw open his coat to reveal a large round button the size of an ashtray that read, "I Love Ducks."

"It's bad for them," the man explained. "That bread is full of sugar and chemical additives that can be dangerous for a duck. Not only that, but they're alarmingly overfed on weekends by all sorts of careless people who haven't the faintest conception of duck metabolism."

As it was, however, the ducks displayed not the slightest interest in the bread tidbits being lobbed at them by Rose. In fact, they evinced a kind of revulsion, the mere sight of the floating bread causing them to swing around on their keels and swim sluggishly away. It was then that McCann noticed that the entire shoreline along the artificial lake was encrusted with a layer of soggy bread. The harder Rose threw, the faster the ducks accelerated their retreat.

"Fucking ducks," Rose shouted. "Eat the goddamned bread."

"Ducks in a park are prey to a host of diseases and

complaints unknown to them in their natural habitat," the duck man said. "I've tried time and again to explain this to the Rec and Park Commission but they're deaf to humane considerations. There should be a buffer, a *cordon sanitaire,* if you will, between the ducks and the public.

"People feed them all sorts of trash, pop-tops, pennies, condoms. . . . In a way, I feel I'm their spokesman . . ."

"Do you talk to the ducks?" McCann asked on a hunch.

"Yes, I do," said the man. "Quack-quack. Quack-quack-quack."

"Quack," said one of the ducks.

"You don't seem to understand," McCann said. "These *ducks,* as you call them, have been unforgivably rude to my girl friend. I don't think I can let that go by."

"You must forgive them," the duck man said primly.

"No, I've been pushed too far."

In the next instant and practically under the duck man's nose McCann's 357 Colt went off with an ear-splitting roar, and down-pond, in the midst of a thirty-inch column of water, a duck disintegrated in an explosion of feathers.

"*What are you doing?*" screamed the duck man.

"Oh, McCann," Rose said. "You don't have to do this."

"Your reputation as a hostess will not be dragged through the mire," McCann said as he cocked the revolver and fired again; once more a deafening report, once more the air was filled with feathers. Panicked but too bloated to fly, the ducks had broken formation and were scattering at captain's discretion.

McCann was sighting a third target when the duck man lunged, colliding with more force than McCann had thought possible and flailing with one arm at the pistol. With all the strength of hysteria, the little duck man grappled with McCann on the lip of the pond as the policeman vainly tried to draw a bead on one of the rapidly escaping birds.

"*Criminal,*" shrieked the duck man.

"Death to all ducks," McCann panted, but with those words the duck man hooked his leg behind McCann's, gave a tremendous push, and toppled them both into the pond. McCann came up sputtering through a veneer of green scum and soggy bread.

The duck man, meanwhile, was wading out to see if anything was left of the victims.

"Dust on the sea," McCann shouted after him.

At the sound of the first gunshot the onlookers near the concession stand had disappeared; only the white paper hat of the concessionaire could be seen peeping over the counter, behind the candy bars and gum. Rose stood alone on the shore, arms akimbo, looking down as McCann, standing knee-deep in scum, returned his gun to its holster.

"That was wonderful," Rose said, laughing. "My honor will always be safe with you around."

"I was thinking," McCann said. "Maybe we *should* run along. If it's okay with you."

As the two of them hurried away toward Lincoln Drive, the little duck man, still in the middle of the pond, was busy gathering up a few stray feathers belonging to his lamented friends.

"*Criminal!*" he shouted after McCann.

Back at their apartment McCann stripped off his wet clothes, smelling of phlegm and frog juice, showered, changed, poured a mammoth whiskey, and then joined Rose in bed, where she was laying out the picnic lunch.

Sitting cross-legged on the counterpane, a napkin tucked in the top of her bodice, a glass of wine in one hand, a chicken wing in the other, Rose was discussing their relationship.

"Other people are reasonable," she was saying. "A picnic in the park presupposes certain modes of behavior. You walk together, hold hands, joke awhile, talk seriously awhile, sit on the grass, smooch a little bit, see the paintings, take in some of the concert. That's Sunday in the park for most people. But you can't do that, McCann. If I were shacking with Professor Haines instead of you —he's let me know he wouldn't mind that arrangement— that's what *we* would have done today. Haines enjoys my company, he enjoys my conversation, he thinks I'm intelligent, he *listens* to what I have to say, and he *appreciates* that I know something about the history and development of social psychology.

"In other words, McCann, he *talks* to me, takes an interest in *me*. When you go someplace with Haines you don't have to worry; there aren't going to be scenes with every jerk that comes down the path. You go to dinner with Haines and he's not going to insult the waiter and dump spaghetti on his shoes like you did at Romano's . . ."

"I know a booger on a spoon when I see one," McCann said.

". . . he's not going to piss in his popcorn box at the movie so he won't miss the cartoon; he's not going to get in an argument at *every* bar he goes in; and he *certainly* isn't going to come home sloshed to the gills every night of the week. Now, really, McCann, why don't you eat some of the chicken? I made it for you, and you haven't had anything to eat since breakfast."

McCann uncorked the wine bottle and took four or five long swallows. "You know I care about you, Rose. Feel this."

"And that's another thing. I imagine that Haines has

a more complex and sophisticated attitude toward fore-play than, 'Feel this.' "

"It all amounts to the same thing," McCann said, beginning to feel weary despite the wine.

"It's *not* the same thing. Haines would be gentle, careful, considerate; if he wanted something, he'd know how to ask."

" 'Suck my freckles' is not good enough, huh?"

"You know I don't mind doing it, but I think you could make it more romantic."

"Well, Rosie, you say this prissy little pedagogue is probably for rent; why not knock on his door?"

Rose, who had been fixing McCann with her steady gaze, suddenly dropped her eyes. "I really don't know. I must be neurotic or fucked-up or something, because I really think I should leave you and yet I can't. The thing is, I know I wouldn't be happy with Haines. I like talking with him and flirting with him, and he's probably good in bed, but somehow he seems to me, in a funny way . . . sort of inhibited."

"A goddamned slave to convention, that's what he is."

"Anyway," said Rose, putting her hand on McCann's head, "I know he wouldn't shoot ducks to save my honor."

McCann emptied the wine bottle and tossed it aside. He looked at Rose next to him, her smooth brown legs tucked under her, her full lips, carmine and slightly parted, her dark eyes now growing lustrous with in-cipient tears, her nose still tipped with red from earlier crying, her neck and shoulders soft and dusky, and her beautiful jet-black hair falling long and straight, glossy and perfumed.

To McCann this woman had always been an alien. She was a hothouse Jew and a classroom cutie who had never taken a breath out-of-doors, never put her delicate foot in mud, never taken any irrevocable step. Before meeting McCann she had delighted in giving little intimate candle-lit dinners to discuss ideas with her college mentors; or she would have other students over for cheese and wine and radical talk. She did not see herself as privileged, nor did she truly feel there was much wrong in life that couldn't be patched up. Like all people who enjoy movies and music, she was an enthusiast, which meant also she was ridiculous. McCann always mocked her openly and treated her ideas as they deserved to be treated.

But now, as McCann watched her earnest upturned face, he experienced an uncomfortable sensation in his chest. He felt all at once that she was growing in size, looming much too close to him, so that his vision started to blur and he couldn't focus on her. And then she began to burn and shimmer like a mirage. It was as if the projector had stopped on one frame and the hot bulb was slowly burning away the acetate, the burned portion smearing but gradually getting larger until it burst into smoke; and there was Rose again, but this time three-times enlarged and alive. He could have reached out and touched her, and he could smell her perfumed hair. This kind of thing had happened before and, as always, McCann felt sick and horrified.

His feelings must have registered because Rose was now looking at him quizzically. McCann felt his eyes begin to water.

"No," he said, putting his hands over his face.

But her image was still before his eyes, as if he were cupping all of that supple body in his hands, and he shuddered as a thought occurred to him that was both terrible and pathetic. *This girl is real and I love her. She is real and I love her and I feel so sorry for her.*

McCann pitched forward on the bed, the whiskey

spilling, his head resting on Rose's knee. He could feel his tears wetting her skin.

"Love you," McCann said.

"Oh, McCann," Rose's voice was so far away. "I love you too. But you're so drunk."

The pain was much worse. His chest was gripped in a vice; bonds were tightening around his heart, squeezing out the blood. Soon his heart would stop, and then there would be no more McCann. At first the thought was funny, but then he was terrified as the pain increased, long agonizing bolts in his chest, until he gasped for breath.

Somewhere in the distance he heard a tremendous crash, as if a heavy piece of furniture had been over-turned, and McCann found himself sprawled full-length on the floor. He pulled up his knees and hugged himself.

"Oh, God, I'm dying." McCann recognized that voice, so piteous and so far away. "Oh, God, don't kill me now." People were always asking for special favors.

"It's not true about Rose," McCann reminded himself as he passed out.

The young doctor appeared perfectly suited to practice medicine for the city. He was lanky and sharp-featured; he had a mop of unmanaged thick hair and a dour demeanor; he wore his white coat carelessly unbuttoned, he obviously tolerated no nonsense, and now he seemed to be suffering with mildly theatrical restraint some minor imposition. But actually, all he was doing was holding McCann's wrist.

"How do you feel?" he asked.

"Dizzy," said McCann.

The doctor's lip lifted a centimeter. "That's because you're hyperventilating. You're taking in too much oxygen. If it happens again, breath into a paper bag."

111

The Stanyan Street City Health Clinic was really nothing more than a first-aid station. Serious cases went by ambulance to Mission Emergency, while the clinic concentrated on the less significant items of bloodletting occasioned for the most part by barroom affairs of honor or by family disputes. After examining McCann, the young doctor had declined to send him on to the Mission.

It was night, and the naked bulbs burned yellow in the hallway. Fifteen minutes earlier, McCann, ludicrously supported by Rose, had arrived in great pain. Now, stripped to the waist, he was sitting with his legs dangling over the examining table. A large round lamp threw a cone of light, illuminating his head and shoulders and leaving the rest of the room in semidarkness, somewhat in the manner of a cartoonist's idea of police interrogation. In front of him was a white enameled case with glass doors inside on which he could see gleaming instruments set out on a cloth.

Rose, who had parked the car, had come back and was now seated in the reception room thumbing through old magazines

"Your pulse is still elevated," said the doctor.

"Tachycardia," said McCann.

The doctor wrinkled his nose; obviously it didn't please him to hear laymen use technical terms.

"Let's say it's a little fast."

When McCann had been brought in, white-faced, terror-stricken, and complaining of chest pains, the young doctor had been in the back office working on a paper he was preparing on the incidence of subdural hematoma by income bracket. He had rushed to the policeman's side and wasted no time in applying his stethoscope here, there, and everywhere he thought it might do some good. The results, in a sense, had been disappointing.

"Well," the doctor had said slowly, "I can't see that there's much wrong with your heart . . ."

With those words McCann immediately began to feel better, the painful weight on his chest lifted more or less, leaving him feeling shaky and exhausted but relieved.

". . . Certainly nothing requiring immediate attention. If you want, in the next week or so, you can go over to General for an EKG. I'll arrange it, but, ah, frankly, I'll bet they won't find anything. Your heart sounds pretty healthy to me, but as I say, it's up to you. I can arrange it."

"That's okay," said McCann submissively.

Although the doctor was McCann's age or younger, McCann felt as if he was being lectured by a vastly older and wiser personage. He knew he should resent this, but at the same time, his panic was gone, his pain was gone, and although his head was spinning, he felt immeasurable relief.

"You drank a lot today," said the doctor.

"Yes."

"Is that a regular thing?"

"Yes," said McCann.

"The reason I ask, I could prescribe some medicine for you, but this medicine doesn't mix with alcohol. You think you might be able to knock off the booze for a while?"

"No," said McCann.

The doctor took up McCann's wrist for another reading. "I'm not going to preach you a sermon. I'm sure you know as well as I do the long-term effects of what you're doing. You may have the constitution of an ox; even so, you'll hurt yourself one day if you keep on with the sauce. You know that already and I don't have to tell you. As for the present, my advice is to sign up for a multiphysic at General, get the results, then if there's nothing organic but these symptoms persist . . ." The doctor released McCann's wrist. "Your heart is normal."

"Thank you, Doctor," McCann said. "I feel better."

"You get my drift, don't you. If there's nothing physically wrong . . ."

"Sure," said McCann, hurriedly reaching for his shirt. "Thanks a hell of a lot."

Tucking in his shirt, McCann backed out of the examining room, repeating "thank you, Doctor," and bouncing off the door frame as he went. A moment later, the doctor heard a woman's voice and then the slam of the front door.

The nurse came in to roll a new section of white paper over the examining table.

"Did you know that guy's a cop?" she said. "What's his problem?"

"I have no idea," the doctor said curtly as he turned on his heel and returned to his office. Seating himself, he immediately took up his pen. He had a paper to write and the flow of his thoughts had been interrupted. Now then: "The socioeconomic aspects of contusion have never really been adequately examined since the time of the Ancients, when Herodotus, for instance, posited that the effeminate life of the East was responsible for the thinness of Persian cranial bones found at Marathon . . ."

Outside, McCann grabbed Rose by the arm and dragged her toward the Bank Club on Haight. After he got a drink he would tell her what he really thought about her.

CHAPTER 11

It was well known to everybody that the community liaison officer for the Teamsters in San Francisco was Jack Apples, head of public relations for the Convenience Drayage Company, main offices Los Angeles. Convenience, wholly run by the Teamsters, was a subsidiary of a shadowy conglomerate whose owners had a vast and far-reaching influence in the marketplace: from lettuce in Salinas, to numbers in Brooklyn, to cotton in Texas, to jukeboxes in Chicago, to ball bearings in Wichita, to prostitution in San Francisco; in short, many businesses of all descriptions clustered under its roof.

Convenience Drayage, however, was slightly different from the other enterprises in that it was meant to be a prototype of the future look in conglomerate subsidiaries. Managerially, it operated in the sunlight and was traded openly on the Pacific Stock Exchange; but it also had an after-hours personality, a distinction that caused its officers the added bother of administering at least two sets of books. This did not mean that Convenience was one of those legitimate businesses used as a cover for illicit activity; on the contrary, Convenience represented a *merger* of two types of business endeavor that in the past people arbitrarily separated on the tenuous grounds that one kind of endeavor was lawful and the other not. With Convenience the managerial concept had matured to the point that as far as possible these two types of activity would be fully integrated into the conglomerate's computerized systems analysis grid. Naturally, this Teamster-operated model for the future did most of its business at the airport and the docks, where oftentimes large shipments of this thing or that thing mysteriously disappeared in transit.

Jack Apples, known to the payroll department as Chief Public Facilitator, began his meteoric rise in Sacramento, where he worked as a legislative analyst for the Senate Transportation Committee. A sensitive politician, Apples had quickly shown an aptitude for reconciling the interests of the unions, the trucking contractors, and the highway lobby, a skill acquired after the basic but determining insight that these interests were exactly the same. Consequently, the legislation he drafted had tremendous clout, with overwhelming persuasiveness and appeal to all but a few quixotic legislators. Everybody in Sacramento (with the exception of the Sierra Club and a handful of other troglodytes who thought Man had been better off during the Pleistocene Epoch) hailed the legislation as progressive, since it benefited trucks and cars, caused freeways to span the state, and allowed the rapid shuttling of goods and an easy tidal action of humanity, except at rush hour. Soon, as a result of his efforts, the haze that filled the hotel rooms where the necessary bargains were hammered out stretched from Eureka to San Diego in one long carcinomatous band.

Apples' efforts in behalf of private transit did not go unnoticed or unrewarded. The Teamsters recognized his value and lured him away from public service with the promise of a substantial increase in salary. He moved from his sterile cubicle next door to the committee room in the Capitol to a suite atop the Bank of America Building in San Francisco. His offices had blue pile carpets, brocade hangings, mahogany furniture, and a gleaming private bathroom.

In his new position as public facilitator, Apples was meant to serve as a buffer between the company's other officers and the outside world. His job included many tasks but one of them was to act as a broker for goods and services being offered to the Teamsters by entrepreneurs outside the organization. It was in this capacity as a broker that he made the acquaintance of William McCann.

Apples admittedly had been a trifle puzzled when his receptionist (a prim little lady whose son was a hit man) had announced that there was a uniformed police officer in the lobby who said he had three million in pure heroin he was willing to sell, at a personal sacrifice, for $750,000. That was an audacious opening, but Apples happened to be a man who didn't care for timidity. Moreover, it had immediately made him believe in McCann's authenticity. His long familiarity with the police mentality convinced him that a nark of any sort would never have the brains to think of sending a patrolman in to see the receptionist. Just to be on the safe side, however, Apples did some checking. The Teamsters, of course, were on good terms with the local authorities, and friends within the department assured the public facilitator that McCann was of good character, meaning that he was not part of any pathetic police scheme to harass the union, the company, or its owners.

It was always possible, of course, that some obscure branch of the Federal Government had instigated some cockeyed plot without notifying the administration. But Washington seemed to think this notion farfetched in the extreme, and had answered his query with an abrupt, "NO UN-UNION ACTION ANY FED DEPT STOP." They were testy, the Washington boys, about the least suggestion that the administration would do anything adversely affecting the interests of the conglomerate.

So, it was obvious that McCann was not part of some fantastic plot to harm Convenience Drayage Company. But what had troubled Apples from the outset was that McCann was so completely beyond the authority and control of any organization. He seemed to put himself first. He had not been loyal to the police department; given a chance, he might prove disloyal to Convenience. It would be embarrassing, for instance, if he should attempt to defraud the company, or if he didn't really possess the merchandise claimed. It would be embarrassing because Apples himself lacked full authority to deal with McCann or any other independent entrepreneur. Apples had to go before the directors (the Committee, as it was called) and make a report, an evaluation, and a recommendation, just as any other business manager did. His hard-won reputation for perspicacity, therefore, was always on the line in these transactions.

Thus, the public facilitator's usual method in dealing with cases such as McCann's was first to establish some kind of leverage, so that the person was not completely beyond authority, before starting to negotiate seriously. It was a good way to weed out frivolous or irresponsible people. That was why Apples had McCann perform a few small tasks before they got down to serious business. McCann had to demonstrate good faith through some act that would also put him in a degree of jeopardy. He had to put his fate, so to speak, at Apples' disposal.

The case of John Smith had been a good test. He had rid the Teamsters of a mildly troublesome person on the strength of a phone call. True, Apples doubted he could prove the murder, even should he want to. Nonetheless, he *knew*. It gave him leverage. Apples was perfectly willing to admit, however, that McCann and his partner had done a very nice job on Smith. The story in the *Examiner*, for instance, had been hilarious.

But at the same time there had been something in the *Examiner* story that had troubled him, amusing though it all might be. Why, for instance, had the coroner's office been so willing to bamboozle the dipsomanic Brannon? Not money, certainly, so what conceivable quid pro quo could have induced the coroner to take the risk? Now *that* was puzzling.

Apples was musing about McCann as he sat in his specially reserved rear booth in the Iron Horse on Montgomery Street, waiting for the police officer to join him for a luncheon date. McCann was not late, Apples was early. He liked to sip a drink and think through a situation for a minute or so beforehand. Muted voices rose sibilantly all around him from the darkened alcoves; the tinkling of glasses and the slapping of dice cups floated back from the bar; and the short black-silk skirts of the waitresses rustled and whispered as they slid by.

Apples was a heavy man, corpulent really, and not much over five feet. He was completely bald and his thick glasses were tilted down over a stubby nose, giving him a lawyerish or professorial look; but in his little eyes shone none of the soft wet luster of academia; those hard agate eyes said "commerce." He wore a light, rough-textured silk suit and smoked a thick green cigar.

He saw McCann entering and snapped his fingers to attract a waitress. The burly policeman hesitated in the doorway a moment, blinking his eyes, before carefully moving his bulk through the closely packed tables toward Apples' booth.

Apples rose slightly and offered a hand as McCann slid in opposite him. He noticed that as McCann seated himself the distinct odor of whiskey, inadequately disguised by Sen-Sen, wafted across the table. The public facilitator made a mental note of this.

"I'm having a martini," Apples said to the girl.

"Double bourbon over with a draft," McCann said.

"So," said Apples, "you drink boilermakers for lunch. That's a sign of virility, isn't it?"

McCann responded to Apples' bantering tone by displaying his erect middle finger for several seconds, long enough to leave Apples the impression that the police officer did not mind making a scene in front of the waitress.

Apples smiled and began chatting aimlessly until the drinks arrived.

"It's frequently been my pleasure to work with law enforcement agencies, both here and in Sacramento. I handled the language last year for the Highway Patrol's annual increment. Everybody was very cooperative, despite some thorny problems, including the matter of tonnage variances for some of my clients; although frankly, between you and me, it was clear to everyone from the outset that my client's good will would be crucial for the success of the bill in committee. The floor vote in the Assembly was fifty-eight to five, and, if I may say so, that final bill was dollar-for-dollar and feature-for-feature the best legislation to come out of the session."

The miniskirted waitress brought the drinks and menus.

"You might as well bring another round," Apples told her, before beginning an examination of the menu. "The sand dabs are excellent here, as is the veal scaloppine."

"I want a ham sandwich," said McCann roughly.

"The ham sandwich is excellent also," Apples said. Putting down the menu, Apples gazed across the table at the hulking police officer, a trace of a smile on his thick lips.

"Listen, my friend, what is to be gained by being surly or belligerent? I appreciate your feeling that we are not progressing as expeditiously as we both might wish. Believe me, I am trying to hurry everybody along. But, as I've told you, it's not up to me to authorize the disbursement of large sums. A committee is charged with that responsibility, and they have to feel secure about everything down to the last detail. You can understand that. Now I like what you've done for us to date and you can be sure the Committee has in hand the pertinent information, including photographic evidence. So be patient."

"Okay," said McCann. "I'll try the sand dabs."

"Thank you for that," Apples said, his enigmatic smile returning.

"By the way, I've been meaning to tell you that somebody over at the bar has his eye on us."

With a golden lighter, Apples sprayed a jet of flame toward the end of his cigar, and in the ensuing smoke cloud his little agate eyes flicked toward the bar.

"Yes," he sighed. "Because of my position in the front office, so to speak, I'm under constant surveillance. That man is an FBI agent."

"Swell. Can I expect my door knocked down in the middle of the night?"

"Oh no, nothing like that. We are getting along pretty well these days with our cousins in the bureaucracy. We like to keep tabs on each other, but they aren't going to *do* anything. Actually, we've been honeymooning with Justice ever since a certain *little shit* was swept from the board by what to my mind is a very heroic Arab. The FBI is not interested in you."

"Nor I in them," McCann said, glancing again at the short-haired man in the dark suit.

More drinks came, followed by the sand dabs and wine.

"You know, Mr. McCann, I've seen a little of your work now, and I'd say there's a place for you at Convenience. And I don't mean driving a semi; I mean somewhere toward the top of the middle echelon."

"But first, I have to do something."

"You're blunt," said Apples, picking at the dabs with his fork. "But I'd say what you have to do is defer an immediate profit on this forthcoming transaction."

"I'm touched by your offer," McCann said, "but, as a matter of fact, I'm not looking for a career. I want money. So do my partners. It's money we're after, Mr. Apples."

"Pardon my saying it, but you're very young. You could do a lot with your life, given the proper structure. But all you want to talk about is money. Every time we've met, you've taken great pains to impress upon me that you are only interested in money. But, Mr. McCann, I'm not entirely convinced that money is so all-important to you. Now why do I say this? Well, let's just take a moment and examine the facts, Mr. McCann, and see if we can determine why you are such an interesting person. First, let me make an observation about the late Mr. Smith of the Argonaut Motel. You were not required to take any special pains in this matter, yet you handled it with admirable finesse, even a touch of humor. The ordinary employee, I'm afraid, would have merely knocked

Mr. Smith on the noggin, and that would have been that."

"How crude," said McCann.

"Crude indeed. So, I think we can attribute your handling of the Smith affair, your putting him on display for a week, your shenanigans with Mr. Brannon, as a commendable attempt to favorably impress a future partner. Still in all, that fails to explain the case of Clayton Thomas."

McCann looked up from his sand dabs and gazed steadily at Apples.

"Yes, Mr. McCann, I'm a careful reader of the newspaper. I couldn't help noticing your name in connection with an incident in the Haight-Ashbury. I admit it was nothing more than a hunch, but in consideration of your penchant for toying with the newspapers, I had someone go out and talk with Mr. Thomas. It was, of course, a person Mr. Thomas knew and trusted from previous dealings. Would you be interested in knowing what Mr. Thomas had to say about you?"

"I'm sure he was overwhelmed with gratitude."

"Well, not quite, Mr. McCann. He says, in fact, that you tried to burn him up. Now why would you want to do a thing like that, Mr. McCann?"

"To tell the truth, I've always been careless with matches."

"Have you? Well I don't think that fully explains it. You are obviously an intelligent man. You have demonstrated an ability to put a complicated scheme in train. You forcefully explain to me now that your only interest is profit. And yet you do something that *really*, Mr. McCann, does not make a lot of sense from a practical standpoint. Do you think I'm right?"

"I think you're in the dark," said McCann.

"Well, yes," Apples laughed. "I *am* in the dark. I cer-

123

tainly am. But you know what I really think, Mr. Mc-Cann? I don't think you had any, shall we say, business reasons for burning up poor Mr. Thomas. I think you did it for a lark. Yes, I think you did it for fun. I admit, I don't understand it as yet, but, really, what other explanation is there? Your behavior makes me think that a life of action might appeal to you."

"Have you ever thought about being an Army recruiter?"

"Very well," said Apples, the wisp of a smile on his face. "I'm meeting with the Committee this afternoon, and your proposal is on the agenda. Now I warn you, the Committee may request some further gesture from you. Furthermore, the members almost certainly will require a fairly explicit description of your operation. Since I assume the shipment is not presently in this country, we would want to assess your means of delivery, to determine if ours might not be more efficient."

"We can talk about that," said McCann.

Apples' porcine eyes studied McCann as the officer drained off a double shot of bourbon in one gulp. Apples had noted that during their brief talk McCann had drunk three double bourbons and most of the wine. And now this uniformed police officer, sitting in a public restaurant, was signaling the waitress for more drinks.

"All right," said Apples, "I'll tell you what. You might as well learn immediately the decision of the Committee. Are you free tonight?"

"No," said McCann, "I have to go to the mayor's dinner."

"Of course. I'd forgotten. I've got to put in an appearance there myself. Tomorrow then. Let me invite you to take a steam bath tomorrow night, as my guest, at the Domino Athletic Club. You know the address? Around eight would be fine. I'll see you there."

Apples carefully edged his portly figure away from the table and waddled out without looking back. The lean man with the short hair detached himself from the bar and strode after him. McCann leisurely finished his lunch and ordered some more drinks, putting them on Apples' bill.

CHAPTER 12

As the new officer-in-charge of the Anti-Terror Unit, Lieutenant Michael O'Riley was the guest of honor at a $100-a-plate testimonial dinner for the mayor of San Francisco, who was engaged in a bitter campaign for re-election.

The mayor's position on the overriding issue of the campaign—the increasing rate of unlicensed violence—had been part of the public record for some time. More than one person had mentioned, however, that the rash of bombings in the city could only act as a brake on the mayor's political ambitions, which, speculation ran, might encompass the governor's mansion, or a seat in the U.S. Senate, or God knows what. His Republican opponent, described invariably as "tough-minded," had been hitting the terror issue for all it was worth at every shopping center and businessmen's luncheon.

Worse still, the GOP incumbent in Sacramento had taken it upon himself to wonder aloud at a recent press conference how San Francisco's chieftain could possibly harbor statewide or national ambitions when he was experiencing such difficulty in keeping his own house in order.

"Local autonomy is the watchword of this administration," the governor had said, "but as a matter of conscience I have told the mayor of San Francisco that I stand ready at any time to authorize the deployment of the National Guard or the state police if he deems this necessary to return peace to this city."

The mayor and his advisers, needless to say, did not think it expedient to accept the governor's offer. Instead, they were banking on the local police, specifically on the mayor's own creation, the Anti-Terror Unit, to dig them out of a bad hole.

The mayor's testimonial was being held in the Columbus Room of Italian Hall, and the room had been draped with red, white, and blue bunting for the occasion. In every corner hung bunches of gaudy balloons, each stamped with a facsimile of the mayor's face. And on a golden banner stretching across the wall behind the elevated head table was the mayor's campaign slogan— "We Can Do It"—spelled out in huge block letters.

The room was thronged with the mayor's supporters, many of whom, admittedly, were not in the habit of paying $100 for dinner. All of the tickets, in fact, had been purchased in blocks by certain anonymous businessmen and legislative advocates, persons who, this year, were nominally Republican and hence had thought it impolitic to appear themselves at a Democratic fund-raiser. Consequently, through some understanding, the tickets stayed in the mayor's office until they were parceled out to the deserving in the local Democratic organizations.

Along with the mayor's precinct workers, the dinner had drawn the cream of the city's bureaucracy: the chief of police, the fire chief, the head of the civil service, and the city attorney; it had drawn all the Democratic politicians, ranging in rank from supervisor to state senator; it had drawn the municipal court judges and every aspiring lawyer in town; it had brought forth the public-relations flacks for all the major firms, corporations, and monopolies; it had gathered in the press, the members of which were segregated at their own table near the podium; and it had even managed to squeeze out one or two of the seven Jewish businessmen who actually run things in San Francisco. It was doubtful that anybody in the room had paid for his own ticket.

By and large, it was a masculine company. With the exception of a few hard-bitten female bureaucrats, the only women present were four or five dancers from one of the Broadway clubs, large-breasted, miniskirted cuties who were selling raffle tickets near the entrance. The dull roar of a hundred conversations filled the air, accompanied by occasional rumbles of boisterous laughter from the bar in the rear, where the men were lined up three-deep.

O'Riley had discovered that he had arrived too early. Dressed in his ordinary brown suit and thin black tie, he was sitting in the back kitchen with one of the mayor's aides waiting for the mayor to arrive. "It'll be better if you two go in together," the aide explained, "as if you've just come from a conference or something." After fifteen minutes of watching plates of shrimp salad pile up on the sideboard, O'Riley saw the mayor come in from the back, trailing a couple of assistants. The mayor made a beeline for O'Riley, grasped him by the elbow, and swept him toward the door.

"How we doing? Do we have the bastards yet?"

"I think we have some good leads," O'Riley said. "It's my theory that . . ."

"The sooner the better, lieutenant." And then O'Riley and the mayor burst into the hall to thunderous applause. O'Riley was bustled up to the head table and found himself holding one of the mayor's large paws as three or four flash guns went off.

"We can do it, we can do it," bellowed the mayor, who had thrown one arm around O'Riley and was waving at the crowd with the other.

O'Riley felt small, drab, and ill at ease sitting next to the full-bodied and immaculately tailored picture of self-confidence that was the mayor of San Francisco. An ebullient man, full of vigor and wit, the mayor from time to time shot pithy comments in O'Riley's direction, never burdening him with the need to reply.

The lieutenant casually put his hand on the coat pocket that held his speech. The speech was the result of a day's concentration, and detailed without histrionics the problems facing the police in running the terrorists to earth: the difficulty in getting reliable information, of infiltrating affinity groups, of hooking the offending fish out of a sea of look-alikes—"WMA hippie type," was the best any patrolman could do.

O'Riley decided to eat something, but unhappily the mayor turned on him just as his fork descended on the peas. The fork clinked, the peas rolled about madly. The mayor, noticing this, said softly, "Don't worry, lieutenant, you can do no wrong."

At least twenty men, all politicians or would-be politicians, were on their feet table-hopping. The politico first would bend forward, placing one hand on the victim's shoulder, and render a prolonged and motionless handshake, at the same time saying a few words and cocking his ear for the response; then he would rock back with laughter, pat the humorist once again on the shoulder, and slide off to the next table.

O'Riley caught sight of his staff, McCann and Henry, seated toward the rear, their blue uniforms conspicuous in the crowd. And beneath him at the press table was Brannon of the *Examiner*. O'Riley was glad to see the pink-faced and disheveled reporter, who, with his spindly legs crossed, was gazing around good-naturedly at the table-hopping politicians. Brannon glanced up at O'Riley, rolled his eyes drolly, inviting the lieutenant to share the joke.

Wine was being served and O'Riley took another look at his staff. He had given them one order for the evening: no booze. They were in uniform and in public. Brannon had not been the first to comment on McCann's alleged drinking. To be sure, O'Riley had never seen the young officer drunk, nor had he smelled liquor on his breath; but McCann always appeared to be under the influence of something, his face suffused with a kind of malicious, gloating look. It might be explained by surreptitious drinking.

From the number of uniformed men in the room, O'Riley could see the banquet was under heavy guard. He had been told police marksmen with infrared sniper scopes were on the roof; and he had seen for himself coming in that a dozen or more officers were stationed in the corridors and lobby. The mayor, apparently, had decided that a bomb going off at his dinner would be a distinct embarrassment. To O'Riley's right, a state senator, handsome, graying at the temples, was suggesting to the mayor that now might be the time, politically speaking, to publicly accuse the governor of a serious moral lapse that, once rumored, was now confirmed, or so the senator seemed to think at least.

The lieutenant turned his thoughts again to his speech.

He had tried to make it as dull as possible. The first five minutes or so contained the few applause lines, some hackneyed sentiments about how law enforcement and an aroused citizenry would soon settle the question of the terrorists and return peace to the city. O'Riley decided he would try to put some hint of emotion in his voice during these passages. Following this came a solid twenty minutes of facts and figures compiled from the Annual U.S. Crime Report of the FBI, which O'Riley felt should be sufficiently stultifying for an audience whose intestines were sorting out a heavy meal. He would drop his voice during this part, so his audience would be brought to the verge of unconsciousness.

Then, just as his auditors drifted off to sleep, he would throw out the bait, hidden in the last few sentences that only the reporters would bother listening to. But these were the only words in his speech that had the remotest news value; and these were the words, O'Riley felt confident, that would be reported in the newspaper and, he hoped, read by the terrorists. He was positive that the terrorists read the newspapers.

The state senator, after telling the mayor about some photographs that had recently fallen into his possession, walked to the podium to begin his duties as master of ceremonies. His task as emcee was to introduce people who already knew each other, without forgetting to insert a joke between each introduction. As the main speaker, O'Riley would be fourth to the podium, a good forty-five minutes away. He allowed his mind to drift.

McCann felt deathly sick. The din of voices in the stifling room did not succeed in lulling him into a reverie, nor did he see anything funny about the table-hopping politicians. Henry, seated across the crowded table, was deep in conversation with a black union official.

The union official, it turned out, had grown up in Henry's neighborhood on the East Side of Chicago, and their grinning dark faces were lit with the pleasure of remembering their bittersweet slum childhood.

Sitting with McCann was the mayor's youth liaison aide, Al Russell, a thickset man of thirty with a large nose, red lips, and a squint. A talker, Russell was directing some thought in McCann's direction. In front of them, the austere figure of O'Riley sat elevated at the head table, as stiff and expressionless as a corpse in state. He seemed to be staring right at McCann.

"Sure you won't have some wine?" Russell was saying, as he poured his own glass to the brim.

"No, thank you," McCann said. He put his hands under the table and felt his pulse. It seemed fast but weak, and McCann guessed it was up to around one hundred and twenty.

"I'm moderate as a rule," Russell said. "It's important to me to keep fit. I play basketball on Wednesday and Saturday, and I work out at the Olympic Health Club every afternoon. You ought to join."

"I work out with my own club."

"That's funny," Russell said without smiling. "It's important to be fit because politics is a competitive sport. All the men here are competitive. This kind of life is very masculine and that's why it's important to be strong. What do you say when you want to flatter any of these men? You say, 'You're tough.' That's the highest honor in politics."

"You're tough," said McCann.

"Ha, ha. Take this dinner tonight. The mayor had no problem unloading his tickets. Why? Because everybody knows he's strong. We sold out in two days. Go ahead, quote all the opinion polls you want; the true indication of political viability is the readiness of the big advocate to peel off a check. When you knock at the door of the third house and nobody's home, baby, you're in big trouble; I mean, *zero* clout."

"I've heard that," McCann said absently. It was very unpleasant. His arms slowly seemed to be turning to lead. He was dizzy and felt an oppressive weight on his chest.

"I'll give you an example of what I mean. Assemblyman Bryant thought he knew all about the banking and insurance bill. 'I don't have to take program on this one,' he says. 'I'll vote my conscience.' He thought he was strong because he took both nominations in the primary. But he confused cunning with strength. So what happened? He couldn't push a ticket for his testimonial. He had to give them away to the Junior Chamber of Commerce and a Boy Scout troop just to fill the hall; and all he wanted was twenty-five dollars a pop. How do you suppose that makes his people feel, when they can't sell a ticket?"

"I just don't know."

"It makes them feel weak; and then the bigger fish start moving in." The mayor's aide, flushed and breathing heavily, poured out another glass and squinted at McCann. "We started to move on him at that point, you see, because we sensed his weakness. Example: Bryant wants to nose in on the SF State locker searches. Last year, all right. This year, *no way.* I called up his aide and I told him, 'Lay off.' That's all I said. 'Lay off. The mayor don't like it, the senator don't like it. State is ours and you stay in your own backyard.'"

The aide rubbed his jowl and then drew a red line across the tablecloth with some spilled wine. "It was time to be hard. And I was."

The pain was increasing in McCann's chest. He was having trouble breathing and the room had slowly begun to revolve. His body was bathed in sweat.

Russell calmly accepted a glass of brandy from the waiter and lit a cigar. "Do you want to hear my philosophy? My philosophy is strength and competition. My motto is, when I meet another man, I want to test him; when I face an opponent, I want to best him. Let me give you an example of what I'm talking about: When I was in Sacramento last month I went to a dinner given by the oil lobby at the El Dorado Country Club. That's *the* exclusive club in the capital. It's an annual bash for the legislators and their aides. We had a beautiful meal, course after course, wine after wine, brandy, cigars, chocolate mousse. And then you know what we did?"

"You vomited."

"We arm-wrestled," Russell said. "And after that somebody found a tennis ball, and we went into the patio to see who could throw it the highest."

Russell peered closely at McCann. "You don't look good. Are you sick?"

"Just a cold," McCann said. To tell the truth, it felt as if steel bands were constricting his chest. And stabbing pains raced up and down his left arm.

Russell puffed up his cigar and craned his neck toward the back of the room. "Have you noticed the raffle-ticket girls? They're from Dino's. I'm a married man and I love my wife, and that's not bullshit. But I really believe that other women are necessary as a form of expression. Freud says that. And in a masculine society it's important to be able to conquer women; frankly, it enhances the reputation. That might be a harsh viewpoint, but it's reality.

"You know," Russell continued, "there are two types of philanderer. One is the type of guy who unconsciously wants to be caught so he can be punished. He's guilt-ridden and being caught is a means of symbolic castration. The other type is a higher type, who recognizes

134

that competitive man needs an outlet for certain aggressive and sadistic urges. You know why I say this? Because, as a matter of fact, I was just now considering going back and hustling one of those tushes right now."

The mayor's aide rose unsteadily and swayed down the aisle toward the rear.

McCann hunched forward at the table, crossed his arms, pressed his knees together, and took a sidelong glance at the head table. O'Riley's eyes still seemed riveted on him. The smell of brandy poured across the table on clouds of cigar smoke. The noise was incredible, and the dapper emcee was trying to get the attention of the unruly crowd by tapping his finger against the microphone, each tap resounding in the room like a knock on a coffin.

Suddenly he heard Russell's voice: "Here she is." And the aide sat down in his chair, dragging into his lap the plump and scarcely clad figure of the admired raffle-ticket girl. McCann looked at the girl and felt immediately as if he were having some kind of seizure; a sharp, burning pain spread across his chest, as if he had been kicked in the sternum.

"McCann," shrieked the girl, and fell forward from Russell's knee, throwing her arms around the policeman's neck. The searing pain in his chest rushed through his arms and legs like jolts of electricity.

"Back," he managed to whisper, and Russell dragged the girl back onto his lap.

"You two seem to know each other," he said, obviously not entirely pleased by this coincidence.

"McCann's my old roomie."

"Shut up," snapped McCann.

The girl was a topless dancer from Dino's who performed under the name Melanie Duggs. She and McCann had met in North Beach a few weeks after he had graduated from the police academy and while he was doing the obligatory stint of undercover work for the narcotics squad. For some reason, one afternoon in Dino's, she had taken a shine to his sullen, congested countenance. By that time, of course, everybody on Broadway knew he was a cop, making it pointless for him to appear on the street and forcing him to meet his quota by paying off informers. One afternoon he had been playing liar's dice with the bartender at Dino's when Melanie came over and nuzzled one of her outsize, perfectly formed breasts against his shoulder. She had asked permission to touch his face, which she said she could see blazing at the bar all the way from the stage. "Oh, it gives me shivers," she said, running her fingers along McCann's pitted neck.

In common with all strikingly beautiful girls born after 1950, Melanie believed absolutely in astrology, the spirit world, reincarnation, and flying saucers. She had started college a dozen times, been to Europe twice, Disneyland once. She had tried, successively, encounter groups, pottery, self-defense for women, organic gardening, gestalt massage, hypnosis, and Zen basketball. She had had occult experiences, such as the time she and her sister simultaneously experienced a sense of dread the very afternoon their mother had fallen off a ski lift; and she liked to tell these stories late at night, holding a candle and sitting cross-legged on the floor, her eyes growing wider and wider. Her vocation had caused her to strain her back, for which she went twice a week to a chiropractor. And, like all beauties of meager intellect, she adored intellectuals, an intellectual being to her any man who chewed gum with his mouth closed.

McCann had stayed at her apartment on and off for several months until he couldn't stand her any longer.

"Oh, what a girl," Russell said, bouncing Melanie on

his knee. "She's a dancer now, but she's studying to be a psychiatric social worker."

McCann was actually gasping for breath. He felt as if he were laboring under several added gravities. Melanie, her full wet lips parted, gazed at him compassionately. "I know what he's going through," she told Russell.

Realizing how close he was to panic, McCann staggered to his feet and pushed his way through the welter of brawling voices until he felt the cool breeze from the opened door. "My heart is going to stop," he said to himself. He listened, and could hear his heart pinging irregularly in his chest. His heart took an agonizing pause after every tenth beat. He suddenly found himself braced against the bar, overcome with fear and dizziness. "Please God, don't kill me here," he said to himself, just exactly as anyone would who thinks he is on the verge of death.

Looking up, his vision blurred, McCann saw the dim figure of the bartender in front of him.

"Double bourbon over," McCann found himself saying.

The bartender seemed surprised at this request for service from a uniformed police officer, but he brought the drink.

"On the house," the bartender said.

In the darkened alcove, McCann felt himself beyond O'Riley's vigilance. The lieutenant, meanwhile, had stepped to the podium and started his speech. McCann noted with satisfaction the nervous catch in his superior's voice. O'Riley, it was clear, was going to botch it. And the lieutenant's thin, wasted body looked so pathetic above this sea of beefy manhood.

McCann greedily swallowed the double in one gulp and ordered another. Fuck O'Riley and his rules! Finally, after the third double, the oppression began to lift from his chest; his skin prickled with sweat and the fires began to melt away the leaden congestion in his veins. His breathing slowed to normal, and his frontal lobes began to stiffen pleasantly. After another drink McCann grinned at the healthy throb of his carotid artery, slow, strong, and regular. The breeze from ouside fanned his cheek and swept away the mist from the dining room, revealing the diners, fuddled by wine and cigar smoke, apathetically gaping at the ceiling, under the pall of O'Riley's droning voice. Every few minutes a hand in slow motion returned a cigar to red lips.

After the fourth double, good humor returned and so did Melanie, who materialized at his side and intertwined her arm with his. In the darkness he could feel her insinuating her hip; her familiar odor wafted up to him, causing another sensation that further increased his sense of well-being.

"I left because he tried to prep my landing zone," Melanie said, smiling. "You're the only one I let prep my landing zone in public."

McCann let his hand drop against her thigh She pressed it and put her arm around his waist.

"McCann," she whispered, "I forgive you for the way you've treated me. I want you to know that. You know, I think it's your bad conscience that makes your heart hurt you. You treated me so bad. But if you were still mine I could make you feel better. Do you know what Melanie would do? First of all . . . Melanie would give you a nice long back rub, the kind you like. And then, do you know? Melanie would pop you in a . . . *bubble bath*. Do you remember how you liked to drink beer in my tub? And then . . . Melanie would squeeze water on your head from a sponge. Oh, McCann, I think about you all the time; every time I see a cop I think of you. And now I wouldn't bother you at all. Melanie wouldn't hug if you don't want to hug; Melanie wouldn't touch your

138

chest at night; and she won't say anything if you want to drink in bed."

"What's your situation now?" McCann was gently moving his hand.

"Oh, we can't tonight," Melanie said. "Somebody is picking me up here afterward."

"Who?"

"He's the guy I'm living with. He works for the Sierra Club."

"Are you his reclamation project, Melanie?"

"He's very honest and sincere. And *very* bright. He's trying to stop development south of Tunitas Creek."

"Your development stopped north of the neck."

"You are bad, Mr. McCann. I don't know why Melanie likes you." She withdrew her arm for a moment to find money for another drink. During their relationship, Melanie had learned that encouraging remarks at her own expense seemed to put McCann in a better mood.

"So you don't want to engage gears," McCann continued.

Melanie pressed against him again and laid her blonde head on his shoulder. "I *do* want to. You're *so* good for me and it's been *so* long. But," she said in a more businesslike tone, "I can't hurt David. He's a very sweet boy and he thinks the world of me. I don't want to disillusion him."

"You can't disillusion his type. They'll be driving a gold spike in Monterey to celebrate the linking of San Francisco and Los Angeles before he gets disillusioned."

"You don't know how sensitive he is."

"I know his type," McCann said.

"I have to help give away the prizes," Melanie said. "If you still work nights we could meet in the afternoon sometime. Call me at Dino's. Okay? Please." Melanie made a kissing sound, and then her velvet-clad hips swung down the aisle, with the heads of two dozen men turning after her.

Finishing his fifth double bourbon, McCann felt his best. He went to the door and looked into the street. A gray Volkswagen was parked a few yards away in the green zone with a young man sitting inside. McCann walked back to the edge of the dining room and waited until he caught Henry's eye. Henry, frowning, shot a quick look at O'Riley, then got up and joined his partner.

He shook his head when he saw McCann's grinning, incandescent face. "You'd better stay away from the mummy."

"Fuck him," McCann said. "Listen, there's a punk outside who's giving Melanie a hard time. We're going to have to take him on."

"Here?"

"It'll only take a minute. Listen, do you want a drink first?"

"No," said Henry, shaking his head.

The two officers walked outside and approached the Volkswagen. The bespectacled youth in the car put aside the newspaper he had been trying to read and rolled down his window. He wore a light blue sportcoat, a wide silk tie, and had allowed his hair to turn curly in back.

"Do you mind stepping out of your vehicle, sir," McCann said politely. The youth obediently climbed out.

"Your operator's license, please." It was passed over and McCann shined his light on it. "David R. Levin. Mr. Levin, where are you employed?"

"I'm employed by the Sierra Club," Levin said affably. "Do you mind if I ask you officers what this is all about?"

McCann smiled. "There's no need to become abusive, Mr. Levin. This is just a routine check."

"I wasn't being abusive."

"Well, Mr. Levin," said McCann, forcing a laugh,

"I'd say that calling me a turd *is* being abusive. At least it is in my book."

"What?"

"And I don't want you calling me no coon, neither," said Henry.

"Just because we ask you to move out of a red zone is no reason to lose your temper," McCann said.

"This is a *green* zone," said Levin, pointing at the curb.

McCann nodded his head knowingly. "His eyes are dilated."

"High as a kike," Henry said.

"This is incredible," said Levin, looking first at one police officer and then at the other.

"Violence will avail you nothing," McCann said. "I see you leave me no choice but to place you under arrest for assaulting a police officer. Turn around and stand on one foot while I tell you your constitutional rights."

Since Levin remained motionless, McCann grabbed him, spun him around, slammed him against the car, and jerked one of his arms up behind him. "You have the right to remain silent," McCann said, twisting Levin's arm until he cried out in pain. "Feel his arm, Henry, he's trying to pull it away. You're my witness."

"Resisting arrest," Henry said.

"Assault on a police officer is a felony, but resisting arrest is only a misdemeanor," McCann explained as he twisted Levin's arm. "So if one doesn't stick we have the other. Of course, everybody we subdue resists arrest because we're not allowed to subdue you otherwise."

Just then a crewcut plainclothes inspector with his coat flapping rushed out of the door and skipped down the steps. He was part of the detail guarding the banquet against the possibility of a bomb or some other embarrassment. Most of this detail was concentrated around the restrooms, but this officer apparently had responsibility for the entrance.

"Say, do you guys need help?"

Levin started to say something, but McCann lifted one huge fist and the ecologist changed his mind.

"This gentleman decided to take us on," McCann said. "I guess we're going to need a wagon. And do you happen to have any arrest slips? I seem to have lost mine."

The inspector shot a contemptuous look at Levin. "Did you check out the subject's vehicle?"

"Yeah, that's the first thing we thought of. It's clean. The gentleman just seems to have a hard on for policemen. Says he belongs to the Sierra Club."

"Figures," the plainclothesman said. "I'll go call the wagon. Do you need a tow?"

"The gentleman says he has a friend inside. We'll wait one on the tow."

While they waited, McCann toyed with the handcuffs, twisting and jerking them while Levin said "Ouch" and "Oh."

"You see how he's fighting me, Henry."

"You bastards aren't going to get away with this," Levin hissed. "I have friends in the ACLU."

"It's good to have friends," McCann said, twisting the handcuffs.

The plainclothesman came back with the arrest slips. McCann decided to book Levin for assault on a police officer, resisting arrest, and failure to obey a lawful order. He would have booked him for possession of a dangerous drug as well, but this was impossible since neither he nor Henry had any. The police van arrived a few minutes later. McCann removed the cuffs and roughly shoved Levin into the back of the van.

"Likes to attack cops," McCann said to the driver as he handed him the slip.

"We know how to take care of him," the driver said, which meant there would be a disciplinary stopover someplace in the middle of Golden Gate Park before Levin got to the Hall of Justice.

McCann took Levin's keys out of the Volkswagen and put them in his pocket.

They walked back into the building and stood in the shadows near the bar, watching O'Riley reach the conclusion of his speech. The room was utterly silent except for the lieutenant's droning voice; all the diners were leaning back in their chairs, torpid and glassy-eyed, cigars dead, glasses empty.

But at the very same time, invisibly, in Henry's mind, a powerfully built man in a derby hat had turned over a heart flush.

"Farts," Henry suddenly shouted, "you're going to die."

A few men at the nearest table blinked and stared over into the shadows at the two police officers.

"That wasn't me," Henry whispered.

"I know it wasn't."

"Do you think that might have been him?"

"Who?"

"The man who talks through my mouth."

"You mean Levin? It might have been. Listen, don't worry, Henry. We're going to find that guy one of these days."

"Die," Henry shouted again.

The black police officer drew back into the shadows, his eyes darting suspiciously around the room. It was even possible that some of the men in this very hall were the ones who devoted themselves to persecuting him. Henry stared hard at the apathetic faces. Were these people mocking him in secret? Was that sarcasm in those inert expressions? Or were they just pretending not to know what was happening?

"I'm going home," Henry said quietly. And lithe as a cat, he bounded down the steps and disappeared into the night.

Keeping in the shadows, McCann carefully edged over to the bar and motioned to the bartender, who brought another double whiskey.

The new officer-in-charge of the Anti-Terror Unit was still speaking. As McCann listened to O'Riley's speech the thought entered his mind that O'Riley seemed to be struggling to make some point. He kept returning to the idea that there was a lack of political purpose behind the bombings. "Mere purposeless acts of fury," O'Riley was saying, "executed by a psychotic too cowardly to reveal his true colors." McCann frowned as he sipped his drink. That, certainly, was not O'Riley's honest opinion. At this point, however, McCann's eye happened to light on Brannon of the *Examiner*, sitting at the press table underneath the podium. Brannon was bent forward and his right arm was waggling. He was taking notes.

Slowly, it began to dawn on McCann what the absurd O'Riley was up to. He was trying to goad the bombers into some act of bravado that would reveal their identities. McCann snorted in disgust, drank the liquor and signaled for another glass. It must be O'Riley's theory, then, that the terrorists wanted to confess, or rather, had a compulsion to confess. They would read in the paper tomorrow that the head of the Anti-Terror Unit said they were nothing more than apolitical screwballs. And consequently, they would feel compelled to issue an immediate manifesto with their names signed at the bottom. McCann shook his head; he didn't care one way or the other, but he recognized that the plan was simple-minded in the extreme.

Melanie materialized again at his elbow and rubbed her

short purple-velvet dress against his legs. She tossed back her golden mane and parted her wet lips in a smile. He could feel her fingers softly tracing the outline of his hipbone.

"I have to go now. You're going to call me?"

"You won't change your mind about tonight?"

"No, baby. But Melanie promises she will be *very* nice to Mr. McCann if he calls her."

They were interrupted by a ripple of polite applause. O'Riley had finished his speech and was seated again, his skull-like head pointed at the podium, where the mayor stood with hands upraised.

"I have to go," she said.

"I'll escort you to the door," McCann said, gulping the last of his drink.

They stepped outside. Melanie, seeing Levin's deserted car, glanced around, but McCann walked straight to the vehicle, got in, and started the engine. He reached across and opened the passenger door.

"I forgot. What's-his-name got tired of waiting and took a cab. He asked me to drive you."

"I don't believe that," Melanie said indignantly. "Where is David?"

"Kidnapped by Arab terrorists. I didn't think you should know."

"Where is he, McCann?"

"Really, we had a talk. I told him how I felt about you, how you were the ace of hearts in my deck and the balm of my old age. He said he didn't mind as long as it's platonic."

Melanie opened the door and got in. "You better not have hurt him."

"No, sweetheart. I just told him I had a message from you that you'd be late and he should leave the car."

"Well," said Melanie softly, pressing against him,

"I'm glad the big policeman will drive me home. I hope he at least remembers where I live."

"The Mission Bell Motel?"

They kissed and Melanie lifted her little skirt above the hips and drew McCann's hand between her knees. He felt once again her smooth flank and rounded buttocks as he dipped inside her panties.

"I knew this was going to happen," Melanie said. "The moon has been in Scorpio and I've had this . . . *tense* feeling all week, like something was going to happen. Don Carlos, my spiritual adviser at Dino's, *said* it would be a heavy week. 'The heavens are going to pounce on you,' he goes; and I go, 'My chart this week has Libra in conjunction with Scorpio'; and he goes, 'That means that something heavy is going to happen'; so I go . . ." As she talked Melanie pulled off her panties and dropped them on the floorboard. "I don't know where we're going, but I don't want to waste any time when we get there."

It was approximately at this moment that they noticed a man standing outside the car on the driver's side with his face pressed against the window. It was a black face and two hands were cupped around the man's eyes as he peered into the car.

Giving a little shriek, Melanie tumbled over against the far door. McCann, also startled at the intrusion, drew his pistol, rolled down the window, and pointed the weapon at the man's head.

"Hi," said the man.

"Hi," said McCann. "Do you know that I'm probably going to kill you?"

"Ha, ha, ha," laughed the little man, slapping his hand against the side of the car. He was a slightly built NMA, about thirty-five years old, with a short, receding natural. A ridiculous smile played across his lips, and there was a strange look in his eyes.

"Gettin' a little?" giggled the man.

"You have every right to ask," McCann said, keeping the cocked pistol leveled at the man's head.

"Aren't you going to get out and slap me around?"

"It'll be a minute before I can stand up."

"Ha, ha, ha," laughed the man.

Opening the door, McCann slid out. The little man, his hands raised over his head, backed away a few steps, still flashing his peculiar smile.

"I know who you are, you know," he said.

"Really?"

"You're William McCann and you're with the Anti-Terror Unit. I saw your picture in *The Clenched Fist.*"

"My goodness, you don't say so."

McCann's anger faded and he regarded the man with curiosity. "What a strange person," thought McCann. The man had such a bland, vacuous smile and such a peculiar expression in his eyes. His eyes looked a lot like Henry's. There was that same kind of madness.

And then, with a sudden rush of insight, McCann understood everything.

"And I guess I know you, too. *You're the bomber.*"

"Ha, ha, ha. You can't prove that."

"How about a little pat down?"

"No, I don't think so. Ha, ha, ha."

As a matter of fact, McCann already had noticed a conspicuous bulge under the man's khaki fatigue coat. Gingerly he lifted the coat with the barrel of his revolver and saw that the man was wearing some kind of home-made leather contrivance. From it hung a fasces of dynamite wired to an alarm clock.

"Couldn't get into a john tonight, could you?"

"No *way,* man. You pigs is all *ovah* the place. You muthafucka jiveass *pigs* . . ."

"Would you mind talking normally, please?" McCann

147

holstered his gun and leaned against the car. "What's your name?"

"I don't have to tell you nothin', pig. I have the right to remain silent; I have the right to a lawyer; and believe me, I'm going to have a gang of lawyers. You think this is a pickpocket you're dealing with? You think this is a purse snatch? Well, you just wait and see. This is going to be a *political* trial. I laugh out loud when I think of you up there on the stand saying, 'Your honor, I thought this was a purse snatch!' Ha, ha, ha."

"You can put your hands down now, if you want." McCann removed his cap and scratched his spiky head. "Do you mind if I see some identification?"

"You have the right to see identification." The bomber fumbled in his back pocket and brought forth a battered wallet from which he produced a tattered driver's license.

"Herbie Simple."

"That's my slave name."

"Is this your correct address, Mr. Simple?"

"Ha ha, ha."

McCann smiled. "What's your correct address, Mr. Simple?"

"You might find something there," said the bomber.

"Oh, Herbie."

"Nine-oh-nine Divisadero."

McCann jotted the address in his notebook and handed the license back to Simple.

"Well, Mr. Simple, your papers appear to be in order."

"I've kept a diary, you know. Everything is in there, for the past year. I'm going to turn it over to my defense committee. And I have some other papers suitable for publication, and I've been working on my statement for my press conference."

"I'll see you around, Herbie." McCann got back in the car.

For the first time the smile left Simple's face.

"You're not slappin' the cuffs on me?"

McCann shook his head sadly. "Can't do it yet, Herb. Insufficient evidence. You know how the courts are these days. The constitutional rights of the accused and so forth. I just don't have a case yet. You've been too damn clever."

"That's true," said Herbie.

"Maybe next time. Now don't fall down on your way home." McCann put the car in gear and drove off, waving good-by to the forlorn little figure standing in the shadow of the building.

"A harmless kook," he explained to Melanie. "Now where were we?"

Early that morning when he returned to his apartment, McCann heard a radio bulletin announcing that the men's room at the Greyhound station had been dynamited, injuring two persons. The Greyhound station was a few blocks west of Italian Hall.

CHAPTER 13

Lieutenant Michael O'Riley was continuing his undeviating habit of taking his lunch at his desk. Many of his brother officers were accustomed to dining across the street at Roscoe's Il Trovatore, a restaurant that specialized in heavy pastas, thick gravies, and a dark red Chianti in which could be tasted the dust of Italy. Other officers took a simpler, liquid lunch at the Inn Justice. None of these bluecoats could claim to have ever seen O'Riley's ascetic visage at noontime.

Neither had O'Riley ever indulged in the camaraderie of the hallway and the squad room. He had never permitted himself to slap a back. Nor had he ever put a vice lock around somebody's ears, nor pretended to commit sodomy with another officer to emphasize some point in a discussion of police politics. In a word, O'Riley was not considered to be one of the boys. Nevertheless, surprising as it might seem at first, O'Riley's brother officers respected him and found they could easily tolerate his deviations from normal behavior. They realized, more or less subconsciously, that certain types of police work require different personalities. Captain Henderson, for instance, officer-in-charge of the vice squad, was certainly strange. So were the slick, jive-talking undercover officers living in the nether world of narcotics. And some of the older inspectors working police intelligence undeniably had that fanatical gleam; they were always sidling up to the people in the hallway with a copy of this or that report from the House Internal Security Subcommittee and pointing out their own testimony underlined in red pencil. In fact, when it came to special assignments, the only people nobody liked were the queers in community relations.

O'Riley's lunch that day consisted of a little packet of Ry-Krisp crackers, a small thermos of watery tomato soup, a wedge of sharp Cheddar, a peach, and three or four lemon drops. Propped in front of him on his desk was a leather-bound book, Spencer's *Principles of Ethics*, which he was intently reading as he ladled spoonfuls of soup between his bloodless lips. Piled high to each side of him on his desk, and stacked in neat piles all around the room, were tabloid newspapers, all from the underground press.

Represented in his collection were *The Tribal Bard* (hippie: sex), *The Red Mountain Tribe* (hippie: political), *The Clenched Fist* (student: revolutionary), *The Haight Oracle* (hippie: narcotics), *The Black Panther* (black: nationalist revolutionary), *Muslim Speaks* (black: cultural revolutionary), *The Hard Line* (PLP labor revolutionary), *Sisters United* (militant lesbian), *Vector* (militant homophile), and *Smash the State* (CIA infiltrated/co-opted).

151

The cubicle in which O'Riley worked was barren except for a street map of San Francisco on one wall and a map of the Ottoman Empire on another. The lieutenant's drab black coat hung on the coatrack; and the lieutenant himself sat at his desk in a white shirt and a thin black tie. In the noontime stillness, O'Riley's body was rigid, his emaciated face immobile, and even in the subdued lighting his eyes were invisible inside their dark sockets: it was the four-thousand-year-old body of Rameses II, his bandages thrown aside, sitting at a desk reading a philosophy book.

But then a soft tapping at the door interrupted his solitude and put a period to his concentration on Spencer's theory of society as an organism.

The door opened a crack and the leering red face of a gargoyle in a crushed hat pushed through, a face reminiscent somehow of a dog with an erection.

"Hiya, big boy," said Brannon of the *Examiner*. "I knew you'd be in here eating your curds and whey. Don't bother to offer me any yogurt, because I've already had lunch across the street."

The flushed face came forward and the rest of Brannon's body arrived. His baggy coat, hopelessly pulled out of shape by years of note pads and gin bottles, was creased and dirty; his vest, also heavily stained by food and drink, sported a vile-looking elk's tooth, leashed to his pocket by a greenish chain; and his pitifully thin ankles were exposed by trousers that were much too short, as if they'd been hiked up his shins as his belly inflated with gas from his degenerating viscera.

"Come in," said O'Riley, sitting back in his chair but remaining perfectly stiff.

The veteran newsman slouched down in the only other chair and rested his feet on a stack of tabloids. His first taste of a cigarette triggered a fit of violent coughing and tears seeped out of the old rheumy eyes. When the attack subsided, Brannon said, "You know, Iron Mike, it's not like it used to be. I've been trying to pump the homicide boys for 'War of the Pimps' but I haven't got to first base. I know all those guys, too. It's 'Hiya, Brannon, how's the kid,' until you ask 'em a question. Then they treat you like a nigger Congressman demanding a citizens' review board."

O'Riley's emotionless face altered slightly as he showed a set of brown teeth. He could see what was coming.

"In the old days it was different," Brannon continued. "You had some pals on the force and they would help you out. Because you were willing to help them. There was more a spirit of trust between the press and the cops. You could count on your pals to . . ."

O'Riley held up a hand. "What do you need, Charlie?"

"Ah, shit, Mike, you dried-up old asshole; you see right through me." Brannon, with a huge drunken grin, was leaning forward in his chair searching for a place to put his cigarette ashes. O'Riley brought out an ashtray from a desk drawer and placed it on top of a bundle of newspapers.

"I'll help you if I can, Charlie."

"Well, my editor has his balls in an uproar this morning, Mike. He wants some kind of follow-up on the Greyhound station bombing; you know, a progress report. It don't have to be much, but something that'll give a little continuity to the story."

O'Riley nodded his head thoughtfully. His two operatives, McCann and Henry, had not reported in so far today, and the lieutenant now regretted having upbraided them for disappearing from the mayor's dinner at Italian Hall. It was only later that he had learned they had been involved in the apprehension of a suspect of radical proclivities found loitering around the doorway of the building, and the suspect had actually tried to put up a fight.

In his desk O'Riley had a memorandum from the mayor's office ordering him in no uncertain language to take bold, decisive steps. It was an election year, unfortunately, and the mayor was up against a law and order opponent who was concentrating on the bombing issue. He had been forced to temporize with the mayor's office, stressing that it took time to infiltrate the radical subculture and so on. But at least McCann's last report had been promising; he and Henry did seem to be making contacts.

O'Riley felt certain it was only a matter of time. Somewhere out there in Haight-Ashbury or in the Fillmore a little collective of four or five anal-sadistic Communists sat behind walls plastered with North Vietnamese posters, tediously debating their next target. True, a dozen collectives had vied with one another for bombing honors in the pages of *The Clenched Fist,* but the crime-lab reports were conclusive; the MO was the same in each incident; even the cheap alarm clocks used to trigger the blasts were of the same brand. It had to be the same collective responsible, and eventually the members would be forced to reveal themselves by the weight of their own desire to bask in the admiration of their peers and perhaps even get a mention in the *Peking Review.*

"Frankly," O'Riley said, "I think we're getting close; my two men are turning up some good leads."

"Listen, I don't like to drop a nickel on anybody," Brannon said, crossing his spindly legs and shooting his grimy cuffs. "But, like I said before, I think that big Irishman drinks."

O'Riley impassively contemplated his friend's florid countenance, his rheumy eyes, the large purple veins throbbing in the porous nose, the pouches of ill-barbered flesh hanging from his cheeks and jowls. Although the lieutenant had never seen McCann looking the worse for drink, perhaps Brannon was able to scent one of his own kind, by means of an aesthetic denied to O'Riley. He remembered also that despite his specific prohibition against drinking at the mayor's dinner he had received a report from an informant within the Bartenders' and Culinary Workers' Union to the effect that a six foot four uniformed police officer with a surly red face had been drinking surreptitiously at the back bar during his speech.

Still, McCann's reports had been very encouraging and seemed to reflect exactly O'Riley's own thoughts. There were imperfections everywhere; it would be over-punctilious to scotch an effective operative because of a minor character flaw. If, in time, it turned out McCann's weakness for the bottle overshadowed his value as an agent, then he would have to go. But O'Riley sensed in his subordinate powerful forces of energy and determination, valuable qualities that only needed harnessing.

"I have never seen him drunk or heard of him being drunk," O'Riley said again for the record. "Even if he was to indulge occasionally during the working day, as many people do in all walks of life, I'm not sure I'd be greatly outraged. Remember U. S. Grant."

"Remember Pope and Butler," Brannon said.

"Of course. Provided it did not impair his ability to accomplish his mission."

"I'm not so sure about his jigaboo partner, either."

"You think he drinks?"

"I think he's loony. How the fuck did he ever get on the force?"

"Affirmative action," O'Riley said, getting out his pipe. Even sophisticated people like Brannon had difficulty grasping the core problem of police recruiting in the seventies. If it was hard to get stable, upright, idealistic young men to join the force, it was triply hard to get any kind of black to join.

The lieutenant struck a match, touched it to the bowl of his pipe, and expelled a heavy cloud of smoke. You simply had to take what you could get and make the best of them. Not to mention that the Federal guidelines dictated that 10 per cent of the force had to be minority by 1980 if Washington was to continue its subsidy to the Helicopter Surveillance Program. In short, the department couldn't afford to be picky.

"I think we're fortunate to have Henry," O'Riley said. "After all, we don't know yet the pigmentation of the people we're after; Henry might prove invaluable."

"Sure, sure. Maybe one crazy jig can catch some other crazy jigs. I ain't trying to tell you your job, Iron Mike; I'm just trying to get you to throw me some fucking *crumb*."

"Well, Charlie—Black Cat again, I'm afraid—we're pretty sure of a number of things. First, that the bombings are being carried out by a highly politicized collective or affinity numbering three to seven members. We can interpolate that these people are youthful, tinged with fanaticism, sophisticated in their appreciation of the weaknesses inherent in the system, yet shockingly naive about how best to exploit the propaganda value of their efforts.

"At this very moment I'm convinced there's a debate raging in their councils: how to make the public aware of their political purpose. They are so maladroit that even *I* don't know exactly what the purpose is, although it hardly matters. Undoubtedly, the collective has written to one of the alternative papers explaining their reasons; unfortunately, as you know, seven or eight other collectives have also written letters, all claiming credit and each for a different reason. In other words, intellectually, they must feel the bombings are dysfunctional unless the political lesson can be hammered home."

O'Riley, warming to his subject, had leaned forward to within a few feet of Brannon. Even so, the lieutenant's eyes, under the high, knobby dome, were still sunk in pools of blackness.

"So," he continued, "they want to deliver their message for a sound, rational, conscious reason. But something is more important. Unconsciously, they want to reveal themselves. You see, Brannon, in their own eyes, they are exceptional people, revolutionary heroes, much different from the cafeteria commandos who talk and talk but never *do* anything, never really pop the enemy in the snout. I'm convinced they want to brag on that. And sooner than later, my friend, this unconscious motivation is going to cause them to make some minor slip, to most people invisible, but to those waiting for it a neon arrow pointing directly at them . . .

"This is inevitable," O'Riley leaned back again in his chair. "And that's why I have decided on a two-pronged attack. First, my operatives in the community, listening posts tuned to the gossip of the street corner; secondly, myself, carefully studying the available material for the one hint that'll be all we need."

Brannon looked around skeptically at the stacks of tabloids in every corner.

"You're still reading this stuff, then?"

"Yes, that's a large part of it. The bombers are going to tell me who they are." O'Riley paused. "Of course, they may need to be prodded."

Nodding his head slowly, Brannon searched for his cigarettes. Somehow, he had managed to sit on his pack and the cigarette he drew out was crushed and bent.

"This is a great insight into police work," the reporter said, lighting up, "but it don't help me."

"It doesn't?" O'Riley leaned forward, his bony fingers pressed together on his desk.

"No, kid. Even if it wasn't Black Cat, you don't want these assholes to find out what you're . . ."

Brannon stopped in midsentence and stared at O'Riley's intent face through a coil of blue smoke. Suddenly, his rumbling, alcoholic laughter broke out, bringing on another paroxysm of coughing.

"Why you miserable little skinny cocksucker," Brannon said, gasping for breath. "I get your message. What do you want me to say? Some more crap about the madman? Why you dried-up little conniving bastard."

CHAPTER 14

Brannon left O'Riley's office and slowly walked down the corridor to the elevator.

"Crumbs," he said to himself. "I have to beg my friends for crumbs."

In many ways it had been a lean year for Brannon. So far the only police stories with any class, other than the bombings, were the Zodiac murders and the War of the Pimps.

Zodiac was a madman collecting slaves for his after-life, interesting only because he liked to correspond with the newspapers in cosmic language. It was really the War of the Pimps that had made Brannon's year. Running for more than a month, it had given him a satisfaction no amount of straight reporting could equal. It was not off the blotter either, so Brannon had a free hand to develop exclusives, which he didn't have to share with anybody.

Since the police were stymied in the case, Brannon had had to do everything himself. The war had broken out in June after the brutal slaying and mutilation of three black prostitutes in the Fillmore. The perpetrator, undoubtedly a maniac, was still at large. But through some all-too-common misunderstanding in the ghetto, the melancholy exit of the three ex-lovelies had blown up into a gang war between rival love brokers.

To Brannon's delight, several of his spirited pieces on "gangland-style executions" had appeared on the front page. And because of the pressure these stories brought to bear on the department, somebody or other had been taken into custody, and was about to stand trial in what promised to be a sensational case.

Brannon got off the elevator at the third floor and walked into the press room. He slumped into his chair and wearily lit a cigarette, tossing the match on the floor, where countless brown burn marks on the linoleum testified that he threw his butts there as well. Pouring a cup of gin, he picked up some 8 by 10 glossy photos from his desk and settled back. The photographs showed the latest victim in the gang war, a handsome young pimp lying in the street, his face disfigured by shotgun pellets. Somebody else might have clucked his tongue over this kind of picture. Brannon, however, thought it a good thing that the coons were knocking each other off. But, like many another who loathed blacks, Brannon got along with them famously. He had even managed to arrange a meeting between the warring condottieri, which was televised on the educational TV station, to the overwhelming disgust of the networks.

Moreover, in an exclusive interview Brannon had talked to the city's most notorious procurer, Dorado Man; and then had topped that by cruising around one night with two of Dorado's radio-dispatched hookers, post-debs in vice, who regarded the misfortune of their knife-dispatched competitors as the breaks of a chancy trade. Although it could only be suggested obliquely, the girls spiked their laconic responses with genial talk of arcane perversion and made all the usual allegations about the city's political figures.

That kind of story had a little class to it. It took skill and effort; it was not like begging a few crumbs from your friends. With a sigh, Brannon put the photos aside, rolled a new book into his typewriter, and began to knock out a quick story on O'Riley and the Anti-Terror Unit.

Examiner Page One Aug. 10.

ANTI-TERROR CHIEF REVEALS
BOMBER'S PROFILE: "MADMAN"

By Charles Brannon
Crime Writer, Hearst Headline Service

The head of the newly formed Anti-Terror Unit has prepared a "working profile" of the bomber responsible for the more than two dozen explosions in public facilities throughout the city, the *Examiner* has learned.

In an exclusive interview with this reporter, Lieutenant Michael O'Riley, taciturn officer-in-charge of the special police unit, said he seriously doubts the terror is politically motivated.

"What we have here is an out-and-out madman," O'Riley said, "who has started this rampage for the sheer pleasure of destruction. The man is a psychopath who commits acts of wanton vandalism without scruple or remorse, and solely for some twisted psychological motive of his own."

The Anti-Terror chief pooh-poohed the rash of

161

correspondence in the so-called alternative press that stridently seeks to attribute political overtones to the bombings.

"The writers of these letters are harmless, stay-at-homes who vicariously use the terror to further their own fantasies," O'Riley said. "There is nothing at all revolutionary about blowing up a toilet."

To date, four persons have been injured, one seriously, in the year-long succession of bombings. The Anti-Terror Unit was formed last week by the mayor to combat the outbreak of violence, which has been centered mainly on public restrooms.

"The bomber undoubtedly is someone incapable of real emotional involvement, who suffers from strong feelings of inadequacy," O'Riley said.

O'Riley likened the bomber to the infamous "Zodiac," although the lieutenant shrugged off suggestions that the bomber and Zodiac are one and the same.

Zodiac, the War of the Pimps, and the Terror make up a crime wave that has plagued and baffled police in past months, occasioning a public outcry and becoming a hot political issue in the current mayoralty contest.

CHAPTER 15

The courtrooms in the Hall of Justice had been modernized as the result of a bond election to expedite the administration of justice. In each court the roof had been raised and the walls covered with shining gray marble, giving the rooms cathedral-like majesty and, it was hoped, imbuing petitioners with a sense of proportion. The lighting, moreover, had been softened and muted by the placing of an arch of pearly glass over the entire ceiling, hiding from view the newly wired rows of neon tubing. The effect was felt to be more dignified than the former arrangement, yellow globes hanging from chains, that announced so distinctly, "police court."

The benches had also been raised in each courtroom, so that now the inky-robed Olympians sat a full three feet above the heads of the supplicating attorneys. Nor had the jury boxes been neglected; in place of the two long wooden benches on which so many generations of jurors had squirmed uncomfortably, each box now held twelve plush swivel chairs that also reclined, so that each juryman, if he wished, could tilt back and count the holes in the squares of acoustic tile that peeped out above the arch of pearly glass. All these improvements no doubt soothed the heart of the petitioner as he waited interminably for his case to begin.

In the hallway outside police court, McCann had crammed his gargantuan frame into a telephone booth. He was giving Henry a list of supplies he thought it might be provident to have in stock.

"Listen, Henry, write all this down," McCann was saying. "We're going to need a couple of AR-15's, one hundred rounds of ammunition, eight phosphorous grenades, a first aid kit, a field lamp, a portable short-wave radio, and a few bayonets. You got it? I'm going to be tied up in court this morning on this Levin business."

McCann sighed. It was going to be a busy day. He ejected from the phone booth, strolled over to the newsstand, purchased a newspaper and a cigar, and then made his way to the john. Tight security in the Hall and on the courtroom floors had made this john one of the safest in town.

Finding an empty stall, he put a half pint of bourbon in the safety liner dispenser, lit the cigar, and settled himself for a leisurely read.

On the front page was the story of the Greyhound bus station bombing, with a photograph of one of the injured janitors, swathed in bandages, being wheeled into Mission Emergency on an ambulance trolley. The other cut showed the interior of the bombed john, a jumble of broken tiles, shivered glass, and twisted metal. Brannon, crime writer emeritus, had hacked out the piece, giving it his usual flourishes: ". . . the case took an ominous turn as . . . the skulking purveyor of wanton destruction . . . previously had confined the terror to unoccupied buildings . . . now spread his cancer to public facilities in around-the-clock use . . . authorities speculated the Greyhound bombing will ratchet upward the level of violence . . . as the list of those senselessly maimed lengthened."

O'Riley was quoted as saying, "No political or social cause can justify endangering innocent lives."

McCann took a swig of bourbon and turned to the funnies, where he read Dick Tracy, Steve Roper, and Gordo. Glancing at his watch, he reluctantly prepared to go to court. On his way out of the john he dropped the empty bottle, wrapped in the newspaper, into the trash bin, and in the corridor he popped some Sen-Sen into his mouth. Then he strode into court.

Approaching the rail that separated spectators from participants, McCann glanced around for the prosecutor. Instead he saw two young fiercely mustachioed lawyers, each decked out in flared slacks, wide lapels, patterned shirts, and botanical ties. The two had their plastic attaché cases open in front of them on the table and were shuffling papers back and forth. Everything about them, from their frowning countenances to their two-tone shoes, said "Federally-funded poverty program."

The door from the holding cell swung open and a plump little lawyer in a rumpled gray suit bounded out and made for McCann. The little man had a bald spot the size of a sand dollar, a moon-shaped face with button features, and a round little tummy protruding over his pants. Despite these physical drawbacks, the man projected a vigorous, aggressive demeanor.

He bounced up and shot out one hairy little paw to McCann as if he were saying, "and *this* is Exhibit A."

165

"I'm Lyle Badger," he said in a high-pitched voice, "the assistant D.A. I've got to prosecute this fucking case. What an asshole that Levin is." The prosecutor grabbed McCann by the elbow and led him a few paces down the aisle.

"You're the arresting officer, right? Well, I'm afraid we have a problem," he said with a barely perceptible nod toward the two fierce young attorneys. "It turns out Mr. Levin is a man of conscience. He won't plead to a lesser count on the advice of those two shysters from Neighborhood Legal Assistance. They want to blow this up into a big police-brutality case."

"What did you offer?" McCann smiled blandly at the two OEO lawyers, who returned him what were meant to be withering looks.

"I offered to walk him for time served with a year's probation. Shit, you can't beat that," said Badger, smacking his hands together. "But they're telling him to hang tough."

"Can he make bail?"

The prosecutor snickered and gave McCann a light punch on the arm. "It's going to be as high as a giraffe's ass. But apparently some rich cunt in the Sierra Club is going to go his bond."

The door from the judge's chamber opened, the bailiff hopped to his feet, yelling "All rise," and the judge sailed in and seated himself on the bench. "Be seated," said the bailiff and the courtroom quieted as the judge rifled through a stack of briefs.

"We got one ahead of us, but it'll be quick," whispered the prosecutor.

A spiraling incidence of assaults against police officers had forced the court into a policy of excessively high bail for those accused of the crime. McCann had assumed that if Levin refused to make a deal he would have to face the prospect of staying in jail until trial, which might be set anywhere from six months to a year in the future.

"This Levin creep is fucking up the works," Badger continued in a low voice. "You should see the calendar. I'm supposed to handle seven cases this morning. Do you know that out of the more than three hundred cases I've handled this year not one has come to trial? Shit, I don't have time to try cases. That calendar's as tight as a bull's ass at fly time.

"And most of the garbage that floats through here *knows* they got us by the balls; they know they can get a good deal. But every once in awhile some Thomas More like this fuckhead Levin comes along.

"Shit, I can't remember what it's like to try a case. And believe me, that's vastly ironic, considering I took this job under the delusion that it might prepare me for the practice of law. It's prepared me to be a used-car salesman."

The judge raised his head, adjusted his glasses, and called the first case.

The defendant was a tall, strapping, nonchalant black kid accused of victimizing the Chinese owner of a Mom 'n' Pop grocery in the Fillmore by robbing him and then beating him senseless with a tire iron.

"Counsels will approach the bench," said the judge.

A heavy black attorney, dressed in a flashy silk suit, diamond rings sparkling on his fingers, confidently strolled up to the bench from the defendant's table, while a drab, lanky assistant D.A. approached from the prosecution side. The judge bent his head into a huddle that lasted nearly a minute before the three heads bobbed in unison. The lawyers returned to their corners.

"Well," said the judge, removing his eyeglasses and rubbing his eyes. "Now if I understand this correctly, it's the defendant's contention that while he committed the robbery he did not commit the assault."

The little prosecutor nudged McCann. "The People of

California ain't got much of a hold on this one. The coon is guilty, of course, but the damn grocer is still in a coma and there are no other witnesses. The coon was caught a block away with a wad of money in his pocket and that's the case. His counsel would laugh at the idea of taking a plea at all, except they're afraid the Chink might come around and still have enough marbles left to make an identification. This way, the coon takes a fall for robbery, but walks."

The flashily dressed black attorney was expostulating with the judge about his client's priors. Many of them, the attorney pointed out, dated from the defendant's minority, and hence should not properly be part of the court's consideration.

"He still has three priors, two for assault," said the judge.

"As I *attempted* to explain to the court in chambers," said the lawyer, with a faintly exasperated air, "we must take into account the background and heritage of my client. His life has been a ceaseless, uphill, Sisyphus-like struggle against the iniquity of American racism. It was racism in the school that forced him into a life of the streets; it was racism in industry that keeps him un- employed; and now I'm beginning to think that racism in the judiciary will force . . ."

"All right, all right," said the judge, "no speeches. The defendant will rise."

The young black got up, put his hands behind him in a kind of casual parade rest, and grinned winningly at the judge.

"How much time have you served, Mr. Carleson?"

"Six months and a few days, judge."

"You were unable to make bail?"

"It was set too high, judge; four thousand is too high, judge."

"All right. Now you understand that you are pleading guilty to the charge of robbery with the knowledge that there have been no previous arrangements with the court regarding your sentence."

The black looked at his lawyer, who nodded.

"Yes, judge."

"All right. And the district attorney's office is prepared to drop the assault charge?"

"Yes, your honor," said the gangling assistant D.A.

"All right. I'm sentencing you to a year in county jail with six months' suspended and two years' probation. Do you understand the sentence?"

"It means I can leave," said the defendant.

"That's right." The judge tapped his gavel. "Call the next case, bailiff."

A bustle ensued in the courtroom as the jubilant Carleson and his attorney made their way to the door. A couple of Carleson's supporters, tall young men in dashakis and narrow shoes, danced up to wallop him on the back, saying, "All *right*." The defendant's mother, a fat woman in a pillbox hat and a veil, grasped the attorney by one of his encrusted hands, tears shining in her eyes. "You *must* come to supper," she said.

Meanwhile, the two fierce OEO lawyers took their places at the defense table, and the little prosecutor sat down at his table and began pulling sheaves of paper out of a battered old briefcase. McCann moved up to sit inside the rail.

Levin, displaying a Band-Aid above one eye, came in from the holding cell, pale and erect. He stiffened when he recognized McCann and quickly looked away when the officer smiled and wiggled his fingers at him. The counsels were called to the bench for several minutes of angry whispering, while the judge looked on with hopeless resignation at the two indignant poverty lawyers.

Smirking, the plump little D.A. returned to his seat and, leaning back, said to McCann: "What'd I tell you? No deals. They want a trial."

With a resigned expression, the judge continued to thumb through the papers in front of him, reading again the police report, Levin's notarized deposition, the contending briefs.

"We'll have a ten-minute recess," the judge said at last. "I want to see all parties involved in my chambers."

"All rise," intoned the bailiff; the judge swept out of the courtroom. Everybody got up and followed him, leaving only the bailiff, the clerk, the court reporter, and a few idlers behind.

Inside his office, the judge unbuttoned his robe, threw himself into his swivel chair. "Sit down, sit down," he said, rotating his hand. He removed his glasses and began massaging his frontal lobes.

"I'm still hopeful that the counsel for the defendant can accommodate the court in some way," he said.

One of the fierce OEO lawyers straightened himself in his chair and shook his mane savagely.

"Our client wishes to plead innocent. For reasons we will make clear in court, this police officer, William McCann, assaulted him and caused him humiliation and caused him to be falsely arrested and imprisoned . . ." He stopped as the judge held up a hand as if he was trying to ward off a blow.

"I've read the brief, of course, but now, let's see . . . Officer McCann, your report states that the defendant lunged at you and struck you with his fist and then resisted your attempts to subdue him."

"That's correct," said McCann.

"Did you incur any injury?"

"No, your honor. You can see he's a lightweight."

Levin bared his teeth and nodded his head, as if to

say, "You'll find out what kind of a lightweight I am."

"You bear no animosity toward Mr. Levin?"

"None whatsoever, your honor; the attack was so feebly executed, in fact, that I would have merely cited the defendant for a traffic violation except that the incident occurred outside Italian Hall during a speech by the mayor. We had strict orders to interrogate suspicious persons loitering in the neighborhood, so . . ."

"Suspicious!" cried one of the OEO lawyers. "Now, your honor . . ."

The judge held up one hand as if he was stopping traffic while he covered his eyes with the other.

"We're not pleading the case yet, Counsel. Mr. Levin, listen to me a moment. I want you to think over your situation and weigh the facts very carefully. Consider, please, the nature of the charge against you; the location of the arrest; the temper of the times; the mood of the public; the likely inclination of a jury of your peers. I want you to consider the dearth of witnesses in your behalf; the sworn statement of the driver of the police van, who deposes that *he too* had to subdue you. I want you to consider if it is possible that those who counsel you have motives of their own . . ."

"*Your honor*," cried out the two OEO lawyers in unison.

"Counsel will allow me to finish my remarks," said the judge. "I want you to consider, Mr. Levin, that the charge against you is a felony, and conviction will bring up to ten years' imprisonment; I want you to remember that you have not been permanently hurt by the incident; that the police department, represented by Officer McCann, bears you no ill will; and that a trial is long and costly, both financially and emotionally.

"I want you Mr. Levin, to weigh all these factors and tell me if you don't think it might be better for your counsel and the district attorney's office to discuss the matter further and perhaps reach a settlement of some kind."

"I want a trial," said Levin, glaring at McCann.

"All right, all right. Don't make up your mind right away. This is merely the preliminary hearing to set bail. We'll schedule arraignment for next week, okay?"

"What is the bail?" asked one of the fierce OEO lawyers.

"Well, I think it ought to be fifty-thousand dollars."

"*What!*" cried out the two lawyers.

"It's a very serious charge. Your client doesn't seem to realize that. Now, Mr. Levin, you think over what I've said to you and see if you haven't changed your mind by next week. That'll be all, gentlemen."

Officer McCann and Assistant District Attorney Badger strolled along the corridor, the little prosecutor lugging his huge battered briefcase. It was lunchtime and the corridor was nearly empty.

"That idiot is going to wind up in San Quentin if he isn't careful," Badger was saying. "As far as I can see, we've got an airtight case."

"That's good," said McCann, absent-mindedly.

"He *did* hit you, didn't he?"

"Sure."

"I mean to say, there were no other witnesses?"

"Right," said McCann.

"I know the judge wants to compete in the Nassau-to-Bermuda race next month, so this may come to trial pretty quick. Say, do you want to have lunch?"

"I can't today," McCann said. "I've already got a date."

"Ho, ho, ho," said Badger, nudging McCann in the ribs.

CHAPTER 16

The Domino Athletic Club has an unprepossessing entrance in an undistinguished building on Stockton Street in North Beach. A small, polished brass plate with the club's name cut in script is the only clue that the door doesn't lead to an upstairs apartment inhabited by six Chinese families.

McCann arrived in a cab, paid off the driver, and stood for a moment in the swirling fog, his blue poplin jacket pulled up around his ears, before ringing the buzzer. The doorman, a swarthy muscular Italian, glared suspiciously at McCann's ugly face and the badge in his hand.

"Mr. McCann? Come this way."

Expensively carpeted stairs led upward, but the muscular Italian, who seemed to be one of those bodyguard-masseur combinations preferred by Southern politicians, took a sharp turn and led McCann down a dank concrete stairway to a dimly lit basement smelling of liniment. The room was utilitarian, a wet bar and television at one end, some tumbling mats, an exer-cycle, and a set of barbells at the other.

"Mr. Apples is taking a steam," said McCann's guide. "The dressing rooms are down the hall. If you want," he added pointedly, "I'll lock up your valuables."

McCann surrendered his wallet, his wristwatch, and his .38 Special and walked down the corridor. He emerged from the dressing room a moment later swathed in a white sheet and waited while the Italian swung open the heavy door of the steam room.

A cloud of steam rolled out and McCann ducked inside. His lungs began to breathe the sodden, hot, palpable air. He tossed the sheet aside and clambered up the wooden banks toward Apples, whose shiny red skin shone out of the mist like a buoy in fog.

"Greetings, McCann. Nothing like a steam before dinner."

McCann cautiously lowered his bare skin onto the thin wooden slats of the bench and drooped his towel across his knees. The thick fetid air made him gasp, and the sweat immediately began trickling down his body.

"I was meaning to ask today whether our little transaction will interfere with your work with the Anti-Terror Unit," Apples said. "I think, indeed we all think, that it is extremely important to curtail political terror in our city. As a matter of fact, the Committee passed a resolution to that effect today, which will be passed along to the mayor. The Committee usually tries not to involve itself in local politics, but the issue is one of such overriding importance. Indiscriminate bombing of public facilities makes it appear that the authorities are not fully in

174

control, and this lessens public confidence in government."

"You don't think the overthrow of the government would be in your best interests?"

"No, indeed, Mr. McCann," Apples said, smiling politely at the feeble sarcasm. "We are staunch advocates of two-party pluralistic representative democracy coupled with free enterprise, as those terms are understood in the higher reaches of corporate capitalism. And unlike the chamber of commerce, we pay those concepts more than mere lip service."

"You put your bets on the table."

"It's only good business, Mr. McCann. Do you like the steam?" Apples' hard little marble eyes were expressionless, but the suggestion of a smile played around his sensual lips.

"How hot is it in here?"

"It's very hot. You know, Mr. McCann, the Committee is very intrigued with you. Yours is one of the few markets still open to the independent entrepreneur. Most of the other commodities have been fairly well organized; and narcotics will be as well, one day; but now there is still room for the individual. I hasten to add, however, that you are running counter to the historical trend. Inevitably, power will concentrate. Business will interface with labor and the two in turn will merge with government; and this is natural and valuable because, you see, there'll be less of a hodgepodge, more cooperation between power bases, more efficiency. I mean, it's obvious. More people are demanding things. Strong government or chaos are the alternatives, Mr. McCann; the future demands centralization. Those who see it will profit; those who fail to see it will inexorably be swept from the board."

Apples gave McCann a sidelong glance.

"But that's tomorrow," he continued. "Today is a

transitional period. We have to determine a means for you, the rugged individualist, to interface with the corporate behemoth. The item you have for sale, you realize, is worthless without the distribution grid provided by our infrastructure. That is why you come to see us, is it not?"

The sweat poured from McCann's body. The steam sucked at his pores like a thousand greedy mouths. He could smell the booze leaking out of him; he could feel the oiliness of it on his skin. His pulse had quickened; in fact, his heart was thumping alarmingly. And suddenly, the first frightened animal scampered through his brain, as he felt the invisible hand clutch at his heart. His pulse raced faster, and the first stab of pain stiffened his left arm.

Apples quizzically examined McCann's hunched body and laboring chest before resuming.

"To recapitulate briefly, you will have shortly a three-million-dollar consignment of the famous Double O Brand from Southeast Asia, for which you need a purchaser. And once again, please, how much do you hope to realize?"

McCann had to fight to keep his hand away from the gripping pain in his chest. "I told you, seven hundred and fifty thousand."

"Well, well," said Apples, patting his bald pate with the corner of his towel. "That's a deal of money. It's like this, Mr. McCann, before any such outlay could be authorized, the Committee would need to have some glimmering of how you envision getting this shipment to San Francisco."

"The Committee can fuck itself," gasped McCann.

Apples had been watching McCann out of the corner of his eye. "Do you feel all right, Mr. McCann? You don't look well at all."

"I don't like the steam," McCann said. "What do you say we have a drink?"

"Why, you haven't been in here ten minutes. Besides, the door won't open from the inside, and Lucky has orders not to disturb us for half an hour."

"Fuck!" McCann bent forward and crossed his arms over his chest. The sweat coursed in rivulets down his face and neck. A hideous familiar terror filled his mind, whirling him in dizzy circles toward unconsciousness. He was weak, helpless, unable to lift his leaden aching arms to throttle the unctuous, smiling Apples. His sinews were disintegrating, and his flesh felt as if it would fall from his bones. As usual when this happened McCann asked God to relent; he begged God not to kill him there, in a steam room, with the mocking Apples.

"We have to know how you plan to do it," Apples said gently. "It's merely good business. We have no interest in taking what's yours; we simply have to know if your plans are realistic, for planning purposes; if your plan is feasible, then we budget accordingly."

"Please let me out of here, Mr. Apples."

"In a minute. I'll try knocking on the door in a minute. But really, Mr. McCann, be reasonable. You served with the Army in Southeast Asia, did you not?"

"Yes," gasped McCann.

"It's safe to assume you made arrangements there for the shipment. You were in the hospital in Long Binh. Did you make the acquaintance there of a surgeon named Baradikian? We know he handles some traffic in that area."

"Open the door, Mr. Apples. Can't you see that I'm not well?"

"In a minute. How is Dr. Baradikian going to send it to you?"

McCann's heart was like a fist slamming against the

inside of his chest. It was a plastic balloon slowly filling with blood until it would burst inside him. It was some small animal being crushed to pulp in a vicelike grip. And the pain was overwhelming.

"A body," cried McCann suddenly, "It's coming in a body."

Apples nodded his head and smiled, patting himself on the face with his towel. "Yes, that's very good," he mused. "I see it now. It would have to come to Travis. Of course, why didn't I realize it? That's why you have the good offices of the coroner, that's why he helped you with the Smith case."

Apples smiled indulgently at the hulking figure of the police officer, bent double and gasping like a landed fish. "Let me see if I can get this door open." Apples waddled over and easily turned the handle. "Why, it wasn't locked after all. Come along, Mr. McCann, and we'll revive ourselves with a drink."

Lucky appeared with fresh towels and sheets. The muscular Italian exchanged a quick look with Apples as McCann staggered from the steam room, still bent forward, the heels of his hands pressed against his chest, and his face contorted with pain.

"I think we'll have a cocktail, if you'll be good enough to open the bar," Apples told the attendant. "Let me help you with this sheet, Mr. McCann."

At the bar, Lucky was mixing a martini for Apples. "What'll the gent have?"

"He'll have bourbon on the rocks," Apples said. "Here, let me pour. There you are, Mr. McCann. Two units of anti-terror." Apples' dull eyes showed a momentary spark of amusement as he poured.

McCann, leaning heavily against the bar, quickly gulped the liquor, and Apples, solicitously standing by his elbow with the bottle, poured out another double shot.

178

"The steam is often hard on a person's system if he's not used to it, but *really*, Mr. McCann, I had no idea." Apples chuckled softly. "Of course. I suspected there was something. There always is when a person drinks; but I couldn't quite put my finger on it. That's why I thought it might be informative to see your behavior under, shall we say, sobering conditions. So that's how it is with you? My goodness, Mr. McCann."

Apples poured some more whiskey. "Well, I must say, your scheme is utterly fantastic: you join the police department to smuggle heroin into the country in a dead body. And as if that wasn't enough, you become a member of the Anti-Terror Unit as well. To give yourself enhanced mobility, I assume. Well, it *is* fantastic, Mr. McCann. But I imagine this hurly-burly life of yours *does* keep your mind occupied. If you keep busy, there's no time for distressing thoughts. And then you sedate yourself quite a bit, don't you? Here, have another."

McCann held out his glass for another drink. "I'll kill you for this," he said at last.

"Hey, that ain't good talk," Lucky said, stopping in the middle of mixing a second martini.

"No, no," Apples said good-naturedly, "I'm beginning to think you won't do anything of the kind."

McCann, after his third double, had partly regained his composure. The pain had stopped, his vision had cleared, he could stand up straight, and the healthy throb of alcohol cleared the lead out of his veins. His strength was returning.

"I have a bad heart," McCann said, draining the glass.

"Do you? And you so young. Well, there's nothing like straight whiskey to ward off a coronary." Apples set down the bottle and made a sign for Lucky to find occupation elsewhere. He then picked up his martini and tasted it. "I don't mean to ridicule you, Mr. McCann. I've taken an interest in you and I'd like to be your friend. This unfortunate allergy of yours to steam baths changes nothing; we'll go right ahead with our partnership. You very graciously have given me the information I need to pass along to the Committee; and I'm sure they'll agree with me that your plan has merit and should be underwritten by the company. So there; do you feel better now? Pour yourself another."

McCann filled his glass. He still felt weak and di-minished somehow. He felt off-balance and unable to defend himself against the probing Apples. He realized that the public facilitator had made him afraid.

"I really do have a bad heart," McCann said, "and for some reason booze seems to be the only thing that helps. I know I'm a dead man, I'm in constant pain, I really don't think I can last a year."

"Of course," said Apples soothingly. "Well, no wonder you're not interested in long-term employment. Poor Mr. McCann. Although I'm afraid it's of no use to you, I understand your predicament perfectly. Without alcohol you suffer what the psychiatrists like to call nervous affects; yes, you suffer anxiety, which is accompanied by a sensation of being small and weak. Am I right? I could even tell you the cause of this, but it wouldn't help you, because you wouldn't believe me. You would be the one most surprised to learn you suffer from attacks of conscience. Did you know you have a conscience, McCann?"

"No I don't," McCann said hastily.

"Yes you do," said Apples. "You have a terrible con-science. Liquor lulls it, but when it wakes, my goodness, what a dragon. In this you resemble a thousand others. But what makes you unusual and interesting, my friend, is that when this terrible ogre is deadened by drink you are free. You escape that hard-faced policeman trapped in your brain and you no longer hear his nightstick of

retribution tapping in your heart and then . . . my goodness, Mr. McCann, why you can do *anything;* you can
act out all those cruel dreams of blood that other people
hardly realize they have."

"This is horseshit," said McCann.

"This is not horseshit. You are one of the few people
able to answer the promptings of instincts that are secret,
irrational, and violent. And *that,* Mr. McCann, is why
you could be so valuable. You are rare. An intelligent,
able man who, under certain conditions, is not fettered
by any scruple. Not by *any* scruple. You have passed
through morality and are on the other side. Convenience
Drayage needs a man like you; I sincerely mean that."

Apples picked up the bottle and poured McCann
another drink before continuing.

"Frankly, Mr. McCann, now that I have more insight
into your personality, I believe more strongly than ever
that money alone means very little to you. In fact, getting
a large sum of money might be the worst thing that
could happen to you; you might find yourself unoccupied,
and that would be bad for you. Believe me, you'd do
much better with interesting and fulfilling employment."

"I want the money," McCann said.

"Allow me to talk with you a moment like an uncle.
Employment in our organization brings many benefits,
not the least of which is a generous health plan. Mr.
McCann, to be perfectly candid, you need professional
help. I am talking about psychiatric help. Now, wait a
minute . . ." Apples' soft little hands fluttered as McCann
started to protest. "There's absolutely no stigma attached
to this. Many of our best people are in some form of
therapy; I've been in analysis myself. It not only can
relieve certain kinds of gross nervous manifestations
such as you experience, but, perhaps equally important,
it can increase one's insight into his fellow man."

"I'm not interested," said McCann, having another

181

drink. "There's nothing wrong with me. I can take care of myself."

"Very well, Mr. McCann," said Apples, the little smile playing again around the corners of his mouth. "Let's drop that for the moment."

Apples knitted his brows and with one finger toyed with the olive in his glass. "But please do me one favor. As I've said, I'm confident our partnership can prosper. The Committee meets next week and I'll deliver a favorable recommendation; so I think that's settled. But I would like you to undertake one more small chore for us, something in the nature of the Smith case but much more interesting. It's the kind of work you'd be doing regularly for us if you were in our employ. As a favor to me, give it a try and see if it doesn't interest you. Of course, this means a bonus; say five thousand for you and your partner for a night's work. We trust each other, so I'll give you the money right now."

Apples summoned Lucky by pressing a button under the bar. He directed the well-muscled factotum to prepare an envelope with the appropriate amount of currency in small bills for McCann when he left.

"Here, let me freshen your drink," Apples said after Lucky had gone. "Now, our problem is this . . ."

CHAPTER 17

"Do you think these might be the ones?" Henry's white eyeballs shone in the darkness a few feet from McCann's head.

"They might be," McCann said.

"They talked to me last night," Henry whispered. "They laughed at me. I could hear them clink their glasses and slap the cards on the table. And when the man won a big pot, he laughed and laughed and pointed his finger at me. And then he turned over his hand and made me say, 'Five spades; you have to die.' But it's not me."

"I know it's not."

The two officers were sitting together in the dirt beneath a huge earth grader in the middle of the OK Construction Company Corporation yard at Half Moon

Bay, twenty miles south of the city. Henry, silently rocking on his haunches, cradled an AR-15 in his arms as he softly crooned the unvarying story of his torment at the hands of the sadistic incubus.

McCann, however, was more relaxed. Sprawled out next to one of the vehicle's large tires, he enjoyed a second old fashioned, his rifle propped against the side of the grader. A mile to the west, the surf rumbled on the beach; and they could see the lights of cars passing along Highway 1. The wind rustled in the eucalyptus grove to the south of the fenced yard; crickets and frogs chirped and grumped; and Henry wondered in whispers why men would want to spend their time ridiculing him from a cardroom inside his brain.

The Teamster intelligence network controlled by Apples had reported that one of San Mateo County's most militant environmental groups, the Defend the Coast League (DCL, pronounced *diesel*) planned to raid the OK compound after midnight, the objective being to deflate tires and pull distributor wires and in that way to prevent the equipment from being used the next day to break ground for a new housing tract south of Tunitas Creek.

The earth-moving equipment, bulldozers, Caterpillars, heavy trucks, were dark masses scattered around the yard, casting long shadows in the moonlight. Apples had retained McCann and Henry to guard the equipment, and to chase off the activists should they come. Their other responsibility, should DCL put in an appearance, was to dynamite several pieces of well-insured equipment. It was hoped that this would make it appear that DCL was linked to the wave of bombings. Apples thought this would discredit the group with the public and at the same time smooth the way for a building project that, as the *Half Moon Bay Review* and *Pescadero Pebble* had noted editorially, was opposed by every coastside resident with an ounce of conscience.

At the same time, of course, they were still members of the Anti-Terror Unit. McCann had informed O'Riley that, acting on an anonymous tip, they would stake out the area during the evening.

Shaking his head and muttering to himself, Henry was deftly twisting detonating caps onto sticks of dynamite, a skill he had picked up in the Army. As a demolitions specialist, Henry had blown up tractors, trucks, irrigation pipes, bridges, water buffaloes, hooches with and without families, roads, rice caches, wells, and, of course, a major in the U.S. Army.

McCann had just opened a fresh old fashioned when Henry touched his shoulder. The crickets and frogs suddenly had fallen silent. Henry quietly put aside the dynamite and turned over on his stomach to peer out from behind the tire. McCann, taking a swallow from the can, reached for his rifle, thumbed off the safety, and moved to the other side of the vehicle.

From the edge of the compound they heard the faint snip-snip of wire cutters.

McCann edged forward a few feet and raised himself slightly. From this position he could make out a dark figure crouching by the fence. A moment later, the figure waved a hand, and four or five shadows stealthily detached themselves from the eucalyptus trees and rushed for the fence. With a screech, the fence was wrenched back and the raiders fanned across the lot.

Apples had suggested they allow the fanatics a few minutes to work before stepping in to break up the raid by firing a few shots into the air. Apples had discarded the idea of shooting any of the pranksters, because much of DCL's membership came from business and industrial families; and it would be hard to know exactly whose

185

son or daughter might be injured during a bout of indiscriminate shooting.

McCann watched his luminous second hand sweep around the dial while he listened to the hiss of escaping air. Then, making sure his weapon was on automatic, he fired a short burst straight into the air, over an adjacent pumpkin field. From the corner of his eye he saw the muzzle flash as Henry fired a stream of bullets skyward. It had been a long time since either of them had heard the sound of automatic fire.

According to Apples' scenario, the ecology pranksters were to flee in panic. Instead, something else happened. A bullet ricocheted off the grader with a twang, and another slug plowed up a furrow a few yards in front of McCann's nose. The far end of the compound lit up with muzzle flashes and resounded with the crash of gunfire.

"Why, those fucking assholes," thought McCann, backing up so precipitously that he spilled his drink. A flat thud and woosh told him a bullet had struck one of the front tires. McCann rolled over and lay flat behind the grader with his arms covering his head and his face buried in the dirt. He remembered now that nobody had even considered the ecologists might shoot back.

Henry, however, stayed in place. He calmly lowered his rifle and fired the rest of his clip in a broad sweep of the yard, the bullets screaming off the flanks of trucks and graders. He then lightly jumped to his feet, simultaneously slamming in a fresh magazine.

"These are the ones," screamed McCann from beneath the bulldozer.

Henry, totally unmoved by the bullets snapping through the air, switched back to single fire, and bracing his left elbow against the grader directed a methodical fire at the raiders—zap, zap, zap—until finally a scream punctuated the shooting.

"They're the ones," screamed McCann again.

"They're going now," Henry said quietly, resting the butt of his rifle on his hip. "I hit one of them and his friends are trying to drag him away. Should I shoot them?"

"No, no," said McCann, hurriedly gaining his feet and carefully peering around the vehicle.

"Hey, you motherfuckers," shouted McCann, "leave that man alone or get shot. Henry, fire a round over their heads."

In one smooth movement, Henry brought the rifle to his shoulder. The weapon cracked and the muzzle flash lit up Henry's calm face for an instant. One of the two dark figures at the fence ducked, bringing a hand up to an ear that may or may not still have been attached to his head. They dropped the wounded man and fled.

"How do you like this?" McCann had dropped to his hands and knees and was searching around in the darkness for his cache of old fashioneds.

Quiet had returned to the corporation yard except for the groans of the wounded man. The crickets and frogs had resumed their interrupted love songs; a car engine started somewhere behind the eucalyptus grove, and then the sound of the motor died away.

McCann had found an old fashioned and was seated by the huge tire. "Do you think they've gone?"

"Oh yes," said Henry, who was checking his rifle and putting in a fresh magazine.

"After I open this drink we'll go see what we got."

The two officers strode across the yard to where the wounded man was groaning softly, sprawled on his back in the mud a few feet from the fence where his comrades had left him. The injured man turned out to be a typical white male hippie type, approximately twenty years old, with his hair tied behind in a pigtail. His face had been blackened with soot or dirt and he wore a military fatigue jacket. A .22 caliber target pistol lay a few yards away.

Kneeling beside the youth, McCann saw that his pant leg was soaked with blood; the bullet had shattered the right leg below the knee, and the youth obviously was rapidly slipping into shock.

"Do you remember what to do, Henry?"

Nodding, Henry pulled a knife from his boot, quickly slit the boy's pant leg and pressed the heel of his palm against the shredded lips of the wound to staunch the welling blood. Then he cut the boy's shirt to make a bandage, elevated his feet, and threw his own uniform coat over him.

"I'll call the ambulance if you'll take care of the charges," McCann said.

With another nod, Henry slipped off to plant the dynamite. McCann walked back to the squad car, slid into the seat, opened a drink, and switched the radio over to the frequency used by the Highway Patrol. Just before he pressed the talk button, two orange, oily explosions erupted and a light rain of debris pattered down on the hood and roof of the car.

"That'll bring them here in a hurry," McCann thought.

He got through to the CHP dispatcher with his request for an ambulance and some back-up units.

"You're Officer McCann with the Anti-Terror Unit?" asked the woman dispatcher.

"Yes."

"I have a message for you. Call Lieutenant O'Riley at his home."

More than an hour passed, however, before McCann had a chance to call O'Riley. They had to wait for the ambulance; they had to fill out an arrest form on the wounded saboteur; and they had to haggle with the locals about whether the hick authorities ought to have been informed of the raid. But most importantly, McCann had to take the reporter Brannon aside to explain to him exactly what had happened. In return, Brannon furnished a clue as to what was on O'Riley's mind.

"While you guys were dicking around down here there was another bombing in the city."

"Is that right? The *Examiner* building, I hope."

"Go ahead, McCann. I'm like Job when it comes to taking guff from my sources."

Finally, McCann and Henry got away from the OK Construction Company yard. They stopped at the first gas station on the highway and McCann wedged himself into the phone booth.

"Listen, Lieutenant," McCann said as his superior's sleepy voice came on the line, "we got one of them in the bag down here. I ran into Brannon and he said something about another bombing."

"That's right," O'Riley said, "but we have a pretty good lead this time. The bomber left behind one of his shoes."

"It must be that old compulsion to confess."

"I think you're right."

The scene of the latest blast was the men's room in the downtown branch of the State Human Resources Development building. A janitor had narrowly escaped injury. Apparently the culprit had somehow managed to walk out of the building undetected with only one of his shoes on. It was the clientele of that agency, one supposed, that allowed him to escape unnoticed.

The two officers drove downtown leisurely. They stopped at Star Liquors at Oak and Fillmore Streets, where McCann spent one of the small bills packaged by Lucky for the purchase of an assortment of thirty canned cocktails and two plastic bags of ice. The two or three young bucks in the store, with their three-quarter-length tan patent-leather coats and their quarts of Rainier Ale or half pints of Johnny Walker Red Label, regarded the giant red police officer with hostility as he elbowed his way to the counter, his arms full of mai tais, margaritas, and whiskey sours.

With fresh drinks in their hands, the officers cruised Webster Street in the Fillmore to look at the whores. It was obvious that the population had been thinned considerably by the War of the Pimps, which still raged in the ghetto districts. McCann's commentary on the whores soon had Henry in a fit of giggles. There was nothing really *wrong* with black women, McCann said, even if their legs do look like burned chicken skin; he might even take one on himself one day, if he could persuade her to undertake a full course of hot water, hexachlorophene, penicillin, a good parasiticide, and if a doctor was in attendance. Henry laughed and laughed; it took his mind off the voices.

At last they arrived at Divisadero Street near Church. McCann parked the squad car in somebody's driveway and dumped a few drinks inside his leather jacket. They walked up some steps and into a filthy hallway solid with trash, broken bottles, bean cans, dog shit, greasy food wrappers; the walls were scrawled with obscenities, and a sickening odor of stale urine floated in the air. As they clumped along the hallway, one of the apartment doors opened a crack and a woman's black face appeared. McCann shook his fist at her, the door banged closed, and the bolt shot into place with a click.

They stopped at Number 7 and McCann hammered on the door with the butt of his pistol.

"Come in," said a soft, feminine voice.

McCann turned the knob and kicked the door open. Herbie Simple, scourge of the city of San Francisco and all its crappers, was sitting placidly in a huge, fan-shaped wicker chair, a spear in one hand, a shotgun in the other. A black beret covered his receding natural and he was wearing a khaki fatigue jacket strung with a hodge-podge of military decorations. He had on a pair of black chino slacks and he was wearing only one shoe.

"Hi, Herbie," McCann said. "What's happening?"

Simple looked up at his inquisitor with the dignity born of a long trial of sufferings known mainly to himself.

"My slave name is Herbie Simple; I'm a major in the People's Liberation Army; my telephone number is 987-3210."

"Not talking, huh?" McCann placed the canned drinks on a table holding a number of scrapbooks.

"Not all the jack boots in Fascist America can stomp more out of me. Not even my brother, John Henry, who has become a running dog."

"Listen, Herbie, do you like mai tais or old fashioneds?"

"Sissy drinks," said the rebel major, laying aside the shotgun and setting the spear across his knees. "I only take liquor neat."

"Aha. Look here." McCann whipped a flask out of his back pocket. "Jack Daniels."

"You can just pass that over."

"Nice place you got here, Herbie." McCann had settled himself on the couch and was taking a look around. A gallery of familiar faces in lurid color stared down at him: Mao, Che, Eldridge, Huey, Emiliano, Stokely. The apartment was small and clean, with a bare, well-swept floor; an army cot with a carefully folded blanket was pushed in one corner; behind Herbie was another table on which lay a partially stripped M1, a ramrod, a bottle of gun oil, and a few rags.

Through a nearby doorway, McCann could see that

the kitchen had been converted into a workroom. Tools were spread on the kitchen table; a vice clamp was attached to the sink; and on the sideboard were thirteen or fourteen alarm clocks. McCann picked up one of the scrapbooks and idly flipped the pages; all the stories, neatly clipped and pasted, were about the bombings; and most of them, he noticed, had been written by Brannon.

"Where do you keep your dynamite, Herbie?"

The cagey saboteur, in the middle of a swig from the flask, waggled his finger at McCann.

"It'll be in the refrigerator," Henry said. "You have to keep that stuff cool. The produce compartment is best."

"That's right," said Herbie, smiling happily at Henry.

"You know, Herb," McCann said, "we've been working night and day on your case, and I think we're getting close to having some evidence a jury would accept. Right now, of course, we'd be laughed right out of court. You know, this could become a big trial."

"Big trial!" cried out Herbie, brandishing his spear. "The trial of the century, you mean. You think this is a liquor store stickup? You think this is some kind of piss-ant strong-arm? You think I slashed my girl friend across the tit with a razor? Get with it, copper, this is no little *nigger* deal."

Herbie let McCann hold the spear a moment while he rummaged through some dime notebooks underneath the coffee table.

"You see this? A diary running from December seventeenth, the beginning of the terror, to date. You see this? The names of my defense committee. You see this? An open letter to the public explaining certain acts. And this is an invitation to Charles Garry to undertake my defense. And here is some correspondence with other black revolutionary leaders around the world."

"Circumstantial," said McCann, examining the spear, which he noted had been made in Taiwan.

"You think this is some kind of *purse-snatch*?" Herbie grabbed his spear angrily and fell back into his wicker chair in a huff.

"We need hard evidence," McCann said, "not conjecture. Do you happen to have a couple of bombs made up?"

"Nothing like that in this house," Simple said, still angry.

"Six or seven of them out here on the table," Henry said from the kitchen, where he was having a glass of water.

"Grab two of them, Henry, and we'll let the crime-lab boys have a look. Well, Herbie, we got to get going; we still haven't given out our quota of traffic tickets."

"Shee-it," said Herbie.

"Oh, and one other thing, Mr. Simple. We'll have to trouble you for your shoe."

McCann and Henry cruised down Van Ness toward the Marina. Herbie's bombs were uncomplicated devices: two sticks of dynamite, of the kind frequently stolen from construction sites and easily procurable in any large city, and a blasting cap, attached to an alarm-clock mechanism. Any twelve-year-old could have put together bombs such as the two Henry held in his lap as they drove over to Melanie's apartment on Greenwich Street.

A familiar Volkswagen was parked outside; apparently, Levin had got his car out of the auto pound. A Volkswagen, of course, is the easiest car in the world to open without a key; that's why so many of them become dune buggies. McCann, with the help of a coat hanger, had the car open in an instant and dumped Herbie's shoe and the two bombs into the back seat. Then they walked up to the iron gate of the apartment building and McCann began hitting buzzers until somebody opened the gate for them.

Melanie lived in a modern plastic building with wall-to-wall mirrors in the lobby and a ceiling covered with some kind of sparkling fluorescent material. McCann's swollen, monstrous body filled the tiny elevator as they jounced upward to the fourth floor. Henry had started muttering and hissing again and opening and closing the fingers of his hands, as if they were two heads conversing. McCann watched him idly and swirled the last swallow of his canned mai tai.

"Melanie knows us, so we can just walk in," he told Henry.

The officers entered the dancer's apartment in much the same way they were accustomed to using to gain entrance in their work, by kicking the door down. Pulling his pistol, McCann stepped back and delivered the door a smashing blow with his heel, splintering the wood around the lock, ripping the chain out of the wall, and tearing the entire door from its hinges.

The officers rushed across the threshold. Melanie and Levin were lying on the living room sofa, their limbs entwined. Both were nude, but Levin still had his glasses on; their twisted clothing was piled in a low ridge across the base of the sofa.

"This is a no-knock," McCann said cheerily. "Hiya, Melanie. What's doing, punk?"

"Die," shouted Henry.

Melanie's eyes and mouth had opened wide, while her consort seemed on the verge of a fainting spell.

"Listen, this is just routine," McCann said, sitting down across from them. "Finish whatever you're doing."

"Whores. Die, die, die," Henry had huddled himself in a far corner, muttering and hissing. The man in his brain had just shown him trip fours.

"Oh, McCann, this is so rotten of you." Melanie scrambled out from beneath Levin and ran into the bedroom. Levin, white as alabaster, trembling in every limb, tried to talk but found that the power of speech had deserted him. He sat up and began sorting through the tangle of clothing.

"Listen, punk. I didn't want to say anything when Melanie was around, but we're here to arrest you."

"For what?" asked Levin in a quavering voice.

"Come on, kid, you know for what; you're parked in a red zone again."

Tears appeared in Levin's eyes and he began sniffling as he put on his socks. McCann relented.

"Oh all right, I'm only kidding. We're really here to arrest you for bombing the welfare office tonight. Now, let's see, you have the right to remain silent, you have the right to counsel . . . Listen, do you care for a drink? I'm having one."

McCann holstered his pistol and brought out a couple of drinks.

"Levin? No? How about you, Henry? Okay, I'll save this other for Melanie then. Listen, I hate to do it, but I've got to slap the cuffs on you; that's regs for dealing with dangerous felons like yourself."

"You just *can't* do this," whispered Levin, blinking back his tears.

"Now don't go resisting again; you know where that leads. Hands behind your back. Thataboy." McCann snapped the cuffs in place and forced Levin to lie face down on the sofa.

"Henry, do you mind watching the suspect for awhile? And remember, unlikely as it seems," McCann added, lowering his voice, "this could be the one."

McCann picked up the two canned drinks and walked into Melanie's bedroom, closing the door behind him.

For more than an hour, Levin lay face down on the sofa listening to Henry's imprecations against the people who gambled with his life. He could see Henry's yellow eyes gleaming with hatred and his lips twitching with spasms of hisses and muttered curses against the ghostly gamblers responsible for his agony.

"That's not me, you know," Henry explained several times.

There were other noises, emitting from the bedroom, that also disturbed Levin: the low murmur of voices punctuated by hoarse laughter; the scraping of furniture; the prolonged creaking of the bed; soft stifled feminine moans; and then the louder rhythmic tumult of a crisis. Levin twisted in dismay on the sofa, until Henry roughly pulled his head back by the hair.

"Are *you* the one?"

Levin's glasses fell off, the room blurred, and Henry became a spectral figure, hunched forward, rubbing his hands together and hissing. At last McCann emerged from the bedroom, buttoning his shirt. His hair was plastered against his knobby skull.

"I've interrogated your sweetheart and I'm glad to say I don't think she's implicated in the plot," he announced. "Well, there's nothing more we can do here. Don't bother getting dressed, Mr. Levin, it's come as you are night at the Hall of Justice."

McCann picked up Melanie's princess phone and called communications, asking them to send a unit to check out the suspect's Volkswagen. Then they dragged Levin to his feet, bundling up all his clothes except his shoes, and set off. Getting out of the elevator in the lobby, the trio, the two officers, and the thin trembling youth dressed only in socks and spectacles, met a chic young couple returning from an evening on the town; McCann courteously doffed his cap and held the elevator door for them.

At the Hall of Justice McCann took Levin up to the sixth-floor lockup.

"So that's the bomber," said the desk sergeant.

"Yeah," said McCann, filling out the arrest slip. "He's a queer, too."

"I thought so," said the sergeant. "We know how to take care of him."

There was only one more thing to do, McCann mused, and that was to find Brannon again.

CHAPTER 18

Lieutenant O'Riley sat rigidly at his desk, sucking meditatively on a piece of rock candy. Spread before him on his desk were several newspapers and half a dozen telegrams. In one hand he held a fountain pen poised over a small pad of notepaper. He was drawing up a list of possibilities, and he had written:

Radicals
Black Nationalists
Environmentalists

Those seemed to be the three possibilities, but he let his pen hover a moment longer while his mind reviewed the evidence culled from a month of assiduous reading of the alternative press.

The events of the previous night certainly seemed to

incriminate the environmentalists. Brannon's latest article, on the front page of the morning *Examiner*, gave a detailed account of the gunfight at the OK Construction Company yard and the subsequent arrest of a prominent employee of the Sierra Club.

There had been strong and immediate reaction to the news. The mayor not only had telephoned his congratulations but inexplicably had sent a telegram as well: "RELAY KUDOS YOUR MEN STOP ATU PAYSOFF STOP UPKEEP FINE WORK."

There were other telegrams from Democratic officials around the state and even one from a private citizen in Los Angeles expressing gratitude; and the police secretary said calls were starting to pour in. The mayor, always ebullient, had been pleased even beyond his usual eloquence this morning. "At last we're getting some movement," he had said. "At last we're *doing* something."

O'Riley glanced again at Brannon's article: "SHOOTOUT WITH TERRORISTS, ONE WOUNDED, SIERRA CLUBBER ARRESTED." He was lavish in his praise of McCann and Henry, "the intrepid young officers," and referred to O'Riley himself as "the gaunt mastermind of anti-terror strategy." He was also calling the Sierra Club suspect "the Cinderella saboteur" because his lost shoe was a crucial piece of evidence.

"The long arduous pursuit of the terrorists who have rocked The City with bomb blasts turned the corner last night as a police net tightened on the bombers in a brilliantly timed one-two punch."

Still, for some reason, O'Riley was vaguely uneasy.

For one thing, the idea that the bombers might belong to environmental groups had never occurred to O'Riley; he did not even take the *Sierra Club Bulletin* or *Ecology Today*. The pen descended on the pad as O'Riley made a note to subscribe to those papers.

The lieutenant's long melancholy face, with the deep seams running from nose to mouth, the grizzled close-cropped hair, the deep-set eyes that were inky pools, seemed chiseled in stone as he sat completely motionless at his desk, contemplating the latest turn of events. His thoughts were interrupted by a rap at the door.

"Come in."

The door shot open and the doorway was completely filled by the hulking figure of McCann; McCann, whose eyes sparkled, whose red cheeks glowed incandescently, whose toothy grin radiated malevolence, whose huge vital chest and biceps seemed to strain the very material of his shirt.

"Hiya, boss," he said, resting one huge paw on the butt of his pistol and with the other holding up the early edition of the evening paper, which featured a large cut of McCann himself on the front page.

"Very pretty," said O'Riley.

McCann threw himself into the empty chair and shook open the paper; an odor of Sen-Sen wafted across the desk to O'Riley.

"Listen to this, boss; the mayor is really making points today; 'MAYOR RAPS CRITICS, LAUDS ANTI-TERROR,'" McCann read. "'The mayor, fighting a bitter contest for re-election, savagely raked his Republican opponent, Jackson Duprey, at a Commonwealth Club speech today for allegedly refusing to support police anti-terror efforts.

"'"Duprey demands law and order for the city of San Francisco," the mayor told five hundred members of the elite businessmen's club, "but he declines to give specifics. Yet the specific and successful efforts of our fine police force to halt the terror are consistently denigrated by my opponent. I'd like to remind you gentlemen that it was only last week at this very podium that Mr. Duprey called the Anti-Terror Unit a 'pathetic last-ditch publicity gimmick by the mayor to stay in office.'"

" 'The mayor said faith and patience in the newly formed unit under the command of veteran police lieutenant Michael O'Riley had paid off last night in the arrest of two suspects, one caught red-handed in the act of sabotage and the other with two explosive devices in his possession.

" ' "The people of San Francisco very rightly demand action and action is what they are given by the police department and by the administration of this city," the mayor said.

" 'Duprey, a prominent San Francisco attorney and restaurant owner, could not be immediately reached for comment, but a staff spokesman denied the candidate had "denigrated" the Anti-Terror Unit.

" ' "Mr. Duprey has always had the utmost confidence in the police of this city," the spokesman said. "His assertion has been that the mayor has been attempting to use the successes of the police to cover his own failings in office." ' "

"It goes on," McCann said.

"I think I get the picture." O'Riley's bony fingers plucked up a number of telegrams and let them flutter back to the desk. "I want to add my congratulations to those of the mayor, the city attorney, and the director of public works. You and Henry seem to be getting results and your devotion to duty is highly commended. Well!" O'Riley leaned back an inch or so in his chair. "So it's the ecologists."

"No," McCann said, "I don't think so."

A moment of silence followed as O'Riley stared at the large, grotesque, apple-red face in front of him.

"You don't think so?"

"No I don't," said McCann. "I think it's the Teamsters."

"The *Teamsters*?"

"It all fits together, boss. This environmental militancy is merely a one-shot deal resulting from the county's decision to okay the Tunitas Creek development. The Sierra Club and DCL were hoping to stop the construction and pin it all on the real terrorists."

"And you think these real terrorists are . . ."

"The Teamsters. My sources in the community, who are unimpeachable, tell me that the Teamsters are trying to organize the heroin pushers in the black and Chicano neighborhoods. Now because of Cesar Chavez and all that, the greasers already have union affiliations, so that's all right.

"But some of the blacks, particularly the Panthers, are not falling in line. The Panthers, as you know, boss, have this *thing* about serving the people; breakfast for pickaninnies, a chicken in every bag, sickle cell anemia tests, *and* . . . a drive against narcotics, all of which they use as a smoke screen for their real revolutionary activities and as a means of shaking down the libs for donations. But what the guilt-ridden libs don't seem to know is that for every doughnut that goes into the mouth of a pickaninny, a bullet goes into the chamber of a pistol; the Panthers take the breakfast donations and go straight to a certain gun dealer in Nevada . . ."

"All right. But what about the Teamsters?"

"The Teamsters, you see, want to discredit the Panthers with their liberal checkbook supporters. The Teamsters realize that these libs will go for feeding darkie brats, and can even stomach community control of the police. But the libs draw the line at terror. So, after they discredit the Panthers and chase off the lib money, the Teamsters will move in and make a deal; *they'll* pay for the Panthers' breakfast program if in return the Panthers will handle the heroin traffic in the ghetto."

"Do you mean to say that the Teamsters are trying to *frame* the Panthers as terrorists?"

"That's right," McCann said, grinning. "That's exactly right."

"How do you know this?"

"Henry. Henry got it from Huey Newton himself."

"Henry knows Huey Newton?"

"Henry knows all those spooks. They're like chickpeas in a pod."

"Please don't use racist expressions," O'Riley said absent-mindedly, as his bony fingers traced a line across his hollow, cadaverous cheeks. To say the least, McCann's theory was startling; but if true, it had even more ominous consequences.

"Then, you seem to be saying, we can expect more bombings."

"I'm afraid so."

O'Riley remembered that there was one black collective that had been writing letters to *The Clenched Fist* for the past two months. The letters had been full of bombastic attacks on racist this and fascist that and had taken credit for all the bombings. O'Riley had dismissed them as being too blatantly pat, the work of a lunatic. But could it be that the Teamsters had planted those letters to point an accusing finger at black militants?

True, they hadn't been signed by the Panthers; they'd simply been signed by a Major Herbie X, of the People's Liberation Army. But the writing, O'Riley had thought at the time, was like a caricature of the Panther prose style, as if it had been lifted straight out of *The Black Panther* newspaper, abounding with expressions such as Mickey Mouse this and Donald Duck that.

The first thing, however, was to gird the mayor for more trouble.

"Are you . . . benefiting from Henry's insights?"

"I sure am," the ruby-faced policeman said. "I'm infiltrating the hierarchy of the Teamsters right now. In fact, I'm late for an appointment." McCann jumped to his feet and yanked up his heavy gun belt.

"Keep me informed," O'Riley said, as McCann lunged out the door.

The sallow lieutenant gazed at the picture of McCann on the front page. The cutline read, "Hero cop shoots terrorist." One might have misgivings about McCann's personal habits, but, like General Grant, he got results. Then, remembering himself, O'Riley quickly jotted down a note to subscribe to *Drayage World* and *Truck and Driver*.

CHAPTER 19

The U.S. Army keeps a small detachment of men at Travis Air Force Base across the bay from San Francisco to operate a receiving unit for the heroes returning from Southeast Asia. This Graves Registration Detail works out of a small square concrete building near the field. When one of the huge c-130's comes lumbering in from the west with its cargo of the month's remains, prisoners from the Travis stockade scamper out, lug the heavy steel caskets from the bowels of the aircraft, then wrestle them aboard fork lifts for the short trip across the apron to the GR building.

There, several morose clerks shuffle the last remaining paperwork dealing with the heroes, and the encapsulated bodies go into a large refrigerated vault behind the building, until arrangements are made for transshipment and final interment in Bristol, Colorado, or Snowflake, Arizona, or wherever the hero happens to come from.

Heroes had once streamed into Travis from Vietnam by the thousands; now, with the formal war over and only the secret war continuing, they trickled in at the rate of only a dozen or so per month; and the clerks had been forced to practice a nervous ingenuity devising ways to multiply the paperwork, so as to forestall any effort to transfer them to other assignments that in all likelihood would be nearer to Big Springs, Texas, than to San Francisco.

Two days had passed since the shoot-out at Half Moon Bay. It was early morning, but McCann was up and driving over to see Henry. He had already phoned O'Riley to tell him that he and Henry would be acting on a tip most of the day.

The tip, of course, actually came from the Armenian surgeon at Long Binh who, in a special delivery letter, had dropped the code message, "give my best to all," which meant that the next unclaimed KIA coming into Travis would have his stomach full of heroin.

Driving an unmarked police car with Mississippi plates, McCann drove over to Henry's apartment on Oak Street. Henry lived in a suitably dreary apartment above a soul food and barbeque take-out that provided him with most of his meals.

Ignoring the cold stares of two bloods on the corner who were sipping their morning Rainier from half-quart cans still wrapped in paper bags, McCann trudged up the dark landing and pounded on Henry's door. After waiting a few seconds, he opened the door and went in.

All the shades were pulled in the apartment and the only light came from the flickering television set, although the sound had been turned down to the faintest buzz. The TV set was one of five in the room, all of them sitting in one corner along with a dozen portable radios, six or seven stereos, a few electric guitars, an assortment of rifles and pistols, some jewelry, and a cardboard box full of wallets and purses, all gathering dust. This stuff, naturally, was stolen property that had not yet found its way to the Hall of Justice.

In another corner was a pile of trash—boxes, wrappers, and paper plates from the soul food place. Littering the floor were clothes, beer cans, wads of cotton, torn pages from the telephone directory, half-burned newspapers, medicine bottles, and expended cartridges. On the mantel were some of Henry's war souvenirs: a Russian AK rifle, some blood-spattered notebooks and a diary written in Chinese, a tattered Pathet Lao flag, and a large Mason jar containing the pickled head of the young North Vietnamese regular who had bayoneted Henry in the stomach.

Henry, his eyes bloodshot, dressed only in shorts, came out of the bedroom with some clothes draped over his arm.

"I couldn't sleep at all, Bill," he said. "They were talking to me all night. They been playing cards in the apartment right over my head. Four men and a woman. They been laughing and yelling all night. They pass the bottle around and deal out game after game of eights. And when the eight comes up the man turns to me and tells me to hate."

"This is the top apartment," McCann said.

"They must be on the roof, then. They follow me, Bill. I turn on my lamp sometimes and the electricity goes right up my arm. But it's not me."

"I know it's not, Henry. Look, I brought you a bloody mary." McCann took two tinned drinks from his coat, gave one to Henry, and opened one himself. Henry regarded the can suspiciously, and then took a little sip.

"Sometimes they come out of the water pipe," he said.

"I know they do. It's not fair, but there's nothing you can do."

"That's right." Henry sat down and began putting on his socks.

McCann, standing at the mantelpiece with the heavy Mason jar in his hand, sipped his drink and gazed into the noncommittal eyes inside the glass, waiting for Henry to finish dressing.

The two officers drove over to Bob's House of Donuts at Haight and Stanyon, where they met Keating, the coroner's deputy. Keating was very nervous.

"Jesus Christ, I sure don't like this," Keating said as he slid up to them in the parking lot. He was wiping his palms on his baggy trousers.

"Listen, it's a cinch. Why don't you have a bloody mary?"

"God damn you, McCann, you know I've got an ulcer."

McCann led the way out to the air base, Keating following in the pastel blue wagon. The AP at the gate perfunctorily waved them through, and they drove up to the small concrete building next to the hangars. A man was standing by the doorway, next to the crossed-shovels insignia of the Graves Registration Detail. The man, in the uniform of a captain, was short and stocky, with dark brown eyes and a flat nose like a doorstop. He wore the Big Red One patch on his shoulder.

"Howdy, fellas, I'm Captain Spicer," he said, rendering a damp hand all around. "You got to excuse me. We had a big shindig last night; a hell of a deal. A bye-bye party for the CO of the Army group here at Travis. I hope I never see the prick again. Now let's see, what is it I can do for you all? I remember something about something."

McCann nudged Keating, who started out of his daydream.

"We've come to pick up Mr. Sizeman," Keating said, pulling a letter out of his inside coat pocket. "Let's see.

Sizeman, Donald. Private first class, Twenty-Third Infantry Division. No known next of kin.

"Yes, yes, I remember," said Spicer, pressing his hand against his forehead. "The unclaimed KIA. Well, he's in storage, if we can figure out which one he is."

Spicer led the way behind the building, across a concrete patio strung with wash lines, to the underground refrigeration unit.

"You wouldn't believe the clerks here," Spicer was saying. "Last month, for instance, they sent a nigger to a Caucasian family in Shreveport, Louisiana. It was a good thing for us they buried him without looking. The only way we ever did find out was that the clerks also sent the white KIA to the nigger family. And *they* opened the casket."

"I suppose that was embarrassing," McCann said.

"No, it turned out all right," Spicer said. "They decided to keep him."

The four men walked down some steps. Spicer pulled back the heavy refrigerator door and they entered the chilly vault. Twenty or so steel caskets were piled on the floor in groups of three. Spicer looked around rather hopelessly.

"Do you happen to know if this guy is a coon?"

"Try to keep a lid on the racial slurs," McCann said, jerking a thumb at Henry.

"God damn, I'm sorry," said the captain, peering at the black officer. "For some reason, with your uniform and all, I didn't notice."

"Never mind," said McCann, clapping the confused cracker on the back. "What difference does it make anyway what color a stiff is?"

"Well," mumbled the captain, "I usually keep colored personnel in the rear."

Spicer went over to a stack of boxes. "See, these little yellow tags are supposed to tell the contents. But sometimes they get torn off in flight, and the flight crews just slap them back on any old way. We've had the bastards play jokes on us, too."

"How old are these guys?" asked McCann, bringing out a bottle of whiskey.

"Week, ten days," said Spicer, refusing the offer of a drink with a wave of the hand. "Because of condition upon receipt, CUR, it's called, there's nothing much we can do for them but stop the orifices, drain, and inject solution."

A throaty "Ahhh" came from the back of the shop. Henry was sitting on the floor in the rear with his ear pressed against a casket. He was hissing and muttering and snuffling deep lungfuls of air.

"Asses," he said, "die, die." The man in his brain had just drawn aces.

"You never know what a jig will do," McCann said under his breath.

The captain smiled faintly and busied himself with looking at the yellow tags.

They found the casket with Sizeman's name on it, at the bottom of one of the stacks in the corner. While Keating and McCann worked to unencumber the box, the captain went back upstairs to get the covering documents, which included a physical identification of Sizeman along with the circumstances of his heroism.

"If we can get rid of the captain for a few minutes, I don't see any reason not to unzip him right here," McCann said.

The captain came back and handed Keating a folder. "That's about it. Just sign this release and I'll get some men to help you carry the box."

"Well," said McCann, "we can't sign for him unless we look at him."

"What?" said the captain. "Why not just take a chance? Who cares? I mean, if he doesn't have family anyway."

"Yeah, well what if some kin show up and can't make an identification because we've got the wrong guy?"

"Oh Christ. Well, go ahead then, but I'll wait outside. I can't stand to look at 'em." The captain, a little wobbly, retreated up the stairs.

"You don't have to bother any of your men," McCann called out after him. "We can handle the box ourselves."

McCann took out his pint bottle and tipped it a few times while Keating opened up the casket. The hero was inside a brown rubber bag.

"Cut it," said McCann.

Keating took out his suture knife and slit the rubber bag down the middle, revealing the body of the dead soldier. Sizeman was in repose, his eyes closed, his forehead yellow, his cheeks white, his neck a blotched purple.

"The sutures should be across his gut," Keating said, pulling out the hero's fatigue shirt. "There they are."

"Okay," said McCann, taking another long drink from his bottle. "We might as well cut him open."

Just then, they heard a noise on the stairs.

"Ha, ha," said a gruff voice, "I've caught you."

It was Brannon, crime writer for the *Examiner*. The reporter was standing on the stairs looking down on them, his absurd old hat pushed back, his hands buried in the pockets of his dirty overcoat. His dissolute old face was lit up with laughter.

"I *knew* you were a lush, McCann," Brannon said. "One boozer can always spot another."

McCann smiled and finished taking a drink. "Well, I hope you won't tell O'Riley about this. It's just that I need a little pick-me-up when I meet a gent like this one," he said, nodding toward the casket. Out of the corner of his eye McCann could see Henry's woolly head sticking out above a pile of boxes; Keating, pale and sweating, quickly pulled down Sizeman's shirt.

"Let's take a look," Brannon said, swagging over, his

overcoat flapping. "So this is Sizeman. Big fuckin' deal. But any excuse for a tiddly, I say." Brannon reached into his own pocket and brought out a pint. McCann could see that the reporter already had had a few.

"Hiya, Keating," Brannon said, "you look like shit."

"Close the lid," McCann said to Keating. What brings you out here today, Brannon? This is kind of no-class for you, isn't it, what with War of the Pimps and the shithouse bomber?"

"So I said to my editor. But he seemed to have some interest in this. Maybe he wants some color on how a dead soldier without folks winds up in potter's field. Something like that, I guess." Brannon took another hit. "You don't have to worry about my telling your boss you're a juicer. I'm obviously not one to judge."

"How'd your editor happen to get on to this?"

"Well," said Brannon, wiping his lips, "it's supposed to be a secret. But I know that Wolinsky touted him on it for some reason."

"Wolinsky?"

"Yeah. He's business manager for Teamsters Local 75; handles the circulation trucks. A cop wouldn't know it, of course, but Wolinsky's one of the biggest gangsters in town. So when he gives a tip, there's bound to be something to it."

Brannon grinned and took another hit. "And now I respond out here on a Wolinsky tip and find the Anti-Terror Unit on the scene. So why don't we stop fucking around, Wild Bill. What's going on out here?"

"Ladies," shouted Henry from the back, "die, die."

Brannon looked around. "Is that your partner?"

"He had enchiladas for lunch," McCann said. "They don't always agree with him."

"It's only ten o'clock."

"Listen," said McCann, pocketing his bottle, "I don't know any more about this than you do. We got a tip same as you. Something is supposed to happen, but honest to Christ I don't know what. We just checked out Sizeman. Nothing. We're just going to wait and see."

"I guess that's it," said Brannon.

Shivering slightly in the frigid air, McCann collected Henry; Keating went off to sign for Sizeman; Brannon had another. Then the two officers, grunting and straining with the weight of the heavy coffin, manhandled the narcotics-laden hero up the stairs and into the coroner's wagon. They started back to the city, Keating first, followed by the two cops, followed by Brannon in his boxy, utilitarian *Examiner* press car.

The little motorcade had just left the main gate when a battered old black hearse of the kind used by rock musicians for carrying instruments pulled out from behind a billboard and forced Keating's wagon into a ditch.

Slamming on his brakes, McCann slewed his car into the back of the hearse and he and Henry tumbled out with guns drawn, then realized that two vehicles full of armed men had pulled up behind them. The gunmen were all hippie types, some carrying Thompsons; others carried sawed-off shotguns. While these men motioned to McCann and Henry to drop their weapons, an Air Force jeep with two plausible looking AP's aboard pulled up. The AP's hopped out, one on each side of the road, and began waving the irregular traffic past.

One of the hippies with a Tommy gun appeared to be the leader. He was a brawny man in his early fifties whose long yellow wig made an odd contrast with his olive complexion. His neck was festooned with beads and macramé; his striped yellow Arrow shirt had been sewn with ribbons; and an outsize pair of purple felt bell-bottoms failed to conceal the tips of his $150 alligator shoes.

He took a couple of 3" x 5" typewritten file cards from

his shirt pocket and began consulting them as he straightened his wig.

"All right," the hippie said, more or less to himself. "Here's the two coppers; here's the meat wagon; now where the fuck is the newspaper reporter?"

Brannon's car had stopped behind McCann's, but nobody seemed to be in it. Another of the hijackers went over and jerked open the door. Brannon, who had collapsed against the dash, fell out and rolled into the ditch.

"He ain't dead, is he?" said the hippie chieftain.

"No, just drunk," said the other hijacker, picking up a gin bottle from the front seat of the car.

While two hijackers propped up Brannon against the side of the ditch, the rest of the gang quickly transferred the casket from the coroner's wagon to the hearse and then stood around stifling yawns or chewing on toothpicks. One of them brought a manila folder for the chieftain, who took from it a couple of damp, freshly mimeographed sheets.

"Give this one to the reporter, will you." The assistant, with the help of a colleague, began shaking and slapping Brannon in an effort to revive him.

"You want to see this?" The hijacker chief proffered the other sheet to McCann.

"Sure." McCann took the paper. "Did Apples write this?"

"I don't know no Apples," said the hippie chieftain.

Henry, meanwhile, with his hands in the air and his back against the car, was muttering and gnashing his teeth, continuing his incessant diatribe against the sleepless cardplayers.

"You should tell your partner not to take it so hard," said the hijacker.

"He hates hippies."

"Yeah. So do I." The hijacker lit an expensive cigar.

The mimeographed sheet was a press release explaining the reason for the hijacking of Sizeman's remains.

People's funeral for victim of U.S. Imperialism
Blood Brothers, a militant collective dedicated to opposing aggression and imperialism abroad and fascism and oppression at home, practiced armed love today in seizing the remains of Pfc. Donald Sizeman, a victim of U.S. bosses and their lackeys.

Sizeman, propagandized into volunteering for Army duty, paid for expansionist U.S. foreign policy with his life. Since the slain soldier is without family, the brothers unanimously adopted him at last night's weekly collective meeting and will inter his body in a pleasant spot, far removed from the serried crosses of a military cemetery.

Funeral services and interment will be private. Contributions to the Anti-Imperialism League. Labor donated.

The balding and paunchy hippie hijackers loaded into their vehicles and disappeared down the highway, leaving only the two bogus AP's to watch over the victims of this bold, daylight stickup. Brannon, stretched out in the culvert, was snoring peacefully, the press release sticking out of his shirt pocket. Cars whizzed by without slowing.

One of the AP's, masquerading as a corporal and holding the stock of a carbine against his hip, told McCann the group would be detained ten to fifteen minutes. Henry, eyes shut, fists clenched, body stiff, muttered his imprecations against the men who hounded him night and day. The other AP came over to get a smoke from his buddy.

The wrenching suddenness of it took McCann so much by surprise that his heart didn't have a chance to quicken before it was over. Henry, seemingly without opening his eyes and in the midst of a muttered curse, bounded like a samurai and kicked, catching the AP corporal in the groin with the side of his shoe; in the same continuing fluid and perfectly timed movement, he hit the other AP squarely between the eyes with the heel of his hand, making a tremendous smacking noise and killing him instantly. It was a trick he had learned while serving with the 101st Airborne Division.

The corporal was down on his knees groaning and Henry was astride him, his hands at the injured man's neck.

"Make him talk," McCann said, just as his heart began to thud sickeningly. "Find out where they went."

In the Army, of course, Henry had been familiarized with techniques for the interrogation of prisoners. While the AP corporal screamed, pleading with Henry for the boon of a quick death, McCann sat dazed in the car drinking whiskey until the pain in his chest subsided and his heartbeat slowed to something reasonable.

"The Vacaville airport," Henry said at the car window. "They're meeting a plane to take the shipment to Los Angeles."

By this time, with the whiskey helping him, McCann began collecting his wits.

"I think they might be the ones," Henry said.

"The ones?"

"The ones who talk to me."

"You might be right." Then McCann, after another swallow of whiskey, made a gesture familiar enough to soldiers in the field. It was the gesture used when a job had to be done for which nobody particularly cares to take credit and that absolves all parties from having given or acted upon a verbal order. Henry stepped over to the AP corporal, whose body was shaken with sobs, and performed the duty with the certainty born of practice and a precise knowledge of the effect of a sharp blow on the medulla. The two officers threw the bodies in Keating's panel truck.

The coroner's deputy, who throughout had been trembling by his van, his face white and his stomach acidic, now began to protest this last operation, the putting of the two corpses in his truck, but a glance from Henry made him suddenly fall silent.

"Now look, Keating, I know this is slightly more than we all bargained for," McCann said, "but if you just bear up this will come out all right yet. You follow us to the Vacaville field. And for Christ sake, let's not wake up Brannon."

They drove to the airport Code Three—red light and siren. As the unmarked car hurtled down the highway, the siren wailing, the red light flashing in the window, McCann's feeling of shock and helplessness dissipated, to be replaced by a growing rage. His brick red face almost glowed, his mouth twisted into a sneer, and his spiky red hair stood up on end. He even began to growl in his throat when he thought of the low trick Apples had played him.

Henry, for his part, sat impassively, his body jouncing and his hat bobbing on his head as the car slewed around startled motorists and careened over potholes while McCann passed long stretches of traffic on the shoulder at 85 miles per hour.

"We're going to kill those motherfuckers," snarled McCann.

"Yes," said Henry, "if they're the ones."

The Vacaville airstrip isn't much to speak of: a few corrugated-iron hangars; a small frame tower on stilts; and a green low-pitched building doubling as the flight service station and coffee shop.

McCann roared up the asphalt approach road. He saw the black hearse and the other two vehicles in the parking lot. A little knot of men stood next to the coffee shop. Farther away on the apron, a DeHavilland twin-engine turboprop was taxiing toward the far end of the field. The police car, still doing 70, smashed through the wooden guardrail of the lot, bounced across a shallow ditch, and hit the apron in full pursuit of the plane.

The DeHavilland, having swung around at the end of the field, had started its takeoff run. McCann, leaving the concrete, shot across the dirt in an effort to head off the aircraft.

"Watch yourself, Henry."

A moment before colliding with the taxiing airplane, McCann slammed on the brakes, swinging the rear end of the car in such a way that it struck the landing gear of the aircraft. The port propeller blade slashed across the hood of the car before detaching itself and looping off into the grass; there was a horrible screech of metal as the plane came to a violent halt and tilted over, the port wing resting on the police car.

McCann was out in a flash, a pistol in each hand.

"Open the door," he screamed at the aircraft's occupants, whose faces were peering out the ports.

Henry, somewhat lackadaisically, opened the trunk, removed his AR-15, and assumed a shooter's sitting position by the rear wheel of the car. The knot of men near the coffee shop had fanned out and started to run toward the crippled aircraft. With the easy accuracy and nonchalance of the expert marksman who has picked off targets at long ranges in the face of such distractions as incoming fire, Henry dropped a round between the feet of one of the onrushing men at a range of 350 yards. The men stopped, deciding to contemplate the spectacle from a distance.

Meanwhile, McCann, in a rage, had somehow managed to claw open the hatch and was screaming incoherently at the frightened men inside who seemed too surprised to offer any resistance. At gunpoint the two passengers and the pilot unloaded Sizeman's coffin from the plane and perched it on the trunk of the car.

"I ought to kill every one of you motherfuckers," McCann was screaming. "I ought to blow your fucking balls off."

"Listen, this is just business," said one of the men.

"I ought to waste you cocksuckers where you stand," raved McCann, brandishing the cocked pistols. Henry sat calmly, his rifle locked on a heart that beat, probably rapidly, 300 yards away.

"God damn you assholes." McCann put his foot behind one of the men and sent him sprawling on the ground. "You fuckers."

The pastel blue coroner's wagon had pulled into the parking lot. McCann, with extravagant wind-milling, waved Keating over, and the truck cautiously bumped over the guard tie and lurched across the ditch onto the apron.

Keating, it turned out, was panic-stricken. "How are we going to *explain* all this."

"Don't worry about a thing," said McCann, catching his breath and wiping his glistening red face with his sleeve. He did feel in need of a drink, however.

"Why don't you guys get your airplane off my car?" McCann said to the three hijackers.

In short order the DeHavilland was righted. McCann sent the pilot over to get the hearse from the parking lot, after reminding him that Henry would kill him if he strayed from his assignment. In the distance, McCann could hear the wail of a siren, and turning, he saw a red light flashing along the highway a mile away.

McCann also noticed that in the Flight Service Station some 400 yards distant somebody was watching them through binoculars, with a telephone cradled under his chin.

"Make that guy in the tower behave, Henry."

In one smooth motion, Henry's rifle trained around and spat, sending a bullet through the green glass of the station, a foot from the observer's head. The man disappeared from view. A few heads in the window of the coffee shop also disappeared.

Under McCann's direction Sizeman's coffin went back into the coroner's wagon, and the two dead AP's, under cover of the squad car, went into the hearse. The back door of the hearse had no sooner slammed shut than two cars from the county sheriff's department appeared on the apron, heading toward them.

"Put your hands down," McCann snapped to the two passengers. "You two guys are undercover narks. You get it? You're cops. And you," he added to the pilot, "you're temporarily under arrest for trying to smuggle dope."

The men, who had been in a precarious line of work for some time and had experienced plenty of vicissitudes, quickly grasped the situation, opened their coats to reveal their guns, and began to push the pilot around roughly in a good imitation of cops at work.

Four or five deputies armed with shotguns and drawn revolvers spilled out of the sheriff's cars. McCann, pushing back his hat, grinned at them, and waved a hand.

"You can Code Four this situation," McCann said. "We caught a gent from the city who wanted to fly a little shipment of coke up north. Sergeants Haig and Hennesy from the State Bureau of Narcotics are interrogating the suspect now, and I guess they don't want to be disturbed."

The two goons from the Teamsters were still roughing up the pilot, shaking him by the lapels, pushing him against the side of the aircraft, slapping his face and pulling his ears, and in general enjoying the experience of learning how the other half lives in a police interrogation. Finally, they dragged the pilot over to McCann's car and made him stand with his hands against the door.

"You can slap the cuffs on this fucker," one of the goons said as he strutted around and brushed lint from his sleeve. "We'll talk to him some more downtown." Then the two newly deputized narcotics officers got into the black hearse and drove away. The men in front of the coffee shop had already departed.

At a nod from McCann, Henry put handcuffs on the pilot and shoved him into the back seat.

"We're going to have to rush this guy to the Hall," McCann said. "We've got a crime-lab unit with a lieutenant on the way. Incidentally," he added, "some shots were fired and a stray went through the station window. You might want to check that out."

Leaving the deputies scratching their heads and looking at one another, McCann jumped in the car and wheeled around toward the exit, with Keating in hasty pursuit in the coroner's van.

"We'll get those cuffs off you as soon as we get to a service station," McCann said to the pilot. "I've really got to drain my lizard."

McCann turned toward San Francisco and sped along the freeway for several miles. Another sheriff's car, red light flashing, streaked past in the other direction. McCann turned off the freeway at a service road and pulled into a Texaco station. Henry leaned into the back seat and removed the handcuffs, and the pilot, as is usual in these cases, immediately began to rub his wrists.

"Let's see what we've got to drink," said McCann, rummaging with one hand in the ice chest beneath his feet. "Here's a margarita for Mr. Henry. I can offer you a bloody mary or a screwdriver."

"A bloody mary sounds fine," said the pilot.

"Listen," said McCann, sipping his drink, "I'm sorry if I got mad back there. I'm new at this game and I guess I let my feelings get the best of me."

"Forget it," said the pilot, shrugging his shoulders. "It could happen to anybody."

"Well, thanks for saying so, but this is strictly business, and you just can't afford to let emotions get involved."

"It could happen to anybody."

"Listen, you know Apples?"

"No. I never heard of him."

"Well, when you see him, tell him to get in touch in the next few days and we'll make the final arrangements about the shipment. And tell him I'm not angry or anything about what happened today. God knows, I can take a joke. Will you tell him that?"

"I never heard of the guy."

"Thanks."

McCann slid the car up to the pumps and a pimply youngster wiping his hands with a rag came over.

"Two dollars worth of Super Chief," McCann said. "And will you look under the hood?" McCann walked back to talk with Keating.

"How's your gas?"

"Fine, I can make it back," said the little coroner, who was staring around nervously. "McCann, is it really a good idea to walk around in public with a drink in your hand? I mean, aren't we conspicuous enough?"

"You're worrying again. The best thing is to act natural. Why don't you pull around next to the john? I've got to take a leak."

After inviting the pilot to help himself to another drink, McCann signaled to Henry and the two were starting toward the john when the station attendant came up, holding the dipstick.

"You're a quart low," he said, "and your air cleaner has been cut in half."

"Fix it up, will you? I've really got to go."

Standing in front of the urinal, playing a steady stream back and forth across the porcelain, McCann explained the next step to his confederates.

When the coast was clear they would bring Sizeman into the john, lock the door, unpack him from his box, snip the stitches, and remove the heroin. Henry and Keating would perform that operation while McCann kept an eye on things in front.

Zipping up, McCann walked outside. Some customers were just leaving. The pimply kid was bent over the front fender struggling with a new air cleaner. It took only a second for the three men to slide the coffin out of the wagon and into the restroom. Then McCann sauntered over to the car, got another drink, and chatted with the pilot while the boy tinkered with the engine. Five minutes later Henry emerged from the john carrying a heavy, evil-smelling package wrapped in oilcloth. After stowing the package in the trunk, McCann and Henry walked back to the john and returned Sizeman to the van. Keating immediately drove away.

In the car they had the last of the canned drinks. The kid finally slammed down the ruptured hood and came over to the window, still wiping his hands with the same dirty piece of rag.

"That'll be fifteen-eighty," he said.

"Fuck, I don't think I've got it," McCann said, searching through his pockets.

The pilot passed over a $100 bill.

"Keep the change," McCann said, "Listen, cops aren't supposed to booze on the job. Do you know what I mean?"

223

"You bet," said the kid.

When they got back to the city McCann let the pilot out at the corner of Union and Van Ness, in front of a cabstand.

"Now remember. Give Apples my message."

"I don't know this Apples," the pilot said as the car pulled away.

CHAPTER 20

"I got your message," Apples said.

McCann was at home. He knew Apples was speaking from a pay booth because he could hear the confused noise of traffic in the background. Cradling the receiver against his ear, McCann stroked Rose's bare legs with one hand and held an iced drink in the other. Rose was lying on her stomach on the couch marking a psychology textbook with a yellow felt-tipped pen, her smooth dusky legs stretched across McCann's lap.

"It's good to hear your voice," McCann said into the phone. "I hope it didn't inconvenience you to get two packages instead of one."

"It didn't inconvenience me," Apples said evenly, "although I admit I am stricken by your cavalier attitude toward the value of human life."

"I hope you're not going to moralize with me. I get enough of that at home." Rose gave his knee a friendly kick as she turned the page of her book.

"No, of course I'm not going to moralize," Apples said. "However, I do want to feel assured that you fully understand the reasons that prompted today's activities. I'm anxious that you might have received an erroneous impression."

"Frankly, I *am* a little puzzled."

"I would say that the operation today was . . . *diagnostic* in character."

"You mean, in the nature of a test?"

"Exactly, Mr. McCann. We, that is, the Committee that handles these matters, met and deliberated several hours last week endeavoring to examine every facet of your scheme, if I may call it that. I opined, as did others, that the scheme had certain . . . *fantastic* elements that did not tend to reassure us of its . . . viability, if you follow me."

"Of course," said McCann. He had drawn up Rose's skirt and was caressing her shapely bottom.

"Moreover, as businessmen, we deemed it necessary to maximize profit if possible."

"That's only good business."

"The consensus following our deliberations, Mr. McCann, was simply that we would devise some diagnostic instrument to determine if you really had . . . had all your ducks in line, as they say in the Capitol, that is . . . that you really held all the threads in your hand."

"Did I pass?"

Apples' stentorian breathing was interrupted by a paroxysm of chuckles.

"Yes, I'd say you passed. The question now, I suppose, is the best way to finalize our arrangements. Would you consent to meet my representatives tomorrow at a warehouse in Oakland?"

226

"No."

"How about someplace down on the Embarcadero?"

"No."

"Am I correct in assuming, then, that you wish to make the arrangements yourself?"

"That's right," said McCann. "I have to be in court tomorrow at the Hall of Justice. Why don't you meet me in the basement cafeteria at noon; you can give me a cashier's check."

"May I ask what guarantees there are of . . . *scrupulosity?*"

"You can bring a technician with you; we can go into the property room and use some contraband testing equipment. Nobody's there at lunchtime so we won't be disturbed."

"The Hall of Justice." Apples was laughing again. "But might not the authorities interfere with us on the way out? I'm thinking of the guard at the door."

"Think it over. The guard changes at one."

"In other words," Apples said appreciatively, "people are only searched on the way in, not on the way out. And the new guard won't know that I walked in empty-handed. I'll just appear an obese lawyer walking out with his fat briefcase. And you, of course, will have no difficulty bringing the goods in."

"You got it. The only people they don't search at the Hall are cops. Listen, I'm expecting another call, so I'll see you tomorrow." McCann hung up. He pulled down Rose's panties to the knees, bent over, and planted a kiss on her behind. She sat up, tossed her panties on the coffee table, and threw her arms around McCann's neck.

"Sweet boy," she said, undoing his shirt. "Who was that on the phone?"

"A dumb asshole that owes me twenty dollars."

"You always make it sound like such a big deal."

"It is a big deal." He made her lift her arms while he

pulled off her knit, revealing her little breasts with their large dark nipples. She had settled next to him when the phone rang.

"Don't answer it," said Rose.

"I think it might be important," said McCann, disengaging his hand. "Why don't you get me a drink while you're up?"

"Fooey," said Rose, flouncing into the kitchen, "it's getting harder and harder to get any action out of you."

McCann picked up the receiver.

"This is Lieutenant O'Riley," said his superior in his customary dry monotone. "I'd like to hear your version of events today."

"I was planning to submit a report first thing tomorrow," McCann said, taking the double gin and tonic from Rose, "but basically here's what happened. Some religious cultists tried to rob a corpse coming to the morgue from Travis. Some of my sources on the street tipped me and we managed to prevent the theft."

"Do you have somebody in custody someplace?"

"No. That was my source. I had to pretend to arrest him to protect him from reprisal."

"Was anybody injured?"

"No."

"Well," O'Riley said doubtfully, "you and Henry seem to be on top of things, although I don't yet see the connection between body-snatching and political terror. In any case, I am being pestered by the press, particularly about a bullet that narrowly missed a controlman at the Vacaville airfield . . ."

"A stray," McCann said, taking a long sip. "Perhaps if you said the incident is still being investigated . . ."

"That's what I *am* saying," the lieutenant said drily. "I certainly don't mean to disturb you at home. We'll talk first thing tomorrow. Good night."

"Was that the call you were expecting?" asked Rose after he had hung up.

"Not really."

Rose had slipped off her skirt. She straddled his lap, facing him, tugged at his heavy blue woolen uniform shirt, and began to pull it off. A powerful odor of sweat filled the air as Rose tugged at the shirt. McCann's body was in the first stages of alcoholic degeneracy. His heavy, brick-red arms were still well-muscled, but his chest, covered by a mat of coarse red hair, had already grown fatty, and his paunch hung several inches over his belt buckle. Still, because of the massiveness of his frame, McCann gave an impression of brute animal strength, an impression accentuated by the malicious expression habitual to his face.

Rose, straddling McCann's huge frame, breathing in his pungent odor, marveled at the insistency of her feelings for a man who to all appearances was brutal, vicious, and immoral. Yet there was something about his acne-marked, congested features, the icy stare from his burning face, his pitted neck and spiky hair, that undid all her intellectual reservations about his character and politics.

Despite the malice stamped on his countenance, she felt in him a vulnerability; she had never feared him, nor was she hurt by his inattention or his sarcasms. The usual rules just didn't seem to apply in their relationship. Although she believed in principle in written contracts spelling out the responsibilities of partners living together, she was repelled for some reason by the idea of such a contract in their own relationship. Consequently, she did everything, he did nothing. She brought him drinks, tried to find out what he liked to eat; she even shined his boots, all the time knowing it to be wrong and unliberated. But she couldn't help herself. As a college radical, she hoped in a vague way for the overthrow of the government, even though the thought of any kind of violence outraged her; and her face took on a very severe expression whenever she thought about the violence perpetrated by the corporations and the government against the inner-city blacks and the farm workers. Yet now she was sitting on the lap of a man who professed a willingness to brutalize a nigger or a spic anytime, without the least provocation, who admitted having killed in war, and who said that genocide seemed to him enlightened policy for all of Asia including Taiwan, the Philippines, and Hawaii.

She just didn't understand it; their relationship was a contradiction of all her principles. During one of the upsets at San Francisco State she had actually seen him clubbing a student lying helpless on the ground; yet in some other compartment of her heart she irrationally believed him to be a kind, compassionate man, despite the fact he had never evidenced the slightest example of these traits. He was not tender or affectionate; and although she liked to ball him, she had known better men. But she had never known anybody else who could make her happy.

It was not that she was stupid. To the contrary, Rose knew herself to be quite intelligent. During the Women's Caucus meetings she was skilled in marshaling her arguments; in school she could make forceful, articulate presentations that thoroughly intimidated the men in her classes. McCann just laughed on the few occasions when she had tried a speech on him. The trouble was that she believed in things and McCann didn't believe in anything. She had tried to explain to him many times that he was being used, exploited by financial interests to maintain a rotting and corrupt system; that he was doing the dirty work for the corporate bosses and getting very little in return; that his true place was with the people.

In her imagination sometimes she could actually see McCann standing astride a barricade amid the din and smoke, in the uncertain light of guttering fire bombs, staring contemptuously at the onrushing police. But in other, more frequent daydreams she involuntarily thought of a quiet life somewhere in the country; he would quit the force and she college, and they would live simply amid trees and greenery and bathe naked in a cool stream.

He claimed he was a racist who would gladly pile all the niggers in the world onto a bonfire; yet Henry, a man obviously tortured and embittered by the outrages of American racism, was his only friend. McCann drank constantly from morning to night yet seldom appeared drunk. He started each morning with a screwdriver that was half vodka, and he might have three or four before the eggs were on the table. He never read anything except the newspapers; he laughed at her studies and had nothing but contempt for learning; yet he was smart in his way.

Rose, with her shining black hair falling over her little breasts, her lively eyes and low convex forehead, gazed happily into McCann's face, massaging his shoulders while he stroked her back. They were lying down together in an embrace when the phone rang again.

This time it was Brannon from the *Examiner*. The reporter was sounding a little sheepish.

"Look here, Wild Bill, I'm sort of between the rock and the hard place on this story about the corpse-napping."

"You were sort of napping yourself."

"Ha, ha. I'm in the unenviable position of having an

eyewitness front-page exclusive without a real clear idea about what happened."

"Well, you've been in tough spots before. Besides, you got the press release, didn't you? I thought that's all you guys cared about?"

Brannon gave a forlorn laugh. "Yeah, I got the handout. Was it really some kind of hippie cult? For Christ's sake, McCann, I don't want to mention it, but I've kind of been a pal to you. I mean, it's not exactly kosher for a cop to lush on the job."

"You mean you'll keep quiet if I talk."

"Well, shit, I don't want to put it that way."

"Listen, Brannon, I'm just having fun with you. When's your deadline?"

"Two A.M. for the home edition. It's already too fucking late for the preview. I swear to Christ my editor's going berserk and I just can't stall him much longer."

"Why don't you come on over and I'll fill you in?"

"No!" whispered Rose urgently.

"Come over in about an hour. You know the address? You can dictate your story from here. I've even got a typewriter you can use."

"*My* typewriter," cried Rose. She was trying to wriggle out of McCann's lap but he held her fast.

"It's a good story," McCann said. "I'll fill you in."

"Well, shit, you're a Christian and a white man," Brannon said.

"See you in a bit." McCann replaced the receiver. "That was the call I was expecting," he told Rose.

CHAPTER 21

When McCann awoke he found Rose snuggled against his chest, one hand across his stomach and a leg thrown over his. With one bounce he tumbled her over to her side of the bed and then, with a groan, put his feet on the floor. Routinely, his head throbbed. His breathing was shallow and his pulse, which he quickly checked, felt weak and irregular. He got to his feet, became dizzy and staggered to the bathroom where he gulped six aspirin and relieved his mouth of its foulness with a swirl of Lavoris. Soon the shower was roaring and his face disappeared as the mirror clouded with steam.

When he got to the kitchen he was dressed in his uniform and the brisk shower had momentarily overcome his spiky hair, which now lay flat against his heavy frontal bone. Rose, sitting at the table with a cup of coffee, was reading the *Examiner*. He could read the banner—"SHOOT-OUT AT VACAVILLE, CORPSE HIJACK FOILED"—and even make out the 14-point bold signer: "Charles Brannon, Chief Crime Writer, Hearst Headline Service."

"Oh, Bill," Rose said, "I didn't know this is why Brannon came over last night. You never tell me anything. I want to *know* what happens to you."

McCann sat down at the table in front of the pitcher of orange juice and the bottle of vodka she had set out for him.

"Read it out loud."

"Okay," said Rose, putting down her coffee cup. " 'Demented hijackers belonging to a cult of necromancy and narcotics attempted to steal the body of a young Army veteran yesterday but were thwarted by alert San Francisco police officers.' "

"That's me," said McCann.

" 'The cult, which styles itself the Blood Brotherhood, may also be implicated in the rash of bombings in the city, the *Examiner* has learned.

" 'Officers from the newly-formed Anti-Terror Unit, acting on a tip, broke up the bizarre effort to hijack the remains of Pfc. Donald Sizeman, 21, as his body was being transported from Travis Air Force Base to the city morgue.

" 'Sizeman, killed August 12 by an accidental mortar explosion, is listed as a native of the City but has no known next of kin. A spokesman for the coroner's office said he will be buried with full military honors at Golden Gate National Cemetery if his body is not claimed within two weeks.

" 'Details of the thwarted hijack, exclusive to the *Examiner*, include these highlights:

" ' • The theft of the body from the coroner's wagon by

young gun-toting hippies driving a black hearse, who forced the coroner's deputy into a ditch.

" ' • A shoot-out at the Vacaville airport as Anti-Terror officers intercepted the body as it was being loaded aboard a rented aircraft for shipment to the cult's mountain headquarters somewhere in Northern California.

" ' • The confiscated plans for a bizarre funeral ritual at the mountain hideout, in which the soldier's body was to be cremated on a pyre amidst chanting and incense.' "

Rose smoothed the paper on the table; her eyes were shining with tears. "You never tell me anything."

"I didn't think you wanted to hear how I oppressed your friends."

"They're not my friends," Rose said, sniffling. "Terror is individualistic and adventurist; besides, it's premature."

McCann poured three fingers of vodka into his glass and added a little orange juice. He picked up the paper and scanned Brannon's article. It seemed to contain all the points McCann had made the night before. The cultists were young; the pilot did not know his clients or his cargo; the plane's destination was a police secret; an undisclosed amount of cocaine was involved (to square the story with the county authorities); several suspects were under surveillance; and finally, the Anti-Terror Unit had all the threads in hand.

The only disturbing note in the piece was the statement by the controlman at the Vacaville field that it seemed to him one of the police officers deliberately fired at him. McCann had countered that, however, by telling Brannon that an exchange of gunfire had taken place between Henry and a rifleman on the roof of a nearby hangar.

In a word, it was a long, outrageous, and confusing story. McCann was satisfied with it.

The phone rang. Since McCann continued to sit musing over the article, screwdriver in hand, Rose got up and brought him the phone.

"McCann speaking."

"You landed on your feet," Apples said and hung up.

"Who was it?" asked Rose, looking up nervously.

McCann shrugged as he poured more vodka. "A threat on my life. One of the cultists, I suppose."

Rose started to cry and came over to put her arms around his neck. Tears ran down her cheeks and her little brown body shook with sobs. A horrible grin had appeared on the policeman's face.

"They're out to get me, Rose. Just because I want to make it safe to take a piss; just because I want to return sanity to the lavatory, they want to scrag me. Sure, I'm defending the boss and the landlord, but I'm also standing up for the little guy: the bum on a rainy day who wants to take a nap sitting up; the pervert who wants a quiet rendezvous; the muralist looking for a wall. Those are the kinds of guys I want to protect; not to mention the occasional citizen who uses a public john for its intended purpose. That's really why I decided on a career in anti-terror; it wasn't just my political beliefs."

After draining off his third glass in a tragic flourish, McCann dramatically thrust Rose aside and swept his hat onto his head.

"That's why I drink, Rose. Because every day I face death. It's true, I drink to keep my spirits up. Sure, you're right, I could quit; I could sell shoes and it would be bliss; I'd never have a drink again. But I'm not that way, Rose, because I think of that wino standing out in the rain, afraid to go into the john. Is that justice, Rose?"

McCann hunched over and stalked across the kitchen floor, preparing for one of his fast draws.

"But you wait. Henry and I will corral the terrorists

one of these days." McCann stalked around the kitchen, pretending his gun was stuck in its holster, before finally covering the blender.

"Reach for the sky, mutha."

The phone rang again. McCann whirled, and cautiously approached the instrument, one finger to his lips.

"Sheriff McCann speaking."

It was O'Riley. He wanted to see McCann in his office promptly at nine.

"They're out to get me, Rose," McCann said as he left.

■■■■■■■■ CHAPTER 22

The fiercely mustachioed poverty lawyer paced back and forth before the bench, sometimes clutching the corners of his vest, sometimes wagging a finger in the air, sometimes stopping to lift a folder of papers from the defense table.

The courtroom was packed. A guard stood at the rear door to keep further spectators out, since every seat was taken. The first two rows, reserved for the press, were packed solid; the newspapers, radio, television, wire services, foreign correspondents, all were there, pads poised.

Seven or eight lawyers clustered around the defense table: the ACLU, the OEO, the Sierra Club, and the prestigious but left-leaning law firm of Kelly, Ross, and Mathews were all represented. Four lawyers from the

238

district attorney's office were handling the prosecution. At the judge's elbows were stacks of briefs, not only from the principles but from friends of the court as well. Beneath him, on the evidence table, were Exhibits A, B, and C, two homemade alarm-clock bombs and a pair of shoes.

In the corridor, bored television cameramen waited, their monstrous Cyclopean eyes mounted on their shoulders; the overflow from the courtroom lined the wall, gabbing about the latest defense efforts, as detailed in the morning *Examiner*. A contingent of the Tactical Squad, clothed in blue jump suits and helmets, guarded the approaches to the courtroom area, searching briefcases and inspecting driver's licenses.

The fiercely mustachioed lawyer was concluding his argument, which ran to the effect that pretrial publicity had made it impossible for his client to receive a fair trial in the City and County of San Francisco, and consequently the defense must ask for a change of venue.

"Motion denied," said the judge.

Brannon, crime writer for the *Examiner*, leaned back from the press section to whisper in McCann's ear.

"This is all horseshit for the press," he said. 'Arraignment isn't the proper time to make a motion for a change of venue."

The focus of this hubbub, David Levin, sat abjectly at the defense table, with lowered head, listening to the whispered words of one of the fierce defense lawyers, whose shaggy mane fell below his collar.

Another team of defense lawyers, armed with more papers, was approaching the bench to argue for dismissal on the grounds of lack of evidence. The assistant prosecutors were all making notes, while the chief prosecutor paced behind them, his hands clasped behind his back and his head bowed in thought.

"Your honor, I would like to draw the court's attention to today's newspaper," said the spokesman for the defense. "There has been yet another bombing since our client has been in custody, the convenience station outside the Market Street BART entrance, which seems to indicate that the wrong man is in custody, since the terror is continuing.

"I further would like to point out to the court that the events of yesterday in Vacaville, obscure as they may be at this point, also suggest not that environmentalists are perpetrating the terror but that a very sinister and demented band of cult ritualists are in fact responsible."

The chief prosecutor, who had been pacing back and forth, responded succinctly to these arguments for dismissal.

"In addressing the court today, I would merely review the findings contained in the grand jury indictment. We are not alleging that the defendant is involved with the bombing that occurred at the BART station entrance; we are charging him with one specific act of terror, the bombing August tenth of the men's room at the Human Resources Development building.

"We are not even suggesting that in this incident he acted alone," the prosecutor added darkly. "We do find the indictment against the defendant sound, to wit: evidence found in the defendant's vehicle strongly links him to the crime; moreover, the same source that supplied police with information about the raid on the OK Construction Company yard supplied the police with the information that led to Mr. Levin's arrest."

The prosecutor held up the indictment, with the huge seal of the grand jury embossed upon it.

"The indictment further states that Mr. Levin was arrested not more than two weeks ago under highly suspicious circumstances while loitering outside Italian

Hall, where the mayor and the head of the Anti-Terror Unit were speaking, and not two blocks from the Greyhound Bus Station that was subsequently bombed that morning by a timed device identical to those in evidence and which could have been planted any time during the previous evening.

"At the time of his arrest, Mr. Levin put up a furious struggle, requiring four police officers to subdue him, even though he was being questioned about a minor traffic violation."

"This is really choice," said Brannon, scribbling furiously.

"What's the defense got on tap?" McCann asked him.

"A rabbit in their hat," the reporter said mysteriously.

"Not a girl by any chance?"

Brannon's ruined, leering face turned around. "That's very good, Officer McCann. As a matter of fact, it's some topless dancer from a Broadway joint."

"That'll make great copy."

"You bet your ass."

Badger, the little prosecutor, who was sitting in front, noticed McCann. He bounced back and slid in beside him.

"Hey, hey, hey, buddy, this Levin character turns out to be a *ba-ad* motherfucker; and we almost cut him loose. I'm telling you, we got the little turd where we want him, with felonies back to back."

"What's the bail?"

"Bail. You got to be kidding. This ain't a bailable offense; he stays put. And not that it makes any difference, but the Sierra Club cunt who posted bond on his four-seventeen changed her mind when she found out her boy is a terrorist."

"What's the timetable?"

"Shit, this isn't going to get on the road for years; there'll be a million motions and appeals. The only funny thing is that the defense is bringing in some surprise witness tomorrow to talk with the judge in chambers."

"Any line on who it might be?"

"Some cunt, I hear. Say, how about a little lunch?"

"Can't today. I've got a date."

"Ho, ho, ho," said Badger, poking McCann in the ribs. When the little assistant D.A. had bounced back to the prosecution table, McCann edged off his seat and picked up the large heavy briefcase that had been resting at his feet.

Apples and another man were waiting when he got to the cafeteria.

"Mr. McCann, Mr. Jones." Apples introduced the chemist, who looked like any clerk in the middle rungs of the civil service.

The three men walked across the basement hallway to the property room, where a police officer in a blue jump suit was standing at the counter reading a copy of *National Review*.

"It's my niece's birthday," McCann told him. "My brother-in-law and I would like to look at the bicycles."

"Sure," said the officer, buzzing the door.

Turning right, they walked through three rooms, each filled with metal racks containing stolen goods of all kinds, but mostly radios, televisions, and stereos, each item tagged with a little card. In the last room nearly a hundred bicycles were lined up against one wall.

"You'll find what you need over there," McCann said, pointing to a cardboard box on the metal shelf. He handed the briefcase to Mr. Jones.

Apples removed a big green cigar from an aluminum tube and rolled the end back and forth in his mouth to soften the tip before applying a jet of flame.

"We all liked the way you handled the OK Construction Company business. The ground-breaking was a huge success. County officials flocked to the ceremonies to tender supportive gestures. The Committee is very pleased with you at this moment."

"Good," said McCann. The chemist, who had quickly assembled the beakers and retorts, lit the burner and expertly ran a test on some of the white powder taken at random from the bricks inside the satchel.

"When's your next shipment arriving?"

"Almost any time now," McCann said, smiling.

Apples elevated one eyebrow, returned the smile, and flicked a cigar ash. "I know you'll keep us informed."

The chemist blew out the flame, deftly replaced the equipment, snapped closed the satchel, and handed it back to McCann.

"Pure heroin," he said.

Apples reached inside his coat pocket and drew forth an envelope that he handed to McCann.

"A cashier's check drawn on the Labor Temple Bank of Commerce. You're familiar with that institution?"

"The Teamster bank."

"Yes," said Apples drily, "I wouldn't advise cashing it elsewhere; at some banks obeisance to Federal agencies supersedes the loyalty a bank owes to its mere customers. That's not the case at Labor Temple. When you cash this, see Mr. Phipps; he handles the Convenience account and will gladly supply you with cash, American Express, or whatever you wish."

After examining the check, McCann set down the briefcase. The chemist picked it up and the three men walked back to the front desk.

"See anything you liked?" asked the jump-suited officer.

"Yeah," said McCann. "There's a blue Peugeot that looks just right."

"Un-uh. Lieutenant D'Arkerly from burglary detail

already has dibs on that for his kid. How about the yellow Schwinn?"

"Too beat-up," McCann said. "I'll wait and see what comes in next week."

In the hallway Apples and McCann shook hands.

"Once again, your efforts in behalf of OK Construction are much appreciated. We hope you do succeed in catching the bomber someday, but the Committee greatly enjoyed your casting of Mr. Levin as a temporary stand-in. I'm Jewish myself so I can appreciate the public predisposition. With the favorable publicity, the Tunitas Creek project can forge ahead without hindrance since, as a matter of fact, we don't expect to hear much from the Sierra Club or DCL in the future."

"I enjoyed doing it. But you can do me a favor. I know the Committee has some influence on Broadway. Mr. Levin's lady friend, a Miss Melanie Duggs, who dances at Dino's, may be called to testify at a hearing tomorrow. It would probably be better if she didn't."

"Would you like her in protective custody?"

"I think that would be good."

"Very well, but it may have to appear something like kidnap and rape."

"She should enjoy that."

"You're an interesting person, Mr. McCann. I think we'll have a profitable association." With that, the public facilitator for Convenience Drayage and the drab Mr. Jones, looking for all the world like two complacent lawyers ambling over to Roscoe's Il Trovatore for a heavy lunch, passed through the maximum security cordon of the Hall of Justice carrying a briefcase containing $3 million in pure heroin.

Putting the cashier's check in his pocket, McCann went up to O'Riley's office.

CHAPTER 23

It was lunchtime and O'Riley was taking his as usual at his desk. He was having some Ritz crackers, a wedge of Swiss, an apple, and some walnuts. Ah he nibbled on a piece of apple, the lieutenant was deeply absorbed in a little tract in front of him, Spinoza's *De Intellectus Emendatione*. Around the room the stacks of tabloid newspapers had grown higher, so that some of them nearly reached the top of his desk.

Although to some Spinoza's life after his excommunication might seem morbid, the countless lonely hours spent in reflection and study in a garret, to O'Riley it had a certain fascination, even charm. O'Riley, of course, couldn't grind lenses to eke out a living; and besides, he felt a moral obligation to participate in life, to contribute to the general well-being of mankind. One couldn't spend one's life turning over the pages of books, no matter how appealing the idea might be.

The lieutenant was cracking his second walnut when a heavy knock sounded on his door.

"Come in," croaked O'Riley.

In burst McCann, like a blast of hot air from a furnace, his spiky red hair like tongues of flame, his congested face burning like molten pig iron. His body heat actually seemed to raise the temperature in the little room. The noncommittal odor around O'Riley suddenly changed places with the heavy damp odor of sweat and Sen-Sen.

"Hiya, boss," shouted McCann, crashing into the one empty chair and panting elaborately. "I came as fast as I could."

"Well done," said O'Riley, in his creaky voice. The lightless eyes sunk in the fleshless skull revolved toward his blazing, radiant subordinate with that misshapen, porous nose, with the eyes at once luminous and evil and that poisonous sneer, eloquent of violence and sadism. Who was this person? O'Riley wondered. Was the raw energy emanating from him benign or dangerous? O'Riley had to remind himself once again that McCann was merely an instrument; his personal merits or demerits were secondary, his value as an instrument of policy primary.

"I'd like you to fill me in on the Vacaville business."

"Just like the *Examiner* says. I tell you, boss, that Brannon is a bloodhound. What a scoop for him—an eyewitness account of a body snatch."

"Mr. Brannon's industry is well known." O'Riley pushed a piece of bond paper with an impressive letterhead. "The Association of Bay Area F.A.A. Controlmen has lodged a protest with the department, alleging that a black police officer—Henry, I presume—deliberately shot at F.A.A. personnel at the field, that there was no exchange of gunfire between police and persons on any hangar, and that the actions of police on the field unnecessarily endangered the lives of all concerned."

"Why those fucking, lying, cocksucking assholes," McCann said, slapping his knee. "Listen, chief, you know how panicky civilians can get during a firefight. Anybody with one walnut shell full of brains would have ducked for cover, but not this asshole; he's gawking around like he's at a tennis match. The guy shooting at Henry was on the hangar *behind* the station; the asshole couldn't possibly see him. Listen, boss, the important thing about Vacaville is that it proves that we're on top of things."

That was true. In many ways, the situation reminded O'Riley of the position of the Union at the start of the Civil War. The people wanted battles and victories, the rebels humbled, Richmond in flames; and all the while McClellan procrastinated and dawdled. McCann, like Grant, however, was aggressive. He pushed; with him there was a sense of movement.

And the mayor had been very specific that morning on the telephone. "The controlmen can take their complaint and stick it you know where," the mayor had said. "How many controlmen are there in San Francisco? Three? The public *likes* the Anti-Terror Unit to shoot it out with hippie cultists. It's the best thing that could possibly happen."

Being a modern police officer meant learning to live with political reality. One might wish that the terrorists could be brought to justice in an orderly, methodical, scientific way. But McCann obviously was all instinct and impulse, a hunch player, a loner, a believer in long-shot tips from unlikely people, secretive, communing more with his own lively impressions than examining the facts coldly and logically. But perhaps that was what was needed. Both of them operated on the psychological premise: McCann, on the psychology of the informer; O'Riley, on the inevitable unconscious demands of the bombers themselves.

O'Riley shelved his speculations for the moment and turned again to the present.

"Let's review the situation," he said. "We have two ecologists in custody, ready to stand trial; we have some kind of necromantic cabal under surveillance; and yet you still hold to the belief that . . ."

"It *is* the Teamsters," McCann said. "Have you seen the latest issue of *The Clenched Fist?*"

"It's right here on my desk."

McCann opened the tabloid to the letter page and laid it before O'Riley's pitchy sockets. He tapped one of the letters significantly.

"*. . . books a white plot . . .*" it said above the letter.

" 'Black people are coming to realize that the white so-called educational system is nothing more than a racist plot to ensnare Black People into mindless obedience to the white power structure,' " O'Riley read.

It has been demonstrated time and time again that IQ tests have been deliberately designed to discriminate against Black Children.

It has been proved time and time again that racist colleges and universities are tailored to manufacture no more than a few tokens and Toms for the front office.

The so-called tracking system shuttles Black Children into menial occupations.

Past attempts by Black *reformists* have aimed at changing the educational system, to make it more responsive to the needs of Black People.

But what is becoming increasingly apparent to *Progressive Blacks* is that the whole *concept* of education is racist and elitist.

In modern-day America education is irrelevant to

the real needs of Black People, which are food, shelter, clothing, and freedom.

Black People are tired and insulted by Head Start Programs and remedial English in the guise of Black Studies. Black People don't need books, or jobs, or food stamps. Black People need complete and total power over their own lives.

The Black People's De-education Coalition has set an action to bring home to fascist America these goals, by striking a blow at the very heart of inequality—*the Public Library System*. (It should be remembered that the SF library has an annual budget of $50,000 while Black People starve.)

At high noon Monday, August 30, the BPDC will mount an action against the Main Library. PROGRESSIVE BLACKS AND JOHN BROWN WHITES HAVE MORE IMPORTANT WORK TO DO THAN SITTING ON THEIR DUFFS IN THE LIBRARY. *A word to the wise.*

For the first time since taking over as head of the Anti-Terror Unit, O'Riley experienced a feeling of rage and bitterness well up inside him. He stared at the letter in horror as a realization of its meaning dawned on him.

"You don't mean to say . . . somebody is going to bomb the *library*."

"Exactly," McCann nodded his head grimly.

"And, and . . ." O'Riley fluttered his hands helplessly.

"And it's not the niggers. There's no such thing as this De-education Coalition. It's the Teamsters. You see, chief, the tip-off is the way they keep referring to *progressive blacks*. That's how the Panthers always style themselves in their literature. The Teamsters are going to bomb the library and pin it on the Panthers, to cut off their support in the liberal community; because if there's one thing a liberal can't stand, it's the idea of somebody burning a book."

"It's horrible," O'Riley said.

"A lot of kikes are liberals; book-burning reminds them of Germany; and the kikes just can't give *enough* to the breakfast program . . ."

"But . . . how are they going to implicate the Panthers?"

"Who knows. Maybe they'll drug one of them and burn him along with the books. The Teamsters are ruthless."

O'Riley looked at McCann's burning face with dismay. It was awful. First the Sierra Club raids a construction company; then a hippie cult tries to steal the remains of a war hero; and now the Teamsters were going to blow up the library.

"This is not acceptable," O'Riley said with agitation. "This is not acceptable at all. We'll surround the library with the Tactical Squad, we'll call up the reserves . . ."

McCann smiled and waggled his fingers, giving O'Riley the unpleasant feeling that his subordinate thought he was letting passion cloud his logic.

"Better, let's catch the bastards in the act," McCann said. "I'm in so tight with the Teamsters I could put my hand on Fitzgerald's nuts. I'll find out how they plan to handle the deal and we'll nab 'em." McCann made a wild grabbing gesture, as if he was catching flies.

O'Riley hesitated. It would be a disaster if they blew up the library. The mayor certainly wouldn't like *that*. But to catch the terrorists in the act! This called for a decision; he had to make an important decision. O'Riley's mind immediately froze. Think of Drake, he said to himself, think of Cortés, think of Grant and Jackson, think of . . . Horatio Hornblower. O'Riley's seamed, hollow, cadaverous face had set as rigidly as a death mask. Then, suddenly, he slapped his hand on the desk.

"We'll do it," he snapped. "Set it up."

"Yes *sir*," said McCann, with the biggest grin O'Riley had ever seen. The young officer leaped to his feet and was gone.

250

The lieutenant's eyes fell again to the *Fist* and happened to light on another letter, shorter than the one purportedly from the De-education Coalition.

> *. . . I'm the one . . .*
> Recently some trash has got abroad about the bomber being a ecogogist. In trut, the bomber is a tall standing hero of the people a man of courage and brillence who loves the people and who would glady die in thier bosum for their betterment. The lies abroad that the revolutionary hero is a ecogogist or hippie are fully false and may the liars be damned in their teeth.
>
> Herbie X
907 Divisadero Apt. 7
987-3210

"p.s. my moth is seeled to cops."

O'Riley smiled wearily at this pathetic effort. If only it were that simple.

McCann lost no time setting things up.

"Mr. McCann for Mr. Apples. Hi, boss. Is this a secure line?"

"Of course. The telephone company always lets me know if I'm being tapped."

"I have another shipment for you. I'll meet you at noon Monday in the periodical room of the main library; we can work out details."

"Very well, Mr. McCann."

"How is Melanie, by the way?"

"Just fine. We have her in a penthouse suite at the Fairmont, being raped continuously. Should we let her go?"

"No, you better keep her a few more days."

"Every truck driver at Convenience is in your debt, Mr. McCann."

Then the ruby-faced police officer drove into the ghetto,

stopped in front of 907 Divisadero Street, and barged into apartment Number 7. Herbie was sitting at his kitchen table, an alarm clock in one hand and a screwdriver in the other. Six or eight sticks of dynamite wrapped tightly together with adhesive tape were by his elbow.

"I'll go quietly," Herbie said softly, laying aside his screwdriver.

"Wait a minute, Herbie. To tell the truth, the district attorney just laughed when I told him what we have so far. 'Do you want us to be the laughing stock of the world?' he says. 'Don't you realize what Nicholas Von Hoffman will do to us?' Listen Herbie, do you mind if I just browse around a minute?"

"You have a warrant of search, no doubt," said Herbie coldly, resuming his tinkering.

"Actually, I don't, Herbie. I was sort of hoping . . . well, you know, man to man . . ." Herbie shrugged his shoulders.

McCann poked around the kitchen, looking for something interesting. Most of Herbie's devices were of a very ordinary type: three or four sticks of explosive attached to an alarm clock.

"What's this, Herbie?" On the windowsill was a small aquarium full of ball bearings.

"Pets," said Herbie.

"I'm going to have to seize them as evidence. Listen, Herbie, do you have anything really . . . sophisticated?"

"Nothing like that here; but don't look in the pantry."

McCann opened the pantry and found a shoebox with a hole cut in the side and two wires leading out. Inside the box were two dry-cell batteries and some kind of solenoid, some electric relays, and a remote-control tuner for a television set.

McCann took out the tuner and pressed the channel

selection button; with a snap, a spark arced across the bare tips of the wires. He put the box under his arm along with two more of Herbie's bombs.

"I'm going to seize all this as evidence," McCann said. "Do you happen to have a paper bag?"

CHAPTER 24

It was just as wet and dreary on Monday, August 30, as it had been the rest of the month. At approximately 11 A.M., an enormous red-faced man in a shabby gray suit, accompanied by a lithe dapper Negro, pushed through the turnstile at the entrance of the main library and clumped up the long flight of marble stairs leading to the periodical room on the third floor.

Stopping for a moment on the second landing, they glanced into the literature-philosophy room. In the back of the nearly deserted room, sitting by himself at a table, was Lieutenant O'Riley, apparently immersed in a massive volume. He didn't look up.

They continued their ascent and soon reached the periodical section, where half a dozen elderly men surrounded the newspaper racks. A young male librarian was the only other person in the room, his head bent over a magazine on his desk. McCann caught his attention and motioned him over with a curt nod.

"You must be the police," the youth whispered. "They told me to be expecting you."

"That's right," McCann said, exhibiting his star. "We're going to set up headquarters here in the john; so if you want to take a piss, go downstairs."

The young man smiled, blushed, and returned to his desk.

Everything had been arranged. According to information supplied O'Riley by McCann, the Teamster bomber would enter the literature-philosophy room at noon and leave a package under one of the tables near the bookshelf marked BRE-CA. At this point, the three members of the Anti-Terror Unit would effect the arrest, the building would be cleared, and the bomb squad summoned to deactivate the device, set to explode at 12:45.

O'Riley, as they had already seen, was in position, reading a book in front of JER-LIM.

Also around noon, Jack Apples, public facilitator for Convenience Drayage, would arrive for his meeting with McCann in the periodical room. A few minutes later, a messenger from Sparky's Delivery would bring in a large package and lay it in front of Mr. Apples. In this package was a bomb: six sticks of dynamite buried in an aquarium full of ball bearings. This bomb would explode when McCann pressed the button of the television tuner in his pocket.

Even now, the Sparky's messenger would be waiting at the Greyhound station for the bus to arrive from Petaluma with the package. The Petaluma stationmaster that morning had received a letter, ostensibly from Jack Apples, explaining that the package had been forgotten by a salesman. The letter also contained a locker key, some money to cover expenses, and a note telling the delivery boy where to take the package. The stationmaster had dutifully put the package on the 10:35 bus to the city.

McCann, of course, had typed the letter himself the day before on Rose's typewriter, the same one he used for his correspondence with *The Clenched Fist*. That typewriter would have to go into the bay someday; he would buy Rose an electric.

"Cocktail hour," McCann said, looking at his watch. He took a sign out of his briefcase that read "Temporarily Out of Service" and hung it on the men's room door. They went inside, locked the door with a key supplied by the head librarian, and opened a couple of canned martinis.

Apples' death in the explosion would demonstrate to O'Riley that the Teamsters really *were* behind the bombings, even though the plans had been changed at the last minute about where to place the bomb.

McCann, fingering the television tuner in his pocket, had nearly drained his can when he noticed something peculiar: a pair of feet were visible beneath the door of one of the stalls.

"Hey, you," shouted McCann, "get out of there."

The stall door immediately opened and a man, fully clothed, stepped out. It was Major Herbie Simple of the People's Liberation Army.

"Herbie! Nice to see you baby. Have a drink."

Herbie looked disdainfully at the canned liquor proffered by McCann but nevertheless accepted.

"I have a grudging admiration for the police," Herbie said. "You knew that planting that fake letter next to mine in the *Fist* would draw me into your net. You can be sure that at the proper time and place I will give credit where due. My honor is intact. But really, it was impossible to dream that a lone man, however brave,

256

however brilliant, could elude forever the snares of the fascist monster." Herbie's yellow fingers played with the canned martini. "I'm sorry to see you here, brother," he said solemnly to Henry.

"Die," said Henry.

"We all have to die, brother; death does not frighten me. The only thing I fear is that my life might pass before I could strike a blow against the capitalist snake whose coils tighten on my oppressed people.

"I have the idea, brother," Herbie said, turning to Henry, "that you are the one truly responsible for my fall. The lackey and the functionary of the white mother country have lured you to treachery with promises of gold. I can dig it; they know fully well that they must use color to fathom color. The Anglo butcher knows the ways of destruction, but only a black mind ever knows another black mind. But it's over. Now my fate is in the hands of the people."

"Die," said Henry, lurching against the wash basin and staring wildly at his own mad reflection in the mirror.

"Listen, Herbie," McCann said, "I told you. The D.A. has nothing on you yet. Go on home and I swear to God I'll arrest you sometime next week."

"I can't go home again," Herbie said, watching solemnly as his words took effect on Henry, making him hiss and mutter. "It's too late to go home. Only the people can save me now. When the people learn my story they will see the impossibility of one man standing alone against the ranged forces of racism, however strong and able he may be. It will be a lesson that may serve to light the road to revolution; perhaps one man's downfall through vanity and individualism will be the clarion call for unity among oppressed peoples."

"Go home, Herbie."

"It's too late to turn back. I'm going now to throw my-self before the feet of Lieutenant O'Riley in the literature-philosophy room and beg mercy; yes, Herbie X will beg mercy." The little bomber's eyes were wet with tears.

"You can't do that just now," McCann said, hurriedly glancing at his watch.

"I'm going," Herbie said, turning to the door.

"Okay, okay." McCann grabbed him by the collar. "You're under arrest. Henry, help me handcuff Mr. Simple and we'll take him downstairs."

"Don't you think you'd better inform me of my rights?"

"I will, Herbie. Down in the car. Okay?" McCann unlocked the door and gently led Herbie into the corridor. The old men still read their newspapers; the youth still bent over his magazine. Apples hadn't arrived yet. They took a quick look at O'Riley as they passed; he was still reading, his compact body rigid as a statue.

They hurried Herbie down a back stairway, through a service door, and into an alleyway. They were buffeted by gusts of rain as they tossed the manacled lunatic onto the floorboard in the back of the unmarked car.

McCann slid behind the wheel and backed the car into the rain-drenched street.

"It's a mistake to throw me on the floor like this." Herbie's muffled voice floated up from the back seat. "The reporters are going to talk to me. They're going to say, 'How were you treated by the police, Major Simple?' 'Thrown on the floor, handcuffed, brutalized,' I'll say, 'but my lawyer, Charles Garry, well known for his brilliant defense of Huey Newton, will have more to say on the subject in court.' I wouldn't want to be you on the stand then, McCann, with Garry pacing up and down and glaring at you with those fiery eyes. 'Just tell the judge, Officer McCann, why you tossed Herbie X on the floor and twisted his arms all up behind him.' And you squirming and wiping the sweat off your face."

McCann glanced at his watch. It was exactly 11:30. He sped down Oak Street to Buchanan and turned into the projects, past long naked blocks where the Redevelopment Agency had torn down hundreds of old tenements to make room for new ones.

"I've got the names for the steering committee of the Herbie X Defense Fund all decided. My correspondence is in order; I've got a two-page statement prepared and an idea for a book and a movie. I've got my diary. And you roust me like I'd stuck up a gas station. You jackanapes are accustomed to two-bit nigger nonsense; you might be able to handle a purse snatch or a pigeon drop, I don't know. But this case involves the man who has thrown a mighty city into a . . . a *fit* of terror."

McCann pulled up behind a condemned building at Buchanan and Hayes. Half the block had been razed, and a crane with its wrecking ball squatted in the middle of piles of debris. The other half of the block was filled with empty buildings. Fog swirled around the two officers as they dragged the bomber behind one of the tenements. McCann kicked open a back door that led into a filthy kitchen littered with broken glass. Herbie stumbled along like an unstable tot as they pulled him through the corridor until they found the bathroom.

Picking Herbie up beneath the armpits, McCann deposited him in the bathtub, feet toward the spigot. Herbie's eyes darted around suspiciously.

"Don't you fools realize who I am? Do you think I was scribbling fuck or shit on the wall of the john? I am Major Herbie X, of the People's Liberation Army. This is not a purse snatch."

McCann pulled an unauthorized Browning automatic from his boot and handed it to Henry. "This is the one," he said.

Henry took the gun and moved behind Herbie. "Die," he said, "die, die."

"I pity you fools when Garry has you on the stand. My mind is too quick to write things down, but I'm strong in debate. I could always talk. I think I might act in my own defense, with Garry as a backstop, to help me over the legal humps. But when you fools are on the stand, I'll let him loose. I was told once that . . ."

Henry put the gun behind Herbie's neck. There was a snap, like a dry stick breaking. Herbie stopped, surprised, in midsentence and looked at McCann reproachfully, the blood dribbling out his mouth. Then he slumped forward in the tub. McCann, his hands trembling slightly, reached in and removed the handcuffs.

Rain hammered on the hollow building and the wind had carried rain through the open door into the corridor, turning the dust black along the floor. The two officers dashed down the back steps. It was ten minutes to noon. They reached the library just as the Sparky's motorcycle pulled up in front.

McCann spun the car into the alley and the two officers tumbled out at a dead run for the stairs. McCann, his face the color of an apple, had started to laugh.

"I think we're going to make it."

The Sparky's boy took his time trudging up the stairs and the two officers, panting and puffing, were waiting for him in the john, where McCann was gurgling down a quick martini. They heard the tapping of his footsteps pass by. McCann took a quick peek, saw Apples sitting at a table inside the door reading a newspaper, saw the Sparky's boy hesitate a moment at the entrance, then turn toward Apples.

McCann stepped into the corridor.

"Now," said Henry breathlessly behind him. "Now, now."

McCann, dizzy, confused, staggered forward a few steps, the channel selector trembling in his hands.

"Now," shouted Henry, and McCann pressed the button.

The roar of the explosion filled the cavernous library like a peal of thunder; the room was completely obscured by smoke and debris; ball bearings by the dozens ricocheted off the walls and bounced down the corridor; a column of powdered marble and smoke gushed toward them; several people were screaming.

"Oh, God," muttered Henry, leaning against the open bathroom door.

The sound of the second explosion was so deafening that later McCann only remembered the echo of it as he lay stunned on the floor. Henry was propelled across the corridor by a blast of fire and smoke that slammed him against the far wall. McCann dimly perceived him lying twenty feet away in a pool of blood.

McCann groped along the shard-covered floor in confusion; he suddenly realized he was choking on vomit, an acrid burning stream of regurgitated gin. Through the smoke and powder, McCann coughed and sputtered on his knees as he tried to think what had happened. Despite his ringing ears, he heard voices and shouts from below and the sound of running feet. He saw the channel selector in front of him and pushed it inside his shirt; he smelled bourbon; the bottle in his back pocket must have broken.

Suddenly a figure loomed out of the smoke before him. A plump little man appeared; and Jack Apples, ashen and trembling, bent over him.

McCann, covered with dust, choking on vomit, began to laugh. That rotten nigger lunatic had got them. Why hadn't he thought to check the fucking stall Herbie had been in? McCann laughed and his stomach pumped up another wave of addled gin.

"That was a nasty trick you played on me," Apples

said. "Do you think I was born yesterday? Do you think I'd stand still and let a Sparky's delivery boy walk up to me with a package? You're a sick and dangerous man, Mr. McCann, and I'm not going to forget this. It's a disgrace, and you can be sure the Committee won't like this a bit."

"The little cocksucker got us." Apples had gone, and he was grinning up at O'Riley.

"Just take it easy," the lieutenant said. "The ambulance will be here in a minute."

O'Riley disappeared, too; and McCann lay among the debris on the floor, laughing silently to himself. Presently he realized that while he was hysterical, he wasn't actually injured. He felt himself all over; nothing hurt, so he tentatively sat up. Actually, he wasn't hurt at all, if only his pulse would slow down.

His nerves were shattered, and soon he felt the familiar pressure in his chest, followed by the stab of pain in his left arm. He quickly scrambled to his feet and, weaving a little, headed for the back stairway.

The ambulance attendants rushed up the stairs to get Henry, who was suffering from a fractured skull, a broken spine, and copious loss of blood. But they couldn't find McCann.

"Another officer is injured," O'Riley said, bewildered. "He's in shock and must have wandered off. Search the building. He's around here someplace."

But McCann was actually across the street at the Pall Mall Club, having a double bourbon over.

CHAPTER 25

September is the best month in San Francisco. The fog lifts and the smog is swept toward the San Joaquin Valley by a brisk onshore breeze. The tourists go away; the sun condescends to shine a bit; the waves grow higher at the beach; and the insolent surfers in the filthy breakers south of the Cliff House are occasionally drowned and their bodies dashed against the rock.

The first two weeks of this glorious month passed in perfect serenity. The odds for the mayor's re-election, as tallied in Reno and Lake Tahoe, gave him a comfortable margin over the Republican restaurateur. The crab catch was up slightly over last year, meaning that crustaceans really do like industrial waste dumped on their heads, just as the oil companies had been saying right along. And the price of a martini stayed the same.

More significantly, there had been no more bombings. San Franciscans, with a sigh of relief, found that the front page once again was devoted to the routine and the commonplace: carnage in Asia, floods in the Philippines, earthquakes in Peru, and famine in Bangladesh.

Meanwhile, the Committee for the Re-election of the Mayor had been busy organizing a testimonial dinner for Saturday, September 14, to honor Lieutenant Michael O'Riley, officer-in-charge of the Anti-Terror Unit, at which the Police Commission would award O'Riley the Outstanding Officer of the Year Award.

It was a gala, of course, held in the Garden Court of the Sheraton-Palace Hotel and drawing a crowd that ran the gamut from glittering Pacific Heights socialites to the mean little neighborhood fixers who adorned Monagan's Ten-High Club.

Absolutely everybody of any political consequence was there: fat Chinese merchants from the Seven Companies; shrill Mexican ladies from the Mission Coalition; ruddy Irish from the police and fire departments, Civil Service, and the Municipal Railway; prosperous Italians with glossy hair and thick eyebrows from the North Beach restaurants and night clubs; beefy, cigar-chewing Negroes from the ILWU; afroed and bedizened slick young blacks from the Office of Economic Opportunity; and salted here and there inconspicuously, three or four of the seven Jewish businessmen who actually run things in San Francisco.

McCann, dressed in civilian clothes, was seated near the front podium, practically under his superior's aquiline but fleshless nose. As guest of honor, the lieutenant, compact, severe, carved in walnut, sat beside the ebullient mayor, and occasionally essayed a corpse's grin when the mayor threw an arm around him in time with a dazzling burst of flash guns. Like most political affairs, the dinner was all noise, smoke, table-hopping, and laughter.

McCann's neighbor was Al Russell, the mayor's youth liaison aide. They had each had five gin and tonics and were working on their second bottle of wine.

"Do you want to hear my philosophy?" Russell was saying. "My philosophy is strength and competition."

"You're a hell of a guy," McCann said.

"*You're* a hell of a guy. You know, frankly, when I first met you I didn't think you were tough enough for the job. But I have to admit I was wrong. You're tough."

"Thank you," said McCann modestly, filling up Russell's glass and his own.

"You and O'Riley did a *hell* of a job," Russell said, bending forward earnestly. "The mayor is just pleased as shit. We have *never* had a program turn out so successfully so soon after inception."

"We did work hard," McCann said, sitting back contentedly and taking in the raucous throng.

Little Badger, the assistant district attorney, came up and clapped McCann on the back.

"Hiya buddy," Badger said. "Big night, huh? I guess you heard about that kike kid Levin."

"No," said McCann.

"It'll be in the papers tomorrow. There was some kind of lovers' quarrel and one of his cellmates stabbed him to death. Apparently the word got around he was queer, but for some reason he was playing hard to get. Well, it's better this way. He didn't have a snowball's chance in hell anyway, when his alleged secret witness didn't show. Yes, the more I think about it the more I think it's just as well. We would have got him, of course, but just between you and me, we were going to have a hell of a problem with the shoes. They were two sizes too small for him; just the kind of thing those OEO shysters would jump on. It's better this way. Besides, I don't have time to try cases."

Badger wandered off.

"I never feel sorry for queers," Russell said. "It's a weakness. Weak people *ought* to be killed; they have no place in this world."

"That's right," said McCann, filling his glass.

"Just a touch for me, thanks. You see that guy over there, talking to Senator Blake?" Russell pointed to a squat, moon-faced man smoking a big green cigar. "That's Jack Apples, a *very* big gun with the Teamsters; and one of the mayor's strongest supporters. Hey, Jack."

Apples politely excused himself and came over to the table.

"Jack, I'd like you to meet Bill McCann, the famous anti-terror cop."

"I've had the pleasure," Apples said pleasantly, taking a seat across the table. "How's your partner, Mr. McCann? I hear he's paralyzed from the neck down."

"That makes his paralysis complete," said McCann.

"Ha, ha," laughed Russell. "Oh, you *are* tough."

"May I?" asked Apples, holding out an empty wine glass. McCann poured. After taking a careful sip, Apples signaled the waiter for more wine.

"Hey, look who's here," said Russell. Charles Brannon, crime writer for the *Examiner,* lurched up to the table, his ruined, leering face burning with drink and his soiled shirtfront soggy with perspiration.

"Apples, you racketeer, how are you? Russell, you punk," Brannon steadied himself with one hand on the table. "But Billie, you're my boy; this good ol' boy helped me a lot." Brannon threw his other palsied hand around McCann's shoulder.

"My heartfelt congratulations to you on your success," Apples said to Brannon, who the week before, had won Press Club awards for Best Series and Best Breaking

Story for his coverage of the War of the Pimps and the terrorist bombings. It was the first time in Press Club history both awards had gone to the same man.

"Shee-it," said Brannon, sitting down suddenly in the chair next to McCann. "You ain't seen nothing. I'm going to get the Pulitzer for my series on the Zodiac killer."

"How's it coming?" Apples asked mildly.

"Another one tonight," Brannon said, wiping his face with the edge of the tablecloth. "I was just down at the morgue viewing the body. A beautiful young girl, big tits. The only trouble with her is . . . her head and hands had been cut off." Brannon laughed hoarsely.

Apples, across the table from McCann, smiled faintly and raised his glass.

"My, my, my," the public facilitator said. "Well, gentlemen, I hope you'll excuse me. These evenings aren't all pleasure for me, you know." Apples, bowing and smiling again at McCann, laboriously got up and waddled over for a word or two with the mayor.

"Jack Apples is the kind of guy you want on your team," Russell said. "He's strong, he's competitive, he's on top of things, he's . . . Hey, hey, my boy, you look like you're starting to sober up. Here, let me pour you out a little of Mr. Apples' kind gift. Now tell me the truth, McCann, have you looked over the raffle-ticket girls tonight? I've had my eye on that little blonde number in the corner. Can you imagine what's going on inside that little skirt of hers? How would you like to have *that* sit on your head? Now, I'll tell you, there are two types of philanderers . . ."

Of course, the papers had been full of the library bombing.

The toll had been severe: one young librarian and three elderly pensioners killed outright; three other

267

pensioners, heavily perforated by ball bearings and in such critical condition that they probably wouldn't be leeching off Medicare much longer; and a police officer, heroically clinging to life although paralyzed from the chin down. But, on the positive side, the bomber had been killed as well.

It had been a difficult task for the crime lab and the pathologists to piece together the fragments of the Sparky's delivery boy. And it had been even more difficult for McCann, aided by Brannon of the *Examiner,* to run to earth the motives that had caused this seemingly innocuous person to terrorize an entire city.

But, bit by bit, just as the pathologists in the morgue were reconstructing his body, McCann and Brannon pieced together the lurid details of how a delivery boy had used his position of trust to plant bombs at will in any part of the city.

Brannon did much of the work in uncovering the real motivation.

The boy's name was Robert (Smiley) Murphy, nineteen, of Redwood City, California. Talking with the boy's weeping parents in their tasteless cramped suburban home, Brannon learned that of late there had been little communication with their son. Most of his friends at Carlmont High School thought he was just an ordinary, normal kid, kind of dumb; but one girl who had known him slightly in the eighth grade said he impressed her as "strange, weird, mixed up." The *Examiner* used her description in the cutline below the front-page picture of Murphy taken from his high school yearbook.

Murphy had dropped out of San Mateo Junior College after one semester and was turned down for Army service because of bad eyes. "He might have felt rejected," said Abraham Schwartz, a clinical psychologist at the junior college who had never met Murphy.

Most of his teachers in college didn't realize he had been in their class even after his picture appeared in all the papers. Brannon hit paydirt, however, when he interviewed Murphy's on-and-off girl friend, Clair Dempsy, who said he frequently had complained that "he didn't seem to be getting anywhere." She also remembered that he had discussed some political ideas while they were watching the Democratic National Convention on television. "I didn't pay any attention to what he was talking about," she said.

"Gradually a picture emerged of Murphy as a frustrated and rejected loner whose ideas for political reform were spurned or misunderstood by his contemporaries," Brannon wrote in his wrap-up of the case. "Unable to form close relationships, he lived more and more in a fantasy world of political revenge."

The clincher, however, came early when McCann, accompanied by Brannon, searched Murphy's small, untidy flat in the Mission District and found several dozen bomb mechanisms, explosives, tools, and political posters of Mao, Che, Huey, Emiliano, Stokely, Eldridge, and a few others.

The landlady said he must have put up the posters recently because they weren't there the week before. Surprisingly, she seemed to recognize McCann.

A few days later, at a press conference called after consultation with his staff, O'Riley announced to one of the largest media crowds in the city's history that the terror had come to an end.

"I think it's safe to say that the bombings were largely the work of Robert Murphy. We believe others that may be involved are already in custody. The terror in San Francisco is over," he said flatly.

The mayor and his aides held their breath after O'Riley said that. Another bombing on the heels of such a statement would be politically disastrous. But nothing happened. Brannon, meanwhile, was hard at work establishing the connection between Murphy and the Sierra Club.

The weeks flew by and nothing disturbed the even tenor of the mayoralty campaign. Most of the citizens in the Bay Area were understandably relieved the terror was concluded. But not everybody. The Berkeley City Council passed a resolution making August 30 "Smiley Murphy Day" in remembrance of those who raise their fist against oppression. Numerous small but vociferous services were held by radical groups in the area supporting Murphy. The Black Panthers issued a statement saying that "much of what Mr. Murphy has accomplished is in the best interest of the people," and Murphy's name was mentioned in communique #117 from the Weather Bureau. And Eldridge Cleaver, from exile in Algeria, termed Murphy "the greatest white man of the century."

McCann and Rose went once to visit Henry in the hospital. He was in the recovery room at San Francisco General following an unsuccessful operation on his spine. Still comatose from the anesthesia, Henry had been lolling back in bed, tubes from the Byrd respirator running down his nose, more tubes from his intravenous feeding bottle drooping into his arm.

"He seems to think he's going to die," said Nurse MacMaster. "Actually his heart is very strong. Now try to cough, Mr. Henry."

"Die, die," muttered Henry.

On the day after the library bombing, on page 46 in the *Examiner,* next to a truss ad, appeared this story:

WAR OF PIMPS CLAIMS NEW VICTIM
The gangland war between rival factions of procurers in the Fillmore continued unabated yesterday with the slaying of a new victim in an abandoned Buchanan Street tenement.

The victim, identified by the coroner's office as Herbie Simple, 37, of 907 Divisadero Street, was found shot to death in a bathtub inside the tenement.

Inspector John Toschi of the homicide detail termed the slaying "execution style, one bullet through the back of the neck," and said Simple's death in likelihood was tied to the rash of killings attributed to a power struggle between rival prostitution rings.

Homicide officers said Simple's apartment had been ransacked, and a playing card—the ace of spades—had been left stuck in the dresser mirror.

Simple's death brings to 11 the number of slayings connected with the gang war. Toschi speculated he may have been a minor figure in one of the rival gangs.

██████████████████ CHAPTER 26

Lieutenant Michael O'Riley and his subordinate William McCann, both of whom had been feted lavishly by a grateful city, walked down the Florentine tile steps outside the Sheraton-Palace and waited on the corner for a cab. The lieutenant appeared weary and despondent but held himself rigidly erect, his hands clasped behind his back. McCann, bilious and dyspeptic, puffed a vile little black cigar given him by one of the mayor's cousins.

They were silent and the street was quiet save for the muffled sound of receding footsteps and a few drunken farewells as the dregs of the testimonial dinner broke up at the door and went home. Behind them, in the shadow of the building, squatted a hippie news vendor who apparently had been selling copies of the first press run of the latest *Clenched Fist* to the departing politicos.

"Feeeee-est," he cried. "Hot off the pr-eeeeees.".

"Want one, boss?"

"Sure."

McCann stepped back, dropped a dollar on the hippie, and took two *Fists*.

"Thankee, gov'nor, thankee," said the hippie, groveling and pulling his forelock.

A cab pulled up and the two men climbed in. McCann handed O'Riley his *Fist*, and his superior folded it neatly and slid it into his coat pocket.

"I'll drop you first," O'Riley said, giving the cabbie McCann's address.

They sat in silence as the car sped through the empty streets. O'Riley, wedged into his corner of the cab, had closed his eyes and was taking a nap. McCann idly opened his copy of the *Fist* and saw on the inside front page a banner headline:

ANTI-TERROR COPS SMUGGLE HEROIN

In the dim, shifting light from passing street lamps, McCann puffed on the foul cigar and read the story.

> Two San Francisco police officers, William Mc-Cann and John Henry, have used their positions on the Anti-Terror Unit to smuggle $3 million in heroin into the United States in the body of a corpse.
>
> Sources within organized crime in the city have revealed exclusively to the editors of the *Fist* that McCann and Henry—two officers infamous in the Haight for their rousting of radical groups—smuggled the heroin shipment into the country in the body of Pfc. Donald Sizeman, a soldier killed in Southeast Asia and later the near victim of a bizarre body-snatch attempt.
>
> The shipment was arranged in Long Binh by U.S.

Army captain D. Baradikian, a surgeon with the 115th Medical Detachment at the base hospital, the sources said.

It was a lengthy article. In the semidarkness of the moving cab, McCann skimmed over the paragraphs. The story said the gunfight at Vacaville had been the result of an attempt by mobsters to steal the shipment; that Levin, of the Sierra Club, had been framed by McCann because of the officer's interest in Levin's girl friend, Melanie Duggs, who subsequently had disappeared; that the library bombing had been staged by McCann in an attempt to frame the Black Panthers, who were trying to crack down on the heroin traffic in the ghetto; that Smiley Murphy was innocent; and that the real bomber was still at large.

The cab drew up to his apartment house. McCann fished out a five for the driver and gently shook O'Riley awake.

"Goodnight, boss."

"Goodnight, McCann, see you tomorrow," O'Riley muttered. The cab moved away, leaving McCann on the curb, a dead cigar in his teeth, looking at the poorly reproduced picture of himself and Henry staring back from the tabloid.

It seemed Apples was taking an awful chance by planting this story, McCann thought. Suppose McCann were to be held. Might he not implicate Apples and the Teamsters? The *Fist* story, of course, was completely unsubstantiated; no responsible official believed anything he read in the *Fist*. And yet, surely there would be questions tomorrow. The only thing implicating the Teamsters was the cashier's check; but McCann had cashed it at Labor Temple Bank ten days before.

Emotionlessly, as he stood riveted in the pale of the

street lamp, McCann tried to weigh his situation. Then suddenly, the problem resolved itself, and he realized what Apples must have realized from the first; that McCann could only do one thing. He would have to take a hike. McCann realized now that, in Apples' game, he was about to be swept from the board.

McCann threw his cigar stump in the gutter and trudged up to his apartment. Apples' Committee in all probability didn't want the election locked up for the mayor anyway. McCann's sudden, unexplained departure on top of an unsubstantiated and unsupportable story in an underground newspaper might prove to be the very thing needed to throw the mayoralty campaign once again into doubt.

The absurd Brannon would read the story in the *Fist* tomorrow, ask O'Riley about it, and, lo, McCann would be gone. It was bound to be embarrassing all around, but McCann could hardly afford to stay in town with $750,000 in his possession and the truth, more or less, in the open. Apples, of course, didn't know the terror was really over. Or did he? And was it? What if a bomb went off somewhere three days before the election?

McCann snapped the light on in the kitchen, got ice, and poured himself a drink. From the bedroom, he heard the creak of the bed and the pad of feet. Rose came into the kitchen, wearing one of McCann's shirts, which fell almost to her knees. She nestled against his chest and threw her arms around him.

"I saw you on TV," she said. "The commentator said the apprehension of the bomber was largely the work of a 'bold young undercover officer, William McCann,' and the camera was right on you when you were sitting with the mayor's assistant. I was so proud of you. You just don't know how it made me feel. I know you're good, despite everything you say; it's acts that count, not words."

McCann took a drink and stroked Rose's long black hair.

"You're the ace of hearts," he said.

"Let's go somewhere, Bill. I don't want to go back to school. Let's take a vacation, go backpacking in the Sierra, or to Lake Tahoe if you want to. I want to be alone with you for awhile."

"Okay," said McCann, "I'll take my vacation and we'll go next week."

Rose stretched up on tiptoes to be kissed.

"You taste like the barroom floor, as usual," she said.

Arm in arm they went into the bedroom; McCann lifted her up and tossed her into bed, seating himself on the edge.

"Here," he said, pulling the Browning automatic from his pocket and putting it in her hand, "I'm through with this for awhile." He smoothed the covers around her neck and stroked her forehead.

"Listen, Rose, I have to meet O'Riley down at the Hall for about an hour to put the finishing touches on our report to the mayor. It has to be submitted tomorrow. But I'll be back, so don't get too sleepy."

"Okay, big boy," said Rose, turning on her side and smiling. The wicked little black nose of the automatic poked out from beneath the covers.

McCann turned off the bedroom light and closed the door. Getting another drink from the kitchen, he walked back to the laundry room on the back porch, where he kept some of his clothes. When he left the apartment, he was carrying a suitcase and was dressed in the uniform of a corporal in the Americal Division.

CHAPTER 27

The Canadian Club clock at the airport said 3:17 A.M. when McCann, ostensibly returned to his former condition as a corporal in the U.S. Army, paid off his cab in front of the main terminal building. Refusing the services of a skycap, he lugged his two suitcases up the linoleum ramp toward the ticket counters.

The second suitcase he had picked up forty minutes before from a locker in the Greyhound Bus Station at Seventh and Market. The suitcase contained $750,000 in cash, well-worn and crumpled bills in the smaller denominations, crisp and fresh in the higher registers.

Ambling up to the Pan American ticket counter, McCann took out a wad of money and paid just over $800 for a one-way coach seat on the 6:30 A.M. flight to Saigon. His furlough papers, although falsified, were perfectly in order. He checked through both bags; if you carried anything aboard, it was liable to be searched.

The bored, thin-lipped clerk perfunctorily looked at his papers, took the money, stamped the ticket. "There you are, Mr. Hallman." Obviously, this was a soldier who had hit a bit of luck in some barracks crap game, a career man who thought nothing of blowing a couple of thousand on a two-week, four-thousand-mile jaunt to Frisco to satisfy his yearning for hamburgers and round-eyed girls.

Feeling relaxed and pleased with himself, McCann wandered over to the observation deck for a few minutes to watch the huge planes roll along the apron toward the runway, their sleek, shiny sides casting reflections on the wet asphalt. He went into the restaurant, had a hamburger and Coke, chatting a bit with a young soldier from Indianapolis on his way to Fort Bragg. Afterward, he bought a copy of *Time* and was going to read it when he felt somebody tugging at his sleeve.

Looking down, he saw the pale, distraught face of Keating, the coroner's assistant. Keating wearing a raincoat several sizes too large, carried a bulging suitcase; a twitch had appeared under his left eye.

"Hi, Keating."

"McCann," Keating whispered, looking all around him nervously. "I almost didn't recognize you. Have you seen this?" The coroner's deputy drew back the edge of his raincoat to reveal the top of a *Clenched Fist* sticking out of his inside pocket. Keating was trembling so violently he could hardly keep the coat open.

"Yes," said McCann, matter-of-factly. "It's pretty accurate for a newspaper story."

"*McCann*. We're in *trouble*. They're on to the whole damn thing. My *name* is in here."

McCann had slowly edged around so that he could

look at the television screen atop the Pan Am counter, where the departure schedule was listed.

"Well," McCann drawled, "have you bought your ticket yet?"

"Ticket? To where?"

"Why, to Mexico City, of course. Didn't I tell you? A guy down there is taking care of everything; he's got forged papers for us and tickets under phony names on a flight to Rio. You have your passport, don't you?"

"Yes, yes." With a shaking hand, Keating withdrew the oblong green pasteboard book. McCann was amused to see that the passport was in Keating's own name.

"Well, you'd better hurry. The plane leaves in forty-five minutes. I've already got my ticket."

"But, McCann," Keating hesitated, his face a study of anguish, "what about the *money*?"

"I've already checked it through. You've got enough for the ticket, don't you?"

"I've only got a couple of hundred," Keating whispered.

"That's enough. You'd better hurry."

Keating scurried off to the ticket counter, bought his ticket, and checked his bag.

"Listen, Keating," McCann said when the little coroner had returned. "You look too nervous; you've got to calm yourself, or you'll draw attention to us. Let's go have a quickie before we board."

They couldn't go to the bar because it was after 2 A.M. closing time, but McCann led the way into the restaurant, found a secluded rear table, and when the coffee came poured a healthy slug of his last half pint into Keating's cup. He remembered that he should have taken out another bottle before he checked his bag through. But Keating wouldn't need much, his ulcer having lowered his tolerance for alcohol.

A few sips of the spiked coffee seemed to stabilize

Keating, although he was still trembling. He managed, nonetheless, to stare accusingly at McCann.

"You were going to leave me behind to take the heat," he said bitterly.

"No, I wasn't. I tried to call your house but you weren't home. I just assumed you'd have the sense to head for the airport. And I was right."

"I talked to my wife half an hour ago. She said nobody called."

"That's just about when I phoned."

"If I hadn't been working the night shift tonight I would never have found out. It was just lucky a hippie kid was selling papers outside Central Emergency."

"Blonde kid that said, 'Thankee, Gov'nor?'"

"How did you know?"

"I know all those punks," McCann said.

"Why did I ever get into this?" wailed Keating. "What's my wife going to say when they start asking her questions tomorrow?"

"You got into it because it made you rich. Who needs a wife? You can have all the little chiquitas you want. You're a rich man. Just follow me and everything will be great."

"Just follow you," Keating said bitterly. "Did you phone Henry to tell him what's up?"

"Now don't be like that, Keating. There's nothing we can do for Henry right now."

Keating, breathing heavily, sipped the coffee; every few seconds he would start around and look at the doorway, as if he were expecting to see a squad of policemen coming toward them.

"Calm down; you look suspicious; just be natural."

Keating turned back to McCann. "What are we going to do about Henry's share? It'll be $375,000 apiece, right?"

"Well, we owe it to Henry to help out with his medical and legal expenses."

"Sure, of course. I don't mean we should screw him; it's just that he can't use it and we're going to need every penny."

"It'll be even Stephen all the way," McCann said, pouring the last of the whiskey into Keating's cup.

The little coroner relaxed somewhat and breathed easier. "I hate to fly," he said. "I'm going to take a piss."

"Well, hurry up. The plane boards in ten minutes."

As soon as Keating disappeared into the john, McCann put a dollar on the table, got up, and quickly strode out of the restaurant. He turned right, hurried up a flight of stairs, and emerged on the deserted observation platform. From this vantage point he could look down through the windows along the corridor to the boarding dock where the Pan Am flight was loading for Mexico City.

McCann had not been breathing the cold, moist night air for more than two minutes before he saw Keating's plump little figure race along the corridor for the boarding dock. From inside, he could hear the metallic speaker announcing the flight. Keating stopped short at the dock, looked about wildly, ran back a few steps, changed his mind, and ran a few steps in the other direction, all the time twisting one hand in the other.

The little coroner distractedly paced back and forth in front of the dock as the other passengers lined up and filed past the boarding officer at his desk. Standing on the windswept platform two hundred yards away, McCann could almost feel Keating's agitation and perplexity.

Finally Keating sidled up to the boarding officer. The boarding officer shook his head, lifted the paper on the clipboard in front of him, and looked back at Keating. Keating turned away and began pacing again while the officer continued to stare at him. McCann could imagine poor Keating asking the officer if a soldier had boarded. "What's the gentleman's name?" says the officer, and Keating's sudden, dumb realization that he didn't know. "McCann," he hazards. No, nobody by that name. McCann grinned ferociously in the darkness as he waited to see what Keating would do.

Inevitably, of course, Keating boarded the plane. And even from a distance, McCann could see his obvious nervousness as he handed his ticket to the boarding officer. Keating was the last passenger to board, and the boarding officer stared after him for several seconds. The little coroner was visibly shaking as he went through the metal detector.

The boarding officer looked down at the last name on his list, rubbed one ear, and then picked up his telephone. Alert the pilot. A suspicious person has boarded his aircraft. McCann waited on the observation platform until the Pan Am flight to Mexico City had rolled out onto the tarmac and lumbered into the sky. In four or five hours Keating, penniless and panic-stricken, would land in a foreign city without the slightest notion of what to do with himself.

McCann had brought out his bottle before realizing it was empty. He set it carefully on the platform ledge and walked inside. He shivered and sat down. It was 4:40 A.M. It had been very foolish to leave the pint in his suitcase; everything was closed now; his only hope would be buying a bottle off a serviceman.

Sitting hunched over in the darkened observation deck before the towering green-tinted glass, McCann felt the first twinge of familiar pain scamper through his chest and down the length of his left arm until his fingers tingled. The pressure built up under his breastbone until he felt nothing but one long spasm of pain. As usual, sweat broke out on his face, his breathing became labored, his vision blurred, his chest throbbed. And as might be expected, he asked God not to kill him there, in the airline terminal, with his money in a suitcase somewhere in the bowels of the building.

He looked around the room for a sergeant or a chief petty officer or somebody who would be likely to have a bottle in his luggage. But the terminal building at that hour was nearly empty, save for a custodian sweeping the shiny floors and a few kids sleeping in chairs, the victims of European charter hoaxes.

The pain grew worse. It occurred to him that he might be too weak to walk, or if he did walk he might pass out and collapse. When he got on the plane he'd bribe the stewardess to put a couple of bottles of whiskey with his breakfast. If not, surely someone on a Saigon flight would have a drink.

Saigon! That magic city! That city where anything was possible; where any kind of passport, any kind of forged document, was easily obtained; where all currencies were available on the black market; where a man could disappear for years in the back streets of the Lon Nol District, a nest of deserters off-limits to the military police.

Saigon! Where a man could change identities or buy a dozen identities; where French citizenship, Peruvian citizenship, anything, could be had for knocking on the right door; where money, however dirty, could be washed through the Saigon banks into unnumbered Swiss accounts. Anything could be arranged in Saigon, absolutely *anything*. And he would be there in twenty hours.

He knew just where to go, the Would You Believe Bar on Quang Tre Boulevard. See Timmy Prosser, a retired warrant; stay at the Biloxi Hotel.

Another spasm of pain passed through McCann's

heart. His shirt was drenched and the skunkish smell of his body wafted up to his nostrils as he sat huddled on the little plastic seat. When he got to Saigon everything would be all right. But for a few hours, at least, McCann had to face his terror.